Lily's Pond

Julane Hiebert

ISBN: 9798731806404

Dedication

A good neighbor is a priceless treasure.
Chinese proverb

To our wee cove's priceless treasures: Marietta and the late Larry Rose, Dennis and Eddie Mae, Shryll and Stony, Robert and Cindi, and the occasional drop-ins, but always welcome, Contractor Mike and Diane. We love you all.

Acknowledgements

While writing can be very lonely, few authors reach their destination alone. My niece, Julie, has been my traveling companion many, many times…always as a reader, but for this book my go-to advisor. Her patience with me and her willingness to answer any and all legalese questions provided invaluable knowledge that I could not have obtained otherwise. Thank you, thank you, thank you, sweet Julie.

And always, always, always, my Bob who has journeyed by my side through sixty-plus years of the worst of times and the best of times.

Foreword

Kansas, to those who choose to travel through mostly at night on the well-beaten paths of interstate driving, is thought to be flat, dry, and devoid of anything worthy of vacation destiny. However, within its borders, cradled within her wheat fields, lush pastures, natural wildlife preserves, and beautiful flint hills, are over 10,000 miles of waterways made up of 120,000 reservoirs, lakes, and ponds. Most of them are man-made. Such is the beautiful body of water that houses the wee cove in which my Bob and I live. Although this story *could* embody the history of this lake, it does not. Rather, it is but a loose composite and reminder of the sacrifice of many for the good of many more. Farms, ranches, and even entire communities lie in watery graves. Sadly, their stories will be lost or forgotten as generations die.

Lily's Pond is pure fiction, yet within fiction often lie truths sometimes too painful or full of fear to voice and wisdom gleaned from bold and healed voices of the past. As it is written: "The thing that hath been, it is that which shall be; and that which is done is that which shall be done: and **there is no new thing under the sun**." Ecclesiastes 1:9 (KJV)

My *hope* is that you will come to love fictional Anderson, Kansas, and the people who inhabit just one story of the many still unpenned.

My *prayer* is that you, dear reader, know the Author who is now penning your life story. The One who knows every story arc, how many chapters it will contain, and how it will end. The One who felt your story worthy for which to die.

One

LILY ARCHER PULLED the newspaper from her back pocket and plopped onto her mama's beloved overstuffed chair. Five minutes is all she wanted. Five minutes out of the heat. Five minutes to gulp down a glass of tepid water while scanning the weekly paper that had arrived yesterday. Five minutes to try to forget the stack of overdue bills arriving daily. She normally turned to the lifestyle pages first, mainly because she didn't want to miss who died or—did she dare hope—who might have returned to Anderson. But today there wasn't time. She leaned her head against the back cushion, gave the paper a shake, and—

JOE KENDALL NAMED FOREMAN OF CITY LAKE PROJECT

A wave of heat surged through her body as she read the front-page headline. She took a deep breath and punched at each word as she read the banner again. Eight words. One for each year since she'd promised Papa on his deathbed that she'd stay on the farm, not leave Mama, make sure her brother finished school.

Lily's feet hit the floor and her papa's old Bible that occupied the top of the small table beside Mama's chair went flying and slid under the piano stool. She'd deal with it later. For now, she was too angry, and the last thing she wanted to be reminded of was Papa's admonition to *hide God's word in her heart*. She wadded the newspaper and hurled it across the room. There'd been rumors of a lake, but until now they'd been only hearsay. Gossip. Something for the neighbors to talk about other than the heat and drought. Eight long years. Eight years of hailstorms, dust, and drought. Wind so fierce you could hardly stand against it, then air so still and heavy you couldn't breathe. Eight years of toil and sweat and looking in the mirror, only to find the eighteen-year-old girl who'd made the promise grow skinny and old. For what? This?

She paced across the room. There must be a way to stop this Kendall person. For a lake to become a lake it needed a water supply. And *her* creek, Willow Creek, was the only possible source. Spring fed. Even now, in this terrible drought, the Willow had water. But it was *her* water. The spring was on *her* land. And she'd never sell.

She turned and peered out the window, trying her best to ignore the dust on the sill, cobwebs in the corner, and streaks on the glass where'd she'd halfheartedly swiped a damp rag the last time she'd attempted to clean house. She had no time or energy left at the end of the day. She'd kept her promise. She'd made sure Bruce finished school, and he'd handed her his diploma and picked up his battered old suitcase the same day. He was eighteen. He was a man. Couldn't she understand? He never intended to be a farmer, he declared. He wanted to see what lay beyond the dirt of Kansas.

They'd fought. Hateful, stinging words. In the end he'd clomped down the stairs. While the slam of the screen door and the *chugga, chugga, chugga* of his battered Model T driving down the lane still rang in her ears, the epitaph of *bitter old maid* he'd chiseled across her heart with his angry words hurt more than she cared to admit. Hurtful utterances that couldn't be retrieved...only remembered.

She knew people whispered behind their hands when she went to town looking more like a man than a lady. She heard their murmurs. *Spinster. Gonna dry up and blow away like topsoil off plowed ground out there on that farm. She drove her brother off, you know.* Their hands didn't muffle one word. Not one. So what? She'd stayed, like she promised. And she'd keep on staying because, like when Papa died, she had no choice.

Mama was sick now...the kind of sick people didn't like to talk about. Something older people experienced when they no longer could remember what they did past the doing of it. But Mama had just turned fifty and the doctor's only explanation of her sickness was...he had no explanation. Mama didn't know there was anything wrong. But *she* knew. Lily knew because more often than not she had to turn Mama's apron right side out and make sure she wore all her underclothing. And most days she had to tell her over and over again that she was Lily, her own daughter. But Mama couldn't remember.

Lily retrieved the wadded paper, smoothed it over her knee, and stuck it in her back pocket. She'd read more later...later, when the chores were done and Mama was in bed. Later, when she could figure out how to tell Ed Murphy at the bank that she couldn't make the mortgage payment again this year. Later, after she once again choked back the tears she'd banked away all these years yet couldn't afford to spend.

For now, she'd better go fetch Mama. It wasn't like she'd have to hunt for her. Mama's routine never wavered, as if she had a clock inside her head. Or maybe her heart drove her down the lane and to the mailbox every afternoon. She'd go that far and wait...wait for Lily to retrieve the mail, hand it to her, then take her by the hand and say, *"Let's go home, Mama."* Then they'd make the walk back to the house, and Mama would sit on the porch until Lily called her for supper. They'd eat in silence. Mama had quit talking a long time ago, except when Lily would put her to bed. Then she'd smile and say goodnight. Only it was always, '*Goodnight Bruce. You've been a good boy today.*'

Lily gave her hair a twist and tucked it under her battered straw hat, then let the screen door slam behind her. She hated the hot, dusty walk to the end of the lane. Hated the ever-present dirt, the crackle of dry, stunted cornstalks, and the buzz of grasshoppers…all constant reminders there'd be no crops again this year. Hated the daily notices of money she owed and couldn't pay. And now, with the newspaper headline screaming at her, she just might hate Joe Kendall.

JOE KENDALL TURNED his car into the lane of the Archer farm. *You can't miss it,* he'd been told. *Look for a mailbox that tilts toward the road.* He smiled at the description. It would've been as simple to tell him to look for the one that had ARCHER painted on the side. As far as tilting, every mailbox he passed tilted. Probably needed some fresh dirt and maybe a rock or two to straighten them again. The drought and wind had taken its toll on almost anything planted in the ground, fenceposts and mailbox posts no exception.

He switched off the ignition and rolled down the window, not yet ready to traverse the long lane that was hardly more than two ruts through the dirt. His task for the day was not an easy one. He needed the job as project foreman for the proposed Anderson city lake as badly as the city needed water but, if he believed what he'd been told, advising Miss Archer that she'd need to vacate her property would be harder than widening the channel with a spoon.

They'd warned him. The fine city fathers had not spared him the details of her expected wrath. *Feisty, hardnosed, angry old maid* was the general consensus. Though her neighbors, who had readily agreed to the purchase price offered—probably because it left them with the bank paid and still some dignity with which to start over—had given a different assessment of Lillian Archer. *Hard worker. Soft-spoken, shy. It's a plumb shame she hasn't found a good man after all these years.* He was too polite to ask why the fact she hadn't found a good man after *all these years* was relevant when her age was not the issue at hand.

He stepped from the car, binoculars in hand. Never hurt to observe the enemy's movements before launching an attack. Miss Archer was not an enemy, but could he convince her that he was not one, either?

Late afternoon heat shimmered across the dust-covered track ahead of him. He widened his stance and brought the binoculars to his eyes. The adjustment of the lenses revealed the approach of a female. Tall and slender, wearing a blue-checkered dress and a white apron, the woman appeared well coiffed. He'd guess her age to be anywhere from fifty to sixty. He'd never been good at discerning the age of a female. It wasn't like he could check her teeth like one would with a dog or horse. He lowered the binoculars and tossed them onto the car seat. A stranger standing in the middle of the road with spy glasses in hand was not the best first impression to give.

Though her gait was steady, her steps were slow. She seemed so intent on her mission that he waited until she was close enough that he wouldn't need to raise his voice, then removed his hat and stepped toward her, his hand and arm extended in what he hoped would be seen as a friendly gesture of introduction. "Miss Archer? I'm Joe Kendall."

She strode around him without so much as a glance to acknowledge his presence. The city fathers should have added *rude* to their description.

He turned to follow her, but the woman stopped when she reached the mailbox. Stopped, but didn't turn around.

Really? "Excuse me, Miss Archer. You must not have heard me. I'm—"

"She's not deaf. You needn't shout."

He swiveled, expecting to see a girl in pigtails but coming face-to-face with a skinny kid in overalls, boots, and a straw hat. No one ever mentioned a hired hand, though by the high pitch of the young man's voice, he'd not yet hit puberty.

"Perhaps I should start over. My name is Joe Kendall." He extended his hand again, only to have the boy ignore it.

"I know who you are, and the answer is no." He moved around Joe and joined the woman at the mailbox.

Joe huffed. The kid was as rude as the older woman. "Excuse me? Do you always answer for Miss Archer?"

"I do. Always." The young man opened the mailbox, withdrew the mail, and handed it to the woman.

"Is she not capable of answering for herself?" It was hot, and he'd lost what little patience he possessed.

The kid removed his straw hat and a mane of auburn hair fell from the confines and settled on *her* shoulders. "Quite capable, sir, had you addressed *Miss* Archer in the first place." She took one of the older woman's hands in hers. "Let's go home, Mama." She glanced at him as they walked past. "You best shut your mouth. It never gets too hot or dry for flies around here."

A new kind of heat hit Joe's face. He closed his eyes and clenched his jaw. If only he'd taken the time to observe the hired hand more closely, he wouldn't have missed the obvious. No young man he knew fit a pair of overalls like this kid. Even too large, they didn't hide the slender curves they held. He ran ahead of them and planted himself in the middle of the lane. He knew his face was red but hoped she would attribute it to the heat. "Please wait. Are *you* Miss Lillian Archer?"

Her eyes snapped. "Whom did you think you were addressing? The hired hand?"

The better part of common sense stifled his answer. He'd faced

14

angry homeowners on more than one occasion, but he'd never had one set his heart thumping like this one. He took a deep breath and hoped she'd give him a chance to start over. "Look, Miss Archer. I apologize. You say you know who I am, but you do realize we've never met, don't you? How was I to recognize you? I'm curious as to how you know me."

She plopped the hat back on her head and pulled a newspaper from her back pocket. "See this?" She waved the paper in the air between them. "Contrary to what you might think about me, I *can* read."

"I...no one is—"

She took a step toward him. "I heard the rumors concerning a lake and now, guess what? It isn't rumor at all. And you, Joe Kendall, chief engineer and project foreman, must be right proud of turning rumor into fact at the expense of others."

"Miss Archer, could we—"

"No. We could not." Her eyes flashed the defiance her stance confirmed.

"You didn't allow me to finish." Feisty, hardnosed, and angry were fast becoming apparent, though he couldn't bring himself to think of her as *old maid.* No siree. That wasn't at all the title her presence elicited.

"Oh, you're finished. My answer is no. I will not, under any circumstances, sell my land. And without my land, you'll not be able to access my creek. And without the Willow, you'll have no lake. Now, I must get Mama out of this heat so I can finish my work. Good day."

She moved to go around him, but he stepped in front of her again. "It's not that simple, Miss Archer. The last thing I want to do is fight with you. But I'm prepared to do so if that's the only course you leave me. You can refuse to sell all you want, but the bottom line is...we can claim the property *and* Willow Creek through eminent domain."

She paled. "What do you mean, eminent domain? You can't just waltz in here and take my land and water away."

He squared his shoulders, ready for the fight that was sure to come. In the past he might've delighted in making the next statement, but not today. She left him no choice but to play his trump card. "Miss Archer, according to the records at the courthouse…technically, this isn't *your* land."

Two

HE'S LYING. JOE Kendall is lying. Lily's throat constricted and silver waves of heat undulated across her vision. "Of course it's my land. Papa left a deed. Surely you found that while you snooped through my private records."

He walked to his car and returned with a folder of papers. "Property deeds are public records, Miss Archer. And according to the records..." He sidled next to her, opened the folder, and underlined with his finger a portion that revealed two signatures. "As you can see, the sole owners of this property are Paul Wilbur Archer and Ruth Marlene Archer. Your parents, I presume."

She nodded, her teeth clamped so tight she couldn't get a word past them.

"I understand your father is no longer living. That leaves your mother as the only person with any right to contest the sale of this property. Should she choose to contest, it would go to court and inevitably end with a verdict against her. Since the property in question will be used for public use, it can be claimed by eminent domain."

She crossed her arms across her stomach to keep it from erupting.

So, he knew Papa was dead. Was he also aware that Mama didn't know her own daughter, nor had carried on any meaningful conversation for longer than Lily wanted to remember? "But can't you…you don't understand. I promised my papa." *Why would Papa ask me to promise if he didn't have everything in order? Did Mama know?* "This place…this land is all…eight years! Eight long years I've worked and scrimped and worked some more to keep my promise. Why? Why didn't I know this? No one ever told me. I pay taxes. I do my best to pay the bank. You can't—" *They can't do this. Can they?* She had to find a way to stop them. First, she must find a way to stop the babbling panic that threatened to squeeze every last breath from her.

"Anderson is a small town. Until the drought, I doubt anyone foresaw the need to accumulate surrounding land so the city would not run out of water. Your name is not on the deed, Miss Archer. However, I assure you your mother will be given a fair price for everything."

His gaze met hers and held a plea for understanding, though she found the intense blueness of his eyes unsettling. Other than her high school sweetheart, she'd never wasted time looking into the eyes of a man, and she had no desire whatsoever to be taken in by the likes of Joe Kendall.

"Fair price, Mr. Kendall? Tell me, who determines what is fair? You? The city of Anderson and its reigning council? How do you put a price on…on all that someone else has ever known their entire life?"

His gaze held steady. "We have appraisers who determine the value." He ran his hand through his hair. "But to answer one of your questions—I don't know how anyone can put a price on another man's legacy. I can tell you this, however. I believe your neighbors will attest to the fairness of the purchase price for their properties."

"And there's that word again. Fair." She shook her head. "*Fair* in these parts is not an adjective. It's a place and a time…an event. *Fair* is where I take my pies to be judged. *Fair* is the one time of year when we can forget the dust storms and the drought. It's where we can still greet one another with a smile and *ooh* and *ahh* over what few vegetables we've managed to eke out of our rock-hard gardens and exclaim over Mrs. Rathborn's latest quilt."

Her cheeks puffed with a long, exhaled breath. She had his attention but couldn't bring herself to voice the real reason *fair* had so much meaning. How did you tell a complete stranger, a man, no less, that the best part of her kind of fair meant a bubble bath, hair washed and styled, and wearing her best dress? The one time every year that she felt like a woman again…down to a puff of powder on her nose, a swish of color on her lips, and a dab of perfume on her wrists. That special evening when even her neighbors seemed to forget she was the farmer next door and allowed her to be Miss Lillian Ruth Archer. That time when she could stroll through the booths and strings of colored lights and remember what it was like to have a beau, be told she was beautiful, and sneak a kiss behind the bleachers of the sale ring and not care who watched. Neither would she divulge how long it had been since she was told she was beautiful…nor that the kiss was nothing more than a bittersweet memory.

"I'll not sell, Mr. Kendall. Now, if you'll excuse us—" She grabbed Mama's hand. "Come, Mama. Let's go home."

She took a step, but Mama pulled against her. Mama *never* refused to walk back to the house after she had the mail in hand. Why now?

Lily pulled again but was once again refrained from taking a step. She swiped the back of her hand across her forehead. "Mama, it's too hot for you to stand out here. Please, let's go home."

Mama smiled at the man standing in front of them and reached for his hand. "Are you ready to go home, Bruce?"

Lily's shoulders sagged. This was not something she would ever have predicted. But what was she to do? Mama couldn't stay out in the heat, and she obviously wasn't going to take a step without *Bruce.*

She raised her eyes to meet Joe Kendall's, expecting to find confusion, perhaps even repulsion. Instead, she was met by a gaze of compassion. "I'm sorry, she thinks you're my brother." Would he understand her plea?

Without hesitation, he gripped her mama's hand. "I'm ready to go home if you are…Mama." He took a step and Lily breathed a sigh of relief when Mama matched his stride. He turned back once and nodded at Lily, then he and Mama walked hand in hand down the lane as though it were an everyday occurrence.

Lily swallowed past an unexpected lump in her throat. She'd not allowed tears since she told Neal Murphy she couldn't marry him because of the promise she'd made to her papa. Why now? Was it learning she had no rightful ownership of the farm? Was it fear of losing everything she'd worked so hard to keep? Or was it because the terrible weight of Mama's illness was lifted just enough to punch a small hole in the dam that held back a pool of tears eight years deep? Joe Kendall, with all the anger he elicited in her, understood…understood her plea for help…and, most of all, understood Mama's need to have Bruce home again.

If only his eyes weren't so blue, or his jaw so square. And if he ran his hand through that thick head of coal black hair one more time, she'd be tempted to smack him.

MRS. ARCHER GRIPPED Joe's hand as if she never wanted to let go. She thought he was her son, and he knew better than to try to persuade her otherwise. There wasn't time to explain to Miss Archer why he could readily take her mama's hand. Perhaps one day he would have the opportunity to clarify his action. For now, he wanted to alleviate any further angst between him and feisty Lillian Archer. Perhaps knowing her mama's behavior didn't embarrass nor repulse him would help. And the bottom line—chances were great that tomorrow Mrs. Archer would no longer recognize him as Bruce.

The lane was dusty and long, and the heat stifling. By the time they reached the house at the slow pace set by the older woman, perspiration rolled down Joe's spine. He hated the thought of looking as though he had a stripe down his back—proof he was the skunk Miss Archer obviously thought him to be—but he should have known better than to wear a khaki shirt.

The two-story home, situated on the west side of the lane, was in need of paint, and the shutter on one upstairs window hung sideways. The yard was well-kept, though the sparse grass brown and brittle. A wire fence surrounded the yard, and stones of various sizes made a makeshift walkway from the gate to a wide roof-covered porch that wrapped around the east and north sides of the house. A white kitchen chair, its paint peeling and rungs held tight by wire, sat beside what he presumed to be the kitchen door. Pipe, rusted with age but smooth from use, made handrails on either side of the wide steps leading up to the porch. What remained of a flower garden, dried stems standing erect like wooden soldiers, stretched on either side of the steps along the porch. One climbing rosebush wound its branches around a corner column and poked red heads through still-green leafy foliage. A sign of hope, perhaps, or a need for beauty.

Mrs. Archer stopped at the gate, and Joe hesitated. A large black-and-white dog lay in the dirt beside the steps. He knew enough about farm dogs that he didn't want to enter the yard until he knew if it would bite. It only took a minute to discern it was probably too lazy to make the effort. The animal raised its head, thumped its tail a couple of times against the dirt, and yawned.

"Dog won't hurt you. He's old and doesn't much care who comes and goes anymore." Lily Archer pushed through the gate ahead of them, then stood to one side while he followed her mama.

"Does he have a name?" He found farm dogs friendlier if he could call them by name.

Her eyes held a mischief that surprised him. "Dog. I call him Dog."

"What? Not Spot or Buddy?"

Her gaze held steady but didn't lose its tease. "Nope. Just Dog."

Ooh, those eyes. He stooped to scratch the animal behind its ears to keep from making a fool of himself for staring. "Then Dog it is."

The older woman pulled her hand from his, grabbed the pipe rail, climbed the steps, and sat on the white chair by the door. She smoothed her skirt and folded her hands atop the mail she'd laid on her lap.

Manners prevented him from addressing the purchase of the property again—at least not today. It would have to be done, but this wasn't the time. Should he turn around and leave? Should he tell Mrs. Archer goodbye? He turned to Miss Archer, who still stood by the gate, her arms folded across her chest. Was that an invitation to leave, or was she waiting to see what he would do next? He had no idea what he would or *should* do.

"Bruce? You better go milk."

The authority behind Mrs. Archer's voice startled Joe, and he didn't miss the flinch of the girl's shoulders. It answered his question as to what he should do next, but it also brought to surface many others.

"Mama, I'll do the milking. Bruce has to...Bruce has to go—" Miss Archer's voice shook.

The older woman jutted her chin. "Girl, you fix Bruce some supper. He'll be hungry after he chores."

Even across the distance that separated them, Joe detected both pain and panic in Miss Archer's eyes. Mrs. Archer had called her *girl*. He knew all too well the hurt of not being recognized. He stepped closer to the younger woman. "Look, I know this is awkward for you, but please believe me when I say I don't want you to be embarrassed. Tell me what to do, and I'll do it without further question. I've milked plenty a cow, so you needn't worry."

Her shoulders drooped, whether in relief or despair he couldn't ascertain. "Only one cow, and she's probably put herself in the barn.

Throw some hay in the stall and she'll stand for you. The bucket is on the wall. Bring it to the house when you're through and I'll take care of it." She rubbed one arm. "I'm sorry. Mama misses him. Once she gets something in her head it's hard to—"

He waved his hand, though he wanted to smooth the wrinkles in her forehead. "You don't need to explain. Is there anything else I can do while I'm here? I was raised on a farm. I know what to do if you'll tell me."

She shrugged and gave a weak smile. "There's a cat in the barn that'll expect you to squirt some milk its direction. I keep it for a mouser, but she's spoiled."

He laughed. "A well-fed cat makes a better mouser, I hear. Please, you go tend to your mama and don't worry about me."

Her shoulders heaved with a deep breath. "I can't pay you, but the least I can do is feed you supper. That is, if you don't need to get back to town right away."

What started out as a disastrous first meeting had fast become one for the books. Miss Archer was as feisty and hardnosed as the city fathers had warned. But she was also beautiful, did not fit the *angry old maid* description in the least, and, he'd have to agree, *it was a plumb shame she hadn't met a good man after all these years.*

"I can't think of any better pay than a good home-cooked meal. I accept your invitation, Miss Archer."

"It will be ready when you get done milking. And you needn't knock. Just come on in when you're done." She ducked her head. "Thank you…for everything. And…and you may call me Lily."

Did she have any idea how much her slow smile lit her face? And who would believe him if he admitted Miss Lily Archer's smile awakened a desire he'd chosen to ignore for a long, long time?

Three

S UPPER WAS SIMPLE and awkward. Simple because all Lily had to fix without killing the fatted hen, which she needed for her egg supply, was potatoes and eggs, although she did have enough flour and lard to bake a fresh batch of biscuits. Awkward because Mama kept calling Joe Kendall *Bruce* and more awkward because the man didn't seem to notice, or mind. He'd dished a portion of the potatoes and eggs onto Mama's plate, spread the jam for her biscuit as though it were an everyday occurrence, and later led Mama to her favorite overstuffed chair as she requested.

Now here she was, Lily Archer doing dishes by herself, again, listening to the bits and pieces of conversation that drifted from the living room. Kendall sat on the piano stool while Mama, the same Mama who'd stopped conversing ever so long ago, rambled about her garden club, which she'd not attended for the past three years. He *ooh*ed and *aah*ed over the description of her once-prized irises and asked about the rosebush twining around the porch column outside the kitchen.

Mama giggled like a schoolgirl. "Silly Bruce. Don't you

remember when you and that girl planted it for me?"

That girl. That girl was Lillian Ruth. That girl was the one who'd stayed, the one who gave up a husband, a home, and a family to keep the promise made to her papa. Lily Archer, that girl who had not paid the mortgage on the farm for two years and would again have to throw herself on the mercy of Ed Murphy, a mercy he'd warned her could only last for so long.

Lily braced her hands on the cupboard and bowed her head. How many times had she prayed, begged, railed for God to do something...anything? And His answer? No rain. No crops. No money growing on trees and certainly none in the bank. Now, sitting in the next room was a man who'd given her a way to pay the mortgage, but it came with a price higher than what she owed. What if she took the offer? Then what? She'd have no home. Mama would still be sick. All she knew, all she'd ever known, was this farm. And she—

"Excuse me, Miss...uh...Lily."

Lily startled and one hand slipped back into the dishpan. She quickly withdrew it and wiped it on her apron. *Her apron.* The same bibbed apparel she'd forgotten to remove before sitting down for supper across from Joe Kendall. What must he think? She'd never baked anything without dusting her apron, the floor, and any work surface with flour. Well, so be it. She turned to face him, only to find her papa's Bible in one hand and Mama's hand firmly entwined with the other.

He handed her the Bible. "I...it was under the piano stool. I'm not sure I put the envelope back in the proper spot."

Lily shrugged. "That's all right. Thank you." She took the Bible and laid it on the counter. "Papa used the envelope as a marker. I don't think it had a special place." She didn't want to admit that since her papa died, she'd not opened the only book she'd ever seen him read. She had no idea where he had it marked or what was in the envelope—most likely old unpaid bills. Nor did she want to confess how the Bible got under the piano stool in the first place.

His eyes crinkled with a smile. "My Aunt Hazel gave me a crocheted cross years ago. I use that to mark my place in my Bible. Not at all manly, I suppose, but it reminds me of what Christ did for me…and also the care and love I received from my aunt."

She didn't really care to carry on a conversation with this man, especially one about the Bible. And if he quoted how *all things work together for good,* she'd scream.

"I'm rambling. I'm sorry." He swiped his hand through his hair. "I do thank you for supper, though. It's the first home-cooked meal I've had for quite a spell." He rolled his lips and took a deep breath. "I'm afraid I really must get back to town. I have…well, I have reports to write and tomorrow is—" He patted Mama's hand.

She understood his unspoken plea for help. How was he to leave with Mama clinging to him like buttons on a shirt? For a mere second, Lily was tempted to feign ignorance in hope he'd experience the same backed-into-a-corner sensation she'd had since reading the newspaper headline earlier, but the genuine concern she detected in his gaze was enough to weaken her revenge. Though she despised the reason he was in her kitchen, it wasn't his fault Mama thought he was Bruce.

Lily stepped to Mama and took her free hand. "Mama, Bruce has to leave now. He has business in town."

Mama nodded and pulled her hand from Lily. "Yes. Yes. Untie my apron, girl. We have to leave now." She smiled at Lily. "We have business."

Lily's shoulders tightened. Visitors to their home were rare and Mama's behavior much more predictable under normal circumstances. From experience, she knew that arguing with her would only provoke a matter. But how was she to free Mama's grip without a scene?

As if he could read her mind, Kendall put one finger over his lips, then turned his attention to her mama. "I have to leave now but I'll be back tomorrow…Mama."

Mama patted Kendall's hand. "You're such a good boy, Bruce." She released her grip and backed away from him. "I think I'll go to bed now, girl."

While the thought of facing him again shot dread through Lily's heart, it seemed to soothe Mama's need to accompany the man into town. One thing was certain. Joe Kendall had wormed his way into Mama's mind in a way that Lily had not mastered in the past three years.

Lily locked her gaze on Joe and tried hard not to let his blue eyes distract her. "You do know this doesn't change my mind about selling the farm, don't you?" The slight flush across his cheeks gave her more satisfaction than a good conscience should allow.

Though a wrinkle slithered across his forehead, his gaze didn't waver. "Perhaps when you get to know me better, you'll understand that every interaction I've had with your mother today has come from a heart of understanding and willingness to help."

"But your job requires—"

Joe gave a curt nod. "Yes, I do have a job to do, and like it or not that job includes purchasing land for a lake which will provide water for the city. However, I have not today, nor would I ever, use another person's unfortunate circumstances to force them to make such a hard decision."

He walked to the kitchen door, then stopped and turned to face Lily again. "I will return tomorrow because I promised your mother I would. Please believe me when I say I will be most disappointed if you don't continue to fight for all this farm means to you, though it won't change the inevitable. I understand you see me as the enemy, but for now my presence seems to give your mama a small bit of hope. We all need hope, don't we?" A soft click of the door signaled his departure.

She could remember only one time she'd been sent to the principal's office, but this would go into her memory bank as the second, and she was no less humiliated. If only he'd raised his voice or slammed the screen door shut behind him. Maybe then she could justify the…the…she couldn't put a name to the tangle of emotions that had her insides tied in knots. Anger that Joe Kendall thought he could waltz onto her property and prove the last eight years were for naught. Fear of what the future might hold for her and Mama. Relief he'd not found Mama's lapses in memory repulsive and had readily gone along with her belief that he was Bruce. And—

No. There was no *and*. No matter how gentle and soft-spoken he was with Mama. No matter if his mere presence gave Mama hope. No matter if his eyes were as blue as a Kansas sky or that she had to look up…way up…to see them. So what if his rolled-up sleeves revealed tan, muscular arms, or—

She rubbed the back of her neck, partly to get rid of the stiffness and partly in an attempt to erase the vain imaginations she'd allowed. "Come on, Mama." She forced a smile and reached for the older woman's hand. "It's time for bed. Bruce will be back tomorrow."

He'll be back, but he won't find us home. Somehow she had to come up with a plan to save her farm, and the only logical place to start was with Ed Murphy at the bank.

JOE STOPPED AT the gate and turned back to peer at the house. He'd not meant for his words to sound so harsh. He'd spoken the truth—everyone needed hope during this time of drought and uncertainty—but he'd made it sound as if Lily were somehow remiss to offer that prospect to her mama.

How could the day have gone so awry? This morning, while still lying in bed, it seemed so simple. Well, as simple as telling someone they really didn't own the land they'd occupied for their entire life. From the description he'd received, he'd believed Lily Archer to be a middle-aged spinster who would be more than happy to get a fair price for land that surely had become a burden to maintain what with no income to speak of because of the drought. While neighboring farmers had voiced regret to leave a lifestyle so familiar, most were more than happy to have money in the bank again.

He clenched his jaw and rubbed his hands across his face. Had he known, or even suspected, that the one piece of land deemed an absolute necessity would constitute such a conflict of emotions, he'd have insisted someone else do the bargaining. A low chuckle worked its way to his lips. Who was he kidding? He'd applied for the job as foreman with bravado, declaring he could talk an auctioneer out of words if it meant money in the man's pocket. While it was good for a chuckle and a job then, it was no longer a laughing matter. He'd stopped smiling over his successes after watching hands calloused and gnarled from years of hard work and sacrifice shake as they penned their names to papers that would essentially bury evidence of their toils under tons of water. How ironic that what would provide life to some would deny a way of life for others.

The rattle of dried cornstalks accompanied Joe's trek back to his car, proof there was air somewhere but not enough to cool the night. His shirt clung to his back and he probably smelled like something from the *Three Billy Goats Gruff*. The image of Lily Archer's pink face as she wiped her hands on her apron skirted across his mind. It was more than knowing he'd embarrassed her. It was seeing her broken fingernails and her hands red and calloused. The fact there were cornstalks standing, though dry and unyielding, gave testament to the woman's hard work. It was observing the shutter that needed repositioning and secured, the bony haunches of the milk cow, the brittle hay left to throw into the cow's stall, the less than half a bucket of milk he carried to the house. And it was sitting in a home lit only by kerosene lamps, sharing food that undoubtedly would have lasted several days had he not accepted the offer of a home-cooked meal.

He leaned against the vehicle's radiator, still warm from the day's heat, and crossed his arms. He'd forgotten how dark nighttime could be in the country, yet how far one could see when their eyes became accustomed to the lack of light. Once her mother was in bed, would Lily extinguish the wicks in the lamps and mull over the day's events? Or was she one of only a handful of women he knew brave enough to wander past the security of four walls to sit and allow the cover of darkness soothe troubled hearts and minds? If he were a gambling man, he'd put his money on her basking in the quiet of the night, her back against the side of the house and her knees drawn to her chest. If only he'd waited to see. If only he wasn't the one who'd added yet one more burden to her otherwise petite shoulders.

He pushed away from the car. He couldn't stop the lake project, but there had to be something he could do to ensure Lily would get top dollar for the farm even though her name was not on the deed. First thing in the morning, he'd visit Ed Murphy at the bank. Though he was rather haughty in appearance, he'd found Murphy to be fair and sympathetic toward the plight of those whose way of life was being relegated to dollars and cents. Surely he could appeal to his good judgment to find a way through the legal aspects of this rather difficult situation.

A sigh of relief escaped his pursed lips as he slid onto the seat. Now, if only he'd be able to sleep without seeing the pain that seemed permanently etched across Lily Archer's countenance—a vision that included eyes of brown velvet and lips he had no business contemplating.

Four

THE INCESSANT HUM of the ceiling fans in the bank pulsed through Joe's head as he breathed to the rhythm… *saWISH…saWISH…saWISH*. Had he never noticed, or was he particularly bothered by the apparent lack of balance the noise represented? At this rate, he'd hyperventilate before getting an audience with the banker. Truth was, he'd never had to wait to have an audience with Ed Murphy before today. While he couldn't put a name to it, there was a definite change of atmosphere in the stuffy, small-town bank lobby this morning. Even Miss Bower, Murphy's personal secretary, seemed harried and pink-cheeked when he asked to see Mr. Murphy. Was she wearing her hair in a different style, or was that one more fact he apparently had never taken the time to observe?

He yawned and gave his shoulders a shake. Between plotting today's meeting with Murphy and Lily Archer prancing through his vision every time he shut his eyes, sleep had eluded him. Now, however, with the heat and the eerie stillness of the lobby, the constant drone of the fan was fast becoming a lullaby and the only thing keeping his eyes open was—

"Excuse me, Mr. Kendall. Mr. Murphy will see you now."

Joe jumped at the secretary's voice. He obviously had not kept his eyes open. He nodded and swiped his hand across his mouth. "Was I sleeping?"

She smiled and leaned so close he could see a dark ring of blue around her even bluer eyes and catch a whiff of something sweet. "I think so, but if anyone asks, I'll say you were praying."

Until this minute, he'd never really thought of the woman as anything but Ed Murphy's personal secretary. But now—well. Miss Bower was suddenly a very attractive young lady and she had indeed done something different with her hair. Held by two combs on the side, honey-colored curls fell loosely to her shoulders.

"You're staring, Mr. Kendall, and Mr. Murphy is waiting for you." An impish smile greeted his gaze. Was she flirting? Were her pink cheeks because he'd been staring, or a reflection of the heat of his face? And why did the image of Lily Archer wiping her hands on her flour-dusted apron decide at this moment to haunt him?

Miss Bower crooked her finger and batted her eyelashes. "Follow me, please. Oh, and you may call me Florence, although I answer to Flo to my *really* good friends."

Florence Bower's tailored suit could no more hide the curves it held than—he flexed his hands at his side—Lily Archer's faded and patched overalls. And since when had Murphy's secretary taken to accompanying the clients to the banker's office? A nod of the head had sufficed in the past.

They reached Murphy's office and Miss Bower gave another flutter of her eyelids before rapping on the frame of the open door. "Mr. Kendall is here, Mr. Murphy." She stepped to one side while Joe sidled past her and came face-to-face with the obvious reason for her pink cheeks.

"Thank you, Miss Bower." A tall, tanned, much-younger-than-Ed-Murphy man with wavy reddish-brown hair pushed away from his desk and stepped forward. His green eyes reminded Joe of a cat, and a tingle of caution scrambled up his back. He had no reason to suspect this person of anything, but years of being in charge of men on the job had given him a good deal of practice when it came to his ability to judge a man's character. This guy had *be careful* written all over him.

The man's ring-studded hand gripped Joe's...hard. "I'm Neal Murphy. My father is taking a much-needed step away from the bank, but I can assure you, your banking needs will be met with the same efficacy." He motioned to the chair across from the desk. "Please, have a seat and tell me how I might be of service of you today. Oh," he turned to the secretary, "perhaps you could bring us some coffee, Flo?"

Evidently Neal Murphy was considered to be a *really* good friend of Miss Bower.

She curtsied. "Of course. I'll just be a minute. Your father apprised me that you prefer a dollop of sweet cream, Mr. Murphy, but how do you take yours, Mr. Kendall?"

While he preferred cream in his also, what Joe needed most this morning was something very strong and very black. His head swam with trying to figure out what was going on, and Florence Bower and Lily Archer were swirling like waters in a whirlpool through his burning, sleep-deprived vision. "Black will be fine, Miss Bower." Any other time he'd consider it rude not to look at a person when he replied, but this was not a normal occasion.

Neal Murphy settled back into his chair and tented his fingers. "So, you're Joe Kendall. I must say I expected a much older man. I understand, by talking with my father, that you're the person responsible for making every farmer along Willow Creek homeless. The foreman, no less."

Caution speared through Joe's chest. While the assessment of his title was correct, Murphy's saying it aloud made it seem something reminiscent of rich bully versus poor boy on the playground. A memory he didn't care to revisit. "I've found the landowners all very cooperative, especially since this project is wiping away years of their way of life."

Murphy waved his hand. "Yes, yes. I know all about their way of life. I also know it has robbed some of what might have been a very fortuitous future had it not been for deathbed promises to keep the sacred farm." He wiped his brow. "Sorry. I grew up here, you know. I'm not without compassion for these folks. It's just that—" He looked up from the desk and motioned toward the door. "Come in, Flo, and thank you for your promptness."

She ran her tongue across her lips, then gave an adoring smile. "I baked muffins this morning. I hope you don't mind that I brought some to the office." She set a tray that held the steaming cups of coffee, a silver carafe, and a small basket of muffins on the desk. "Oh, you should know that Lillian Archer is waiting to see you. And her mother is with her."

Why was there a hint of sarcasm in her voice? Could it be jealousy? Joe tucked that question away. Time would provide the answer.

"Lil…Miss Archer is…is here? Did she have an appointment? She's…she's in the lobby? Now? With Ruth?" Murphy's hand holding the basket of muffins shook so hard he set the basket back onto the tray.

It was obvious by the wrinkle on her forehead and her lips drawn bowstring-tight that Murphy's shaky hand and nervous questioning did not elude Florence Bower's observation. "She doesn't usually have an appointment. I've told your father over and over again she shouldn't just show up and expect to be seen, especially with her mother being like she is. She brought the usual pint of fresh cream and a dozen eggs. Shall I have her make a later appointment?"

Murphy ran his fingers across his forehead and left a wrinkle in their wake. "Her mother being like what? You say she brought cream and eggs? Why? Wait. No, no. It's fine. Please assure her I'll be with her as soon as I finish with Mr. Kendall." He shooed her away with a flick of his wrist.

Joe stood and extended his hand to the banker. "Look, I'll come back another time. I hate to keep a lady waiting." He especially hated to keep Lily waiting. He knew from experience that her mother's actions could be unpredictable and having to wait in a hot lobby would not help.

"What?" Murphy ran his hand around his collar. "Yes. Of course. Let's say, perhaps, first thing in the morning?" He stood and shook Joe's hand. "I'll make sure Flo clears my schedule. I'm sorry. I…I had no idea—"

"First thing in the morning is fine. I'm afraid I'm also guilty of dropping in without an appointment. In the future, I'll make sure I schedule a time to discuss problems as they arise."

Murphy thrust his hands into pockets. "I've spent most of my banking career in Kansas City. I'd forgotten how impromptu a small town can be. I'm hoping I can maintain the same level of community that my father endeared while at the same time implementing a few more boundaries. Thank you for understanding, Kendall."

Joe let himself out of the office, leaving behind an obviously flustered banker. If he could only make it past Florence Bower and Lily Archer without the same level of frustration. To his surprise, the lobby was empty, and the secretary seemed too busy to acknowledge his presence. "I thought there was a client waiting for Mr. Murphy."

Florence gave a dismissive swipe of her hand across the desk. "There was, but she left when I told her you were with Mr. Murphy and gave her Ne…Mr. Murphy's message. Her mother obviously couldn't sit still long enough to wait until he was ready for them."

The hair on the back of Joe's neck bristled. Why did Miss Bower feel it necessary to tell Lily that he was with the banker? Did the younger Murphy's *new boundaries* include announcing who was in the banker's private office? Knowing he had an audience with the banker might well have prompted Lily Archer to leave. "Did you happen to see which direction they went?"

35

The secretary laid her pencil on the desk and crossed her arms. "No, I didn't see which direction they went. I don't keep track of customers once they leave this building."

"In the future, Miss Bower, you will refrain from divulging such matters as to whom is in my office. I expect you to make *all* our clients feel welcome and comfortable while they wait."

They both jumped at Neal Murphy's gruff voice, and there were immediate tears in Miss Bower's eyes. At least that answered his previous question.

Murphy shouldered past Joe, opened the door, and stepped out onto the sidewalk, then took off running. He must have spied Lily.

With no idea how to soften the tense atmosphere that now permeated the lobby, Joe followed him out the door. Though he had a good idea why Lily Archer was at the bank, he was curious as to why it seemed to put young Murphy into such a dither. Was there more than a casual history between the two? And if so, why should that question cause him to feel as though he'd been kicked in the pit of his stomach?

Did she leave because she knew he was in Murphy's office or because her mother got restless? He gave his shoulders a shake to relieve the tension and hopefully remove Lily Archer's image from rendering him weak in the knees. He'd worked too long and too hard paying his way through engineering school to allow himself to get snared by a pretty face, no matter how dire the circumstance.

Thankful the sidewalks were void of pedestrians, Joe shoved his hands into the pockets of his britches and shuffled across the street to the drugstore. He had to admit it was much more than a pretty face. It was work-worn hands and broken fingernails swiping across a flour-dusted apron. It was fried potatoes and eggs shared when the cupboards were more than likely bare. It was the rattle of dried cornstalks. And, truth be known, it was being called Bruce.

Joe took a long, deep draught of air. He'd promised Mrs. Archer he'd visit her again today. He doubted she'd remember, but Lily would, and he intended to keep his word. If he was lucky, the apothecary would be as empty of customers as the city street. And if he was even luckier, the hometown druggist would have something to ensure he would have a full night's sleep tonight.

NEAL SHUFFLED HIS way back to the bank, aware that other business owners—what businesses were still open for business—were peering at him through their storefront windows. No doubt a banker running down the street waving his arms and yelling *Liillyybuug* like a madman was not a normal sight for the small town of Anderson. He didn't much care. What he did care about was why Lily left without being seen. Why did Florence deem it necessary to mention Ruth Archer was with her daughter? His first day at his father's desk and he had more questions than he'd ever had while in Kansas City. Maybe because here they were personal…too personal.

He stopped at the door and took a deep breath. The last thing he wanted to do was return to his office and wait for Florence to usher in the next client. In fact, if he had his way, he'd get in his car and go directly to the Archer farm. This wasn't at all the way he wanted to let Lily know of his return to Anderson. Had he known she'd be in town this morning, he would've arranged a private meeting, a surprise, followed by a romantic candlelight dinner—

And where would you have taken her for this romantic dinner? You're no longer in Kansas City. This is Anderson. The only place open in this town past six o'clock is Ernie's gas station. She'd be quite impressed with a bottle of orange soda and a bag of peanuts.

As frustrated as he was at not finding Lily, he couldn't help the smile that pushed against his cheeks. That bottle of orange pop and its accompanying bag of peanuts was exactly what he would take her as soon as the bank closed. How could she deny the memories that combination should revive?

And what will you do about your daughter? Leave her with your parents again? Take her with you? You can't leave town without some kind of explanation. Running after Lily Archer might not be the light you want to shine yet.

Neal ran his tongue across his teeth. He'd address that later. First, he needed to tell Florence he would not be working late this evening. He'd spend the rest of the day going over Lily's bank records. There must have been some reason she was waiting to be seen. Could it be that her farm was one threatened to be swallowed by the new city lake? Would that be so bad? Maybe, just maybe, that would convince her to reconsider a proposal he was ready to extend once more.

LILY STOPPED AT the house long enough to get a jug of water and a blanket. It was too early to eat lunch, but she grabbed the one banana left from last week's grocery purchase, the only luxury she allowed in the meager budget and wouldn't have indulged in if it weren't for Mama. Thank goodness she'd bought them greener than usual so it was still firm enough for Mama to clutch. Now, if only that one yellow piece of fruit would satisfy her long enough to give Lily a few minutes of respite. In retrospect, she should have waited for Joe Kendall to emerge from Murphy's office. At least then she could have told him he needn't keep his promise to return today…hope or no hope.

Her eyes burned from the lack of sleep last night and her crying jag all the way home from the bank this morning. Hot wind, dust, and tears were not a good combination for a lady's complexion. Unless, of course, one could afford a fancy spa where rich women paid top dollar for a mud bath, guaranteed, they advertised, to draw out all impurities from stressed bodies and leave them baby's-bottom soft and smooth.

Not exactly the description she would want to be remembered by, but she was not rich, and few would attest to her being a lady.

It was still hot, but the overhanging branches of the willow beside her favorite spot along Willow Creek—the place Papa dubbed Lily's Pond—would provide a shady spot. It wasn't anywhere near a pond, but rather a small bend in the creek where the water pooled. But it was the one and only place on their entire forty acres Lily could be herself to think, cry, or dream. Today would be given to thinking. There had to be a way she could keep the farm, keep Mama in familiar surroundings, not lose what she'd fought so long and hard to keep. Besides, she'd already had her quota of tears for quite a long time, and her dreams had long ago turned to nightmares.

Thankful Mama had not balked at walking to the creek, Lily spread the quilt under the willow tree and sank to its softness. She clutched the hem of Mama's dress and pulled her down beside her. Though determined to keep one eye open, the tug on the fabric should be enough to alert her if the dear soul decided to wander away. How long had it been since she'd been able to close her eyes and not worry about Mama, the crops, the bills? Where was Bruce? Was he well? Would he ever return? And if he did come home, would he stay and help with Mama? She wouldn't ask him to help with the farm, but, oh, it would be so nice to have some relief from the constant worry of…life.

An even bigger concern—would Joe Kendall keep his promise to return today? And if so, would he tell her what he and Ed Murphy talked about? To be sure, their conversation centered around the poor Miss Archer and her lack of funds. But then what?

Oh, Papa. I'm so angry with you right now. Why didn't you make sure everything was in order before you left me here alone? What would you do about Mama if you were here? What's going to happen to us, Papa?

Five

THE AROMA OF bacon, fresh-baked cinnamon rolls, and brewing coffee pleasantly assaulted Joe's senses as he entered Milly's Diner, a reminder he'd skipped breakfast. He nodded at the few locals seated around a long table as he made his way to the counter. Some returned the gesture with a smile, most did not. He understood. For now, he was either the savior or the enemy, depending on what side of the city limits you called home.

"Well, you're either late for breakfast or early for lunch, Joe Kendall." The middle-aged proprietress smiled, pulled a pencil from her bleached blonde hair, and leaned across the counter, order pad in hand. "What can I get ya?"

He'd formulated a plan between the drugstore and the diner but wasn't sure how to pull it off without raising suspicion. "What do you have that would travel well? I'll be out most of the afternoon and I'm already hungry." He pulled a menu from between the salt and pepper shakers.

"You won't find nothin' lookin' in there, darlin'." She took the menu from him and stuck it back where he'd found it. "As hot as it is out there, I wouldn't recommend anything but a bread-and-butter-with-a-slice-of-cheese sandwich on my special oatmeal bread." She straightened and winked at him. "One won't do a man your size, though. How many ya think ya can hold in that—" She waved her hand up and down. "That there big ole handsome body of yours?"

He laughed and folded his hands atop of the counter. "Oh, I don't know, Milly. Let's say three." That would be one apiece for him, Lily, and her mother, but he had to be careful it wouldn't look as if he were bringing charity to the Archer household. He had an inkling that Lily wouldn't take a bite of anything, even if she were starving, if she thought for one minute that it was given out of pity. "Oh, I'll also take three slices of whatever kind of pie you have today."

She cocked her head. "Coconut cream, but that'll spoil quicker than ya can say howdy-doody. I do have some cinnamon rolls left, though. Would that do?"

"That'll do fine. I think you make the best cinnamon rolls of any restaurant in town."

She slapped the air between them. "Smart aleck. I'm the *only* restaurant in town and you know it. You want coffee while I make your sandwiches?"

He shrugged. "Is it free?"

She leaned across the counter again. "One cup, no refills. And if you breathe a word about it being free, I'll pour it in your lap. By the way…you have any luck buying the Archer place?"

He frowned and gave a quick glance at the table of locals. "You know I can't divulge that information, Milly. We've discussed this before."

She plunked a coffee cup on the counter in front of him. "Now, don't get your britches in a wad. I'm saying if you're havin' trouble, you might wanna let Neal Murphy help ya out. You'll meet him if you go to the bank. I heard he was here to take over for his father."

"I did meet him, and I have an appointment with him in the morning. Is there some reason you think he might be able persuade

Miss Archer to sell better than I can?"

She rolled her eyes. "You take a good look at him? Could you say no to a specimen like that?"

Joe laughed. "Well, he's not exactly my type."

Milly winked and shook her head. "No, I don't suppose he is. They were sweethearts, you know…Neal and Lily." She reached behind her for the coffeepot, then turned back. "Don't know where you were comin' from when you came through the door, but you missed quite a spectacle. Young Mr. Murphy ran down the street hollering for Lily like they were still in high school." She poured the coffee and set the pot back on the burner.

So that was the reason for the banker's shaky hands at the mere mention of her name. "Did he find her?" There was that punch to the stomach again. He took a sip of coffee, then made a face at Milly. "This stuff is as bitter as an old maid and about as cold, too. Good thing it's free." Anything to change the subject. He really didn't want to hear about Lily's past romances, especially with Neal Murphy. He couldn't put his finger on why the man caused him to doubt his character, but nevertheless, doubt it he did.

Milly crossed her arms across her chest and looked over the rim of her glasses. "Anybody ever teach you it was rude to complain about the food? You sit there and sulk while I make your sandwiches." She gave an exaggerated sway of her hips as she went to the kitchen.

He took another sip of the coffee and made a face. He liked Milly, but this stuff was awful.

JOE TUCKED THE paper sack of sandwiches and cinnamon rolls on the seat next to him. One last stop for gas, then he'd head for the Archer farm. Though the morning had not gone as planned, he was thankful he'd not discussed the reason for his visit to the bank with

Neal Murphy. He had no intention of mentioning the younger Murphy to Lily, nor was he going to approach the purchase of the land again. Today's visit was merely to fulfill the promise he made to Mrs. Archer.

Keep telling yourself that lie long enough, Kendall, and maybe you'll finally believe it. If Lily were named Lyle, you'd waste no time in pushing for a sale…ill mother or not.

It was pathetic that the voice in his head knew him better than he knew himself. If only he could stuff a rag in it.

The gas station was void of customers when Joe pulled in. With his dilapidated green chair tipped on its back two legs, Ernie leaned against the side of the station under the overhang, swigging on a bottle of orange soda. "Ya here for gas or is ya needin' directions to another farm around Willow Creek?"

Joe stepped out of the car and smiled at the older man. He liked Ernie. "Gas for sure, then I was hoping you could give me some information. Fill it up, Ernie, and I think I'll take three bottles of that orange soda if you can spare them."

"I'll pump the gas, you can help yourself to the sodies. Three of them you say?" He gave a low whistle. "You're drinkin' heavy today, Kendall. Now, what kind of information is ya needin'?"

Unlike Milly, Ernie was about as close-mouthed as anyone Joe knew when it came to any kind of gossip, but would this question qualify? "Went to the bank this morning to talk with Ed Murphy."

"Ed weren't there, were he?" Ernie tipped his chair away from the building and stood. He pulled a bandana from the rear pocket of his greasy green coveralls and wrapped it around the bottle of soda and gave his one-leg-shorter-than-the-other shuffle to Joe's car.

"No. Met his son, though."

Ernie unscrewed the gas cap from Joe's car and lifted the hose from the pump. "And I reckon you're wantin' the lowdown on Neal Murphy. Well, I don't chinwag, ya know."

Joe leaned against the side of the car. "I do know that, Ernie, and I appreciate it. Just tell me this one thing…can I trust him?"

The older man chewed on his bottom lip and Joe counted the dings of the bell on the pump as it rang up the gallons. Had he asked what Ernie would consider gossip?

At last, Ernie removed the nozzle from the gas tank and hooked it back on the pump. He leaned close and wrote down a number on a piece of paper he dug from the pocket on his chest. Finally, he turned to Joe. "Now then, young fella. You pick up this here motor vehicle of yours and give it a toss. Then you pace off the distance. That's how far you can trust Neal Murphy. That's all I'm gonna say."

Joe pushed away from the car. "That's fair enough. You've answered my question. Now, how much do I owe you?" He pulled his wallet from his back pocket.

"You gonna get them bottles of sodie?"

Joe nodded.

Ernie checked the paper in his hand. "Well, ya got five gallons and it's twenty whole cents a gallon, plus a nickel apiece for the sodies." He shut his eyes and wrote in the air with his finger. "That'll be one dollar plus a dime and a nickel."

Joe pulled a dollar from his wallet and dug in his pocket for the change. "Thanks, Ernie. I'll get the sodas and go on my way."

"Yep." Ernie stuffed the money into his pocket, grabbed his rag-wrapped orange drink, and sat back onto his chair. "Gonna get hot as Grandma's fryin' pan. Sure could use some rain."

Joe laughed as he grabbed the sodas from the icebox in the station and hurried back to the car. In the few weeks he'd known Ernie, his parting words were always the same. But then, so was the weather…hot as Grandma's fryin' pan, and they could sure enough use some rain.

LILY FOLDED THE blanket over one arm, grabbed the jug of water, and wiggled the fingers of her free hand toward her mother. "Grab my fingers, Mama. Let's go get you some lunch."

Her mother gave a wan smile but at least she didn't balk leaving the shade. There was little in the cupboard to fix a quick lunch…some biscuits left from last night's supper and maple syrup she could drizzle over them. That would have to do.

They hadn't walked far when her mother tugged on her hand. "Bruce is coming, girl. See?" She pointed toward the barn. Coming toward them in the long strides she remembered was none other than Joe Kendall. What was he carrying, and how did he know where to find them? Did he make it a habit to wander around someone's property without first receiving permission?

He stopped a few feet in front of them and smiled at Mama. "I hope you don't mind. I brought lunch." He held a paper sack toward them.

A shiver shinnied across Lily's shoulders. "Why?"

"Uhh. Why what?"

Oh, those blue eyes. Even clouded with confusion they poked through her reserve. She couldn't let that happen. "Why did you bring us lunch? Do you always feed your prey? Fatten them for the kill?"

His eyes snapped, the blue becoming ever bluer. "Had you not been so quick to leave the bank this morning, I would have visited with you there. I promised your mother I would return today. You'll learn that I keep my word."

She straightened her shoulders. He'd not raised his voice, but his words stung. She deserved his rebuke, but could he understand her fear? "How did you know I was at the bank this morning?"

His gaze softened but didn't flinch. "Miss Bower announced your presence to Murphy. I'm also aware that she made it known to you that I was with the banker. What I don't understand is why you left."

"Do you have any idea how uncomfortable it is to know that two men who have the power to take from you everything that has ever meant anything are sitting in the same room discussing your fate?"

"First of all, Miss Archer, we weren't—"

"I left, Mr. Kendall, because I wasn't ready to see the satisfaction written across your face once you knew that even if I don't sell, I'll lose this farm. Have you ever suffered such a loss, Mr. Project Foreman?"

"Stop, girl." Mama pulled her hand from Lily's. "Don't yell at Bruce." She sidled next to Joe and hooked her arm through his.

Is this the game he wanted to play? Take advantage of Mama's muddled mind? Get Mama on his side by pretending to be her long-lost son? And how was it that after ever so long of not talking, she now babbled like a schoolgirl?

"I did not come here to talk about buying this farm, Miss Archer." He smiled down at her mama. "If it helps at all, the banker and I did not discuss even for one minute this farm or anything pertaining to it. Once his secretary announced that you were waiting, I suggested we postpone our meeting until another time so you wouldn't need to sit in the hot lobby."

Mama pulled at the sack Joe held.

"Are you hungry?" He unwound his arm from Mama and opened the paper bag. "Bread-butter-and-cheese sandwiches."

Lily stomped her foot and dust flew. "That's not fair. You know she thinks you're her son and you're taking advantage of it."

His head jerked and his eyes blazed. "And you, Miss Archer, prefer to see everyone as evil and thus miss out on something that might be enjoyable." He handed the sack to her mother. "There are three sandwiches in there, plus three cinnamon rolls. Three bottles of orange soda are wrapped in my shirt. I'm not asking for anything in return except the shirt." He lifted his arms as if to surrender. "You win." He turned and shuffled away from them, his head down and his arms limp at his sides. A few yards away, he turned back. "Just so you know, this is not at all how I wanted this day to end."

Lily groaned. If only he hadn't used the very phrase that Neal

Murphy uttered the night she refused his proposal of marriage. Would she come to regret this day as much as she regretted that night? Would she really miss out on something that might be enjoyable? Did she dare take the chance?

"Wait. Please. How did you want this day to end?" Could she bear to hear it?

His shoulders rose and then fell as he expelled a long, shuddering breath. "I simply wanted to prove to you that I am a man of my word. Nothing more. Nothing less."

"Then why the…the—" She pointed at the sack her mother held like it was her most prized possession. "After your meager supper last night, did you think we needed food but would be too proud to accept anything more than a sack lunch?" *Oh, Lily. Why such venom?*

In three giant strides, Joe closed the gap between them, his hands fisted at his side. "Oh, there's more. You see, I didn't sleep last night. You invaded every thought and, believe me, I fought it as hard as you're fighting me right now. Yes, I'm aware you shared food you could have saved for yourself and your sweet mama. I also saw the shutter that needs to be nailed back in place, and the house that could use a coat of paint. I saw the dry cornstalks and the brittle hay and the wilted flowers by the porch."

She tried to turn away, but the burning gaze of his blue eyes held her captive.

"But more than that, I saw you, Lily Archer, a beautiful young woman who has worked harder than most men to keep a promise few would have kept. I witnessed the panic written across every fiber of your body when you learned the deed on this farm was minus your name. I saw the fear in your eyes when you didn't know how I would react when your mama addressed me as Bruce. And I saw the relief you hoped I wouldn't see when I allowed her that memory."

"She doesn't…she thinks—"

He nodded. "I know. Believe me when I say I know all too well

47

how it feels to no longer be recognized for who you are, not even your name. Now, for the first time, in a long time—longer than I want to remember—I find myself caring for something, someone, more than myself. You can spout all the hurt and anger you've harbored over what you've constantly reminded me to be eight long years, but it won't change who continues to dance through my every thought or twists my heart into knots at the memory of her."

He stepped away, but his eyes seemed to burn through her. "I think it best if you go back to the bank tomorrow and plead your case with Murphy. I have a very good hunch that things will work in your best interest."

Lily closed her eyes against the pain she saw in his eyes, the slouch of his shoulders, and the dust that rose with each shuffle of his feet as he walked away without so much as a glance backwards. Why did it hurt so much?

JOE FELT AS pummeled as if he'd kicked his own behind all the way back into Anderson. Why, after only one meeting, did the likes of Lily Archer manage to get under his skin, into his line of vision, and wrap herself around his every thought? It wasn't like he was desperate for female companionship. All vanity aside, he knew he wasn't hard to look at, had a job that would provide well for a family, and was mature enough to dismiss silly advances by even sillier species of the opposite sex. He'd had plenty of opportunities to have a beautiful woman at his side. He'd even been tempted to stand before a congregation and declare *until death do us part* a couple of times. It wasn't as if he didn't have thoughts of coming home to a frilly-aproned partner, a house smelling like fresh-baked bread, and children shouting for his attention. But in the end, always in the end, God would reveal a different plan. Because he believed that God's thoughts for him were to give him peace, not of evil, he never doubted His leading. But where was God now? Why was He allowing such crazy thoughts that most certainly did not offer him anything that even remotely resembled peace?

He stopped his car in front of the boardinghouse, threw his hat onto the cushion next to him, and leaned his head against the back of the car seat. If he was so handsome and wise, why did one skinny, feisty, farmer-woman tie him in such knots and cause him to lose all decorum? Whatever made him confess he hadn't slept, couldn't stop thinking about her, and whatever else might have come forth without any forethought whatsoever? What was that old saying—*It's better to keep your mouth shut and appear stupid than open it and remove all doubt*? Well, he'd opened his wide and definitely removed all doubt. He rubbed his eyes with the heels of his hands. Would she take his advice and go see the banker in the morning? And what would she do when she realized it was none other than Neal Murphy?

He leaned his forehead against the steering wheel. Lily Archer and Neal Murphy was not a combination he even wanted to consider. Thank goodness the druggist had given him a sleeping potion. Maybe he could at least make it through the night without a farmer-woman with faded overalls and brown-velvet eyes chiding him.

Six

NEAL LOOSENED HIS tie and pulled his shirt loose from his britches on the way into the house.

"Oh, good, son. You're home early. Rosie will be thrilled." Mother looked up from the needlepoint she held on her lap. "She's in her room planning something special for you, so please act surprised."

He pulled his tie from the collar. "I...I don't have time, Mother. I have an appointment."

A look that signaled both disappointment and disapproval flashed across his mother's countenance and he braced himself for the questions that were sure to come.

"An appointment at this time of day? Oh, Neal. What or who could possibly be more important than your little daughter? She misses her mother so much and now you—"

"You think I'm not aware of how much Rosie misses Helen?" He threw his tie over the back of the nearest chair. "I miss her too, Mother. But life goes on. You told me that yourself. 'Life must go on, Neal, for Rosie's sake.' Remember? Well, here I am trying my hardest for life to go on." He sank into the chair, pulled the tie from the back, and folded it over his hand.

Mother laid her handwork on the table beside her and leaned forward. "You're trying hard for life to go on for you, Neal, but not for Rosie. You said you moved here so she could experience growing up in a small town."

"I did. That's exactly what I want."

"But you've not taken her from this house in the two weeks you've been here. Most of her toys are still packed in boxes in the storage shed. She doesn't know there's a park. She doesn't even know there are little girls her age right down the street."

He involuntarily ducked his head to avoid the guilt his mother hurled his direction. "What are you doing all day, Mother? Needlepoint? Couldn't you take—"

"That's enough, Neal." Father lowered the newspaper he'd held in front of his face this entire conversation. "You'll not speak to your mother with that tone of voice. You and Rosie are welcome here as long as you care to stay but only if you treat us with respect and take the responsibility of raising your own daughter. Is that understood?"

Neal jumped to his feet. "I thought you wanted to help." Had they forgotten how they'd encouraged him when he voiced his desire to return to Anderson to raise Rosie?

Father methodically folded the newspaper and Neal cringed. If the man folded it once, it meant he was through reading for the moment. If he folded it in fourths, the action relayed agitation, and if he rolled it and stood with it in his hands, it signaled a lecture, with the daily news punching the air like exclamation points.

"Help, yes." Father gave the paper a final fold, then rolled it and stood. "But we have no intention of raising Rosie. That. Is. Your. Job."

Neal winced with each jab of the paper. "I'm no longer in high school. I didn't know I would be required to ask permission to leave the house of an evening."

Father's face reddened and he stepped closer. "Then stop acting as if you're still a teenager. You're no longer the local hero, Neal. Like any other high school big shot, your reign as *most popular* ended as soon as you walked across the stage and got your diploma. It no longer makes a difference who scored the winning touchdown, made the last basket from center court, or how many cheerleaders you could claim as your girl. What matters now is what kind of man, husband, and father you've become."

Neal rankled. "I never once collected cheerleaders, Dad. Until I met Helen, there was only one girl in my life, and you know it."

Father waved the newspaper in the air. "Oh, I know. I also know you left Anderson in a huff because Lily Archer was bent on keeping the promise she made to her papa on his deathbed—something that most men wouldn't do, by the way. And now you've come back because you promised Helen, on *her* deathbed, that you would raise your little girl as if her mama were still alive. Do you really think this is what Helen would want for Rosie? Holed up with two old people while her daddy keeps himself too occupied to be bothered?"

Neal unbuttoned the top button of his shirt. Even for Father, that was a long-winded lecture. He didn't have time for this, though he'd pay dearly if he didn't spend at least fifteen minutes with Rosie. It wouldn't be enough to satisfy his parents but it would be a start. "I'll go see what Rosie has planned for me, and I promise to act surprised. I will also keep my appointment for tonight. We can talk about my neglectful parenting another time."

He turned on his heel and hurried up the steps. He didn't want to give his father a chance to continue his oration, and he didn't dare look at his mother. He'd never been able to hide anything from her, and if given enough time she'd know his real reason for returning to Anderson. He did want his daughter to grow up in a small town. That part was true. What he had yet to admit to anyone, and it took Helen's death and driving back into his old hometown to admit it to himself—

he took a deep breath and exhaled it through pursed lips—was that he'd never stopped loving Lily.

NEAL SLAMMED ON the brakes and blew his horn three times as he drove under the overhang of Ernie's gas station. If he hadn't had to argue so long with his parents, he'd have been out of town and halfway to the Archer farm an hour ago. Rosie cried when he left, until he promised her a new dolly. It was bribery, but it had always worked for him. What could it hurt?

"Ain't no need for ya to honk at me like I was a fat lady crossin' the street." Ernie ambled out to the gas pump. "I seen ya a-comin'. Hard to miss a bright red Cadillac convertible in this town. Thought ya was a firetruck or somebody important at first, all red and shiny. How much ya want?"

"Fill it. I'm in a hurry. Oh, I'll take two bottles of orange soda and a bag of peanuts, too."

Ernie grinned, his gold-tipped tooth shining like a medal. "Whew! Got me quite a run on orange sodies today."

"What do you mean, quite a run?" Neal pulled a dollar from his wallet. "This should cover it. Put the rest on my ticket."

"I mean lotsa folks thirsty for orange sodies today." Ernie waved the dollar bill in the air. "This won't cover it, and ya don't have no ticket."

Neal pounded on the steering wheel. "What do you mean I don't have a ticket? I've had a ticket here since I was in high school."

"Well, ya don't have one now. Ya ain't been in high school for eight years, and your daddy paid the one you had. Ya take it up with him if ya want, but for now ya owe me two dollars and fifteen cents."

"Two dollars and fifteen cents?"

"Yep. Two dollars for ten gallons of gas, ten cents for two bottles of soda, and a nickel for the bag of peanuts. I ain't no banker but God done blessed me with a mind to do sums." He held out his hand and rubbed his thumb and the next two fingers together.

Neal pulled out another dollar and dug in his pocket for the fifteen cents. "Start me a ticket for next time."

Ernie scratched the back of his neck. "Things have changed since ya was here last, Neal. Don't do tickets no more. Ya ain't got cash, I don't got gas, or soda, or peanuts. I thank ya for stoppin' in, though. Always good to see a young'un come home again."

Neal's tires squealed as he pulled away from Ernie's. *Doggone old man, anyway. Who does he think he is? 'Don't do tickets no more.'* Well, maybe the bank wouldn't allow late payments, either, though he'd found ample evidence that his father had been more than generous to most everyone in the county. He'd check tomorrow on Ernie's status. For now, he had more important things to worry about.

Like how Lily would react to seeing him again.

LILY SLIPPED TO the floor of the porch and drew her knees to her chest, careful not to knock over the bottle of soda. It was no longer cold, or even cool, but the sweet tanginess made up for it. How could Joe Kendall know that the fizzy orange drink would bring back memories she'd not allowed herself to visit for ever so long?

Too hot to sleep upstairs, she'd drug Mama's mattress from her bed and put it on the floor of the living room. She'd tied the curtains in a knot to get them out of the way and propped the windows open with the ever-trusty broom handle she'd cut for such a purpose to allow the maximum amount of air to circulate into the room. Circulate, that is, if she also kept the kitchen door open and if there happened to be a breath of air.

Though it wasn't yet dark, Mama had curled up on her makeshift bed on the floor and fallen asleep as soon as her head hit the pillow.

Lily would make a pallet on the floor beside her later. For now, she'd take advantage of the quiet and go over the day's events. One thing was certain, she'd allowed stubborn pride to explode into harsh, hateful words. Though Mama couldn't, or didn't, voice her disapproval of her daughter's behavior, dismay and disappointment had co-authored their messages across her countenance, and it hurt more than if she would have or could have put it into words.

Lily rubbed her fingers in circles on her forehead. Maybe she could rub some sense into today's events. Why was she so stubborn? At a time when she longed for someone to talk to, someone who would listen and laugh and say words back to her, why did she spurn the one opportunity she had with Joe Kendall? She took a drink of the soda and leaned her head against the house. If she stayed out until it was dark enough, maybe she'd find the North Star. Then what? Make a wish?

A low growl from Dog tensed her shoulders. Though supposedly a watchdog, he hadn't so much as given a snuffle for years except…

Lily's chest tightened as she slowly rose to her feet at the roar of a car coming down the lane. *No. It can't be.* Before she could test whether she could take a step without crumpling, three honks of the horn confirmed what her heart told her was impossible. Neal. Only Neal Murphy's presence would make Dog bare his teeth and crouch for an attack. Neal had kicked him once, and Dog had never forgotten.

Lily clutched her bottle of orange soda in one hand and wound her other arm around the corner post of the porch, afraid if she turned loose her legs wouldn't hold her. What was he doing here?

There was no mistaking the swagger as the occupant of the car walked to the gate waving two bottles of orange soda in one hand. "Guess what?" He patted his shirt pocket. "I've got a bag of peanuts."

Dog bared his teeth and gave another deep growl.

Neal stopped in his tracks. "Dog still mad at me, is he?"

She nodded. Her mouth was so dry she couldn't get a word past her lips.

"You going to call him off, or am I going to have to take a chance he'll chew my leg to the bone?"

There was that lopsided grin that used to melt her heart. But not tonight. His swagger and grin were eight years too late. She licked her lips. "What are you doing here?"

He clinked the two bottles together. "Brought our favor...Wait." He leaned across the gate, the frown between his eyes visible even from her vantage point. "Where'd you get that soda?"

Caution tingled across her shoulders. This was probably not the time to tell him about Joe Kendall. Not that there was anything to tell. "Do you really think I've not had a soda pop since you left? You haven't answered me. What are you doing here?"

"You want me to yell across this fence all evening or are you going call off that mutt and let me come talk to you?"

From years of prior history, Lily knew he wouldn't leave until he'd said whatever he came to say. "Come here, Dog. Let him in."

Dog flopped to his belly, and a surprisingly subdued Neal walked to the edge of the porch and looked up at her.

She clung to the post, not ready to give him the satisfaction of seeing her visibly shaken by his presence. If only she'd known he was in the area, she wouldn't be standing here in her chore clothes, barefoot, hair tied back with one of her papa's old bandanas. Why was he staring at her? She could only imagine what was going through his mind. *Poor Lily sure has let herself go over these past years.* He hadn't, that was evident. Hair still perfectly groomed. The rolled sleeves of his white shirt revealed the tan, muscular arms she was familiar with. And the open collar...

He tilted his head and shot her a smile that in past years would make her heart do flips. It still worked. "You going to let me come up there beside you, or am I going to have to stand here and get a permanent crick in my neck?"

Stars and stripes. The dimple on the left side of his mouth was still there. She couldn't let his nearness sway her. "Does your wife know you're here, Neal?"

He fumbled with his collar. "My...how do you know about my wife?"

"Really? You don't think I've seen the picture of your little family on your father's desk?"

His eyes narrowed. Before she could stop him, he set the sodas on the ground and hurdled onto the porch beside her. "Look at me, Lily." His voice was soft but demanding. "I don't want to stand here all night with you avoiding me. All I ask is that you listen to me, then I'll leave if that's what you want."

She reluctantly turned toward him and gripped the porch post tighter. Neal Murphy was like a magnet and if she wasn't careful, he'd pull her right to him. She couldn't let that happen ever again, but his gaze held her captive.

"Remember the little bunny you rescued from your barn cats?"

She had no idea where he was going with this question but knew better than to stop him. He never rambled. "I remember."

"Do you remember what I did when that bunny died and you came running to me on the playground the next day, crying?"

She nodded.

"Say it, Lily. Tell me what you remember."

He was so close she could feel the heat of his breath. "You...you hugged me and kissed me on the cheek, then told me it would all be okay because you'd catch me another bunny."

He ran his finger across her forehead. "And did I keep that promise?"

She flinched at the warmth of his hand. "You did."

He put his fingers under her chin and forced her to look at him. "And then what did you do?"

The dimple beside his mouth deepened, a sure sign he was going to smile...or laugh. "I...I kissed you and called you my hero."

He stepped closer. "And where did you kiss me, Lilybug?"

She closed her eyes. If she looked at him one minute longer, she'd weaken. "On the lips. I kissed you on the lips."

"And that's when I knew…" He ran his fingers down her cheek. "Look at me, Lily, please."

She opened her eyes but bit the tip of her tongue to remind her of the pain this man caused her all those year ago.

Oh-so familiar eyes full of desire met hers. "That's when I knew you were my girl. We were six years old, and I knew. I knew when we were six. I knew when we were twelve, and I knew…I knew right up until the night we graduated and you told me you wouldn't marry me." His lips trembled.

So, this is where he would make his stand. Bring up the past to justify showing up without so much as a fair warning. She pushed his hand away. "That's not fair, Neal. I didn't say I *wouldn't* marry you. I said I *couldn't* marry you. There's a difference. I made a promise I couldn't break. I thought you'd understand. Instead, you walked away."

Neal locked his hands behind his head. "You broke my heart, Lily. I walked away because I knew I could never be a farmer and I couldn't bear to stay and watch someone else—some man in overalls with a tractor and a plow—sweep you off your feet."

She shook her head. "No, Neal. You don't get to pin your broken heart on me. I never asked you to be a farmer. Look around. Does it look to you as if I've been swept off my feet by anything other than wind and dirt? You left. Now leave again. Go home. Go home to your wife and child, wherever home is for you now. Please."

He bit his lower lip and shook his head. "Oh, Lily, if only you knew." His shoulders drooped as he retrieved the sodas and made his way to his car. No swagger this time. And no goodbye. Only the dust he left behind as he made his way back down the dirt lane.

If only she knew what? Would he have explained had she given him a chance? She loosened her hold on the porch post and waited until she could make sure her legs would hold her before taking a step. With luck, she'd not have to face Neal Murphy again any time soon. After flexing her knees, she finally felt steady enough to go back into the house. She walked around to the kitchen door and found Mama with her nose pressed against the screen door, clad only in her panties. She must have gotten too warm, or decided it was time to get dressed. Who knew what made Mama do the things she did? *Oh, Mama. Why? Why tonight of all nights?* She swallowed past the growing lump in her throat. How long had Mama stood at the door? Had Neal seen her? She'd shed more tears today than she'd allowed herself over the past eight years. They had to stop. "Let me in, Mama."

Mama backed away as Lily opened the door. "Papa knows."

Lily stopped, one hand on the door-pull. Didn't she remember that Papa was dead? Did she see and recognize Neal? Papa had never liked Neal Murphy. Did his presence trigger a memory? "Papa knows what, Mama?"

A vacant stare was Mama's reply, a sign she'd retreated once again into a world that forbade Lily's presence.

Lily edged into the house and took her mother's hand. "Let's go to bed, Mama."

Long after her mother went back to sleep, Lily lay with her eyes wide open and her mind whirling. The only thing that made any sense at all was for her to go back to the bank again tomorrow. This time she'd wait until she had an audience with Ed Murphy, and nothing or no one would deter her.

Seven

JOE CRINGED WHEN Lily and her mother walked into the lobby, though she didn't acknowledge his presence. While he'd urged her to return to the bank today, it hadn't occurred to him that she'd be here so early. Would she leave again if she saw him?

Miss Bower looked up from her desk. "Oh, you're back, Lily." She ran her finger down the open appointment book in front of her. "I'm sorry. I guess I forgot to pencil in your appointment time."

Lily paled. "I...I didn't make an appointment. I've never had to make an—"

Joe rose from his chair and walked to the desk. "She can have mine, Miss Bower."

Lily startled. Maybe she hadn't ignored him after all. Perhaps she was so intent on her mission to see Murphy that she hadn't even noticed his presence.

Lily plucked at the collar of her dress. "I...I can't do that Mr.—"

"Bruce." Mrs. Archer grabbed his hand.

Lily's cheeks turned as red as if she'd been slapped. "Mama, don't—"

Joe patted the older woman's hand. "Would you like to take a walk with me while Lily talks with Mr. Murphy?" He gave a quick shake of his head to Lily and hoped she wouldn't argue.

Miss Bower frowned. "But Mr. Murphy is expecting *you*, Mr. Kendall."

Joe leaned across the desk and peered at the open appointment book. "Hmm. It looks as though there are *no* appointments penciled in, Miss Bower. In fact, I don't see my name anywhere." He tapped his finger on the page. "Perhaps you can put Miss Archer's name right there on that…top…line." He smiled at her. "That should satisfy Mr. Murphy. Don't you agree…Flo?"

The secretary's forced smile did not reach her eyes, which darkened and darted between Lily and the hand clasped in his. "Mr. Murphy has not yet arrived. I'll apprise him of Miss Archer's presence as soon as he's ready to receive clients. In the meantime, perhaps you would like to take a seat, Lillian." She waved her hand toward the bank of chairs against the far wall.

Joe winked at Lily and leaned toward her. "I'm going to take your mama for a walk. Don't worry about her."

Lily clutched her purse. "Why are you doing this after the way—"

He placed a finger over her lips. "Shh. Someday I'll explain. For now, plead your case with Murphy. I have an idea he'll listen more intently than ever."

He didn't look back as he led Mrs. Archer from the bank. Encouraging Lily to spend any time alone with Neal Murphy took every ounce of willpower he could muster. But Murphy had a wife and child, evident by the picture on his father's desk and the proud explanation that went along with it. *'Our only grandchild, and she's a princess.'*

Ruth Archer seemed perfectly content to walk alongside him. If she noticed people looking out their store windows, she gave no indication. For some reason, it gave him a sense of comic satisfaction to nod at each inquisitive face. Ahh, small towns. Neal Murphy thought he could implement a few boundaries. Well, that would be most interesting to watch. Joe smiled down at the lady beside him. "You and I have a few boundaries of our own, don't we?"

She smiled up at him. "You're a good boy, Bruce."

He returned the smile. "Yes, I am. Yes, I am…Mama."

NEAL SLIPPED OUT of his suit coat and hung it on the back of the chair. This weather was much too hot to stick to more business-like attire, at least not in Anderson where the only other person to maintain such rigid appearance of propriety was the undertaker.

He loosened his tie and unbuttoned the top button of his shirt. Undertaker. The role of banker was not unlike that of the mortician and he grimaced at the comparison.

Years of depression, drought, and dust storms had left a wide swath of the country's once-productive wheat fields barren. Other crops, if they sprouted at all, stood stunted and dead, their death rattles heard even on the stillest of nights. Farmers couldn't afford to buy food or clothing for their large families, let alone seed or equipment with which to maintain their livelihoods. Without the farmers' money, other businesses succumbed one by one, evidenced by the drawn shades on their storefront windows and the handwritten CLOSED signs taped to their doors. The town was dying and, like it or not, the banker was the one seen to declare death to their ability to continue to borrow life-sustaining monies and ultimately close the coffin on their hopes and dreams after years of toil.

Neal opened his top desk drawer and withdrew Lily Archer's file. He'd spent hours after his shortened visit to her farm last night going over and over the information he'd gleaned. Until then, he'd attributed Father's stooped shoulders, shuffling gait, and wrinkle-etched face to his advancing age. He propped his elbows on the desk and buried his face in his hands. Only now did he understand the bitter agony those signs of aging represented.

"I'm sorry, Neal, but you have a client waiting."

Florence Bower's voice broke his reverie. He ran his hands down his face and crossed his arms on the desk. "Yes, yes, I know. Kendall is here." He wasn't at all ready to discuss the lake project with him, but maybe the man could help come up with a solution regarding the Archer property. "Send him in, Flo."

A wrinkle of disapproval slid across her forehead. "Mr. Kendall *was* here but he forfeited his appointment to Lily Archer."

Neal's hands involuntarily balled. As much as he wanted to see her again and as badly as he hoped she'd had a change of heart after seeing him last night, this wasn't the time. He wasn't ready to face the inevitable questions. Her name wasn't on the deed. Period. "Is Mr. Kendall still here? Wait. Never mind. Please send…No." He slipped Lily's file back into the drawer and stood. "I'll greet Miss Archer myself. Thank you, Flo." He stepped past his secretary, fully aware of the deepened frown and the glare she directed at him. Perhaps working late with her several nights had sent the wrong signal.

The woman Neal observed sitting in the lobby was not the same one he'd encountered on her porch last night. Last night's Lily was angry, suspicious, and—if he allowed himself enough imagination— even hinted that had he not walked away, she might have married him. The Lily he observed today sat with her shoulders slumped and her eyes downcast, as if her future were written on the clenched hands in her lap.

Last night's Lily was dressed more like a hired hand than the girl he'd known and loved. This morning…His chest tightened as the seconds ticked by without him being noticed by the one woman he knew better than he'd ever known his wife. She looked…He fought back unexpected tears. He hadn't cried since the day he buried Helen.

Why now? Why did the sight of this long-ago sweetheart stir such a war of emotion? Was it because she was clad in the same dress she wore the night he walked away? Was it because her once shiny auburn hair no longer bounced on her shoulders or curled around her face but was pulled into a tight bun low on her neck? Or could it be because she looked so defeated and alone?

"Lily." Her name rolled from his lips before he had a chance to quell his thoughts. It was more an exclamation of pain than an acknowledgement of her presence.

She looked up and paled. "You? Really, Neal? I…I thought—" Her eyes darted between him and Florence Bower, who had sidled next to him.

He moved away from his secretary and steeled himself for the daggers she'd throw his direction. "That will be all, Miss Bower."

He wasn't wrong. Flo's spears of anger were hurled with great accuracy. It was a good thing looks couldn't kill, although they telegraphed quite clearly a desire to do great bodily harm. No doubt, she'd misinterpreted their after-hours work as much more than his intent to become acquainted with Father's business as quickly as possible. His introduction back into small-town life just became more complicated.

All the past regrets lodged in his throat as he took a deep breath and willed his voice to remain steady. "Please come in, Lily."

LILY STOOD AND tried hard to ignore the head-to-foot perusal and pinched mouth of Florence Bower. Facing Neal was hard enough. She didn't have the strength nor the time to worry about how she must look in the eyes of the one person who'd been her nemesis since grade school. The years had mellowed their relationship somewhat, at least to the point that they could greet one another in a civil manner. But now she understood Florence's obvious disapproval when Joe Kendall forfeited his appointment, and even the look of mixed pity and disgust when he offered to take Mama for a walk. Poor Florence, having to make such a difficult choice at whom to bat her eyelashes. Would it be Joe Kendall or Neal Murphy? Both, maybe.

"Lily. It's good to see you…again. Please…" Neal motioned for her to follow him.

Lily plastered on a smile as she walked past Florence.

"Oh, Lily dear," Florence called after Lily. "I couldn't help but notice your shoelace is untied. Be careful you don't trip and fall."

Neal stopped so suddenly, Lily bumped against his back. The last bit of dignity she could muster was stripped to bare bones, and she turned to face the secretary, determined to maintain at least a modicum of pride. What Neal did as a result was up to him, but she wouldn't and couldn't let this pass. "My shoelace is not untied, Florence. It's broken. But thank you for noticing and for kindly and discreetly drawing my attention to it." She brushed past the wide-eyed, open-mouthed secretary and shuffled her way to the front door lest her shoe fall off for sure. One thing was certain…she couldn't take much more humiliation.

Neal rushed to her side and grabbed her arm. "Wait, Lily. Please don't leave. At least give me a chance to understand what is going on here." He turned to Florence. "Perhaps you would like to explain?"

The secretary's red face didn't hide the stiff neck nor the roll of her eyes. "I merely noticed her shoelace was untied and didn't want her to fall. I'm sorry I raised my voice. I think she mistook my friendly warning as being rude, but I wanted to make sure she heard me. That's all." She folded her arms across her quite ample chest and gave Lily a warning smile, as if she dared her to counter her explanation.

Neal waved his secretary away. "Look at me, Lily."

The gaze that met hers was so full of pain she turned away. "You didn't know it was me and not my father visiting with Joe Kendall yesterday, did you?"

She couldn't trust herself to speak. A shake of her head would have to suffice.

"And until I showed up at your house last night, you had no idea I was back in town, did you?"

She started to shake her head again, but he cupped her chin in his hand and forced her to look at him.

"That's why you told me to go home to my wife, isn't it?" The breathless quiver of his voice belied his steady gaze. "*If* someone would have informed you that Father is retiring and I'm taking his place, and *if* anyone would have told you that I agreed to come back to Anderson to raise my daughter because her mother, my wife, died three months ago, *if* you would have had all that information, would you have welcomed me differently last night?"

Lily pulled away from him and blew into the palms of both hands, then closed her fingers to make tight fists. "All those *ifs*, Neal, are like the air I've captured in my hands." She held her hands, palms up, and opened her fingers one by one. "See? Nothing. Empty. Not even the air I blew into them. *Ifs* aren't tied to the past like some kind of magical rope that can be pulled into the moment and change everything."

Neal stepped toward her. "Lily, please. Come back to my office and let's talk this—"

She squared her shoulders. It would give her a minute of satisfaction to be behind closed doors with Neal while Florence Bower had to remain on the outside. While the *ifs* weren't tied to a magical rope, a thread of hope had wrapped itself around her heart the night Neal walked away. She'd always dreamed, but never dared believe, that he'd return for her one day. Now, here he stood, all glorious six-feet-something of him. Whether his return had anything to do with coming for her or not made little difference. His voice held a plea and his eyes held—no, she couldn't allow herself to think beyond this very minute and this minute was too full of anger, fear, and regrets. "No, Neal. I should have never let Mr. Kendall forfeit his appointment. Ultimately my future rests in the hands of what you two decide. But I want you to know this…I will fight with every ounce of energy I can muster to keep my farm. I know my name isn't on the deed and I have no idea how it will work, but I won't leave quietly. You will have to move me off with whatever big machinery it takes to build a lake."

As soon as the door clicked shut behind her, Lily regretted her hasty departure. She should have at least waited to see if Neal would pay her for the cream and eggs. Her car had sputtered and died as she turned onto Main Street, but she'd been able to coast it into a parking spot right in front of the bank. *Well, Lily. You've managed to avoid the inevitable and now are faced with the impossible. You have no money, no gas, and what pride you had has been reduced to a broken shoelace. What are you going to do?*

Eight

LILY SHUFFLED TO the car and slid into the driver's seat. If only Joe Kendall would show up with Mama so they could…

She released a huff of exasperation. So they could what? Leaving wasn't an option. Neither was sitting in a hot automobile for the rest of the day. It's what she got for counting on being paid for the produce she'd delivered yesterday. Had she known it was Neal who needed to give permission for the payment, she'd never have taken the chance on driving to town and not being able to return home.

Hope deferred makes the heart sick. She clenched her teeth. The truth of the long-ago memorized scripture couldn't be denied. She was heartsick all right. Heartsick. Sick to her stomach. Her head pounded and her foot cramped from trying to keep the stupid shoe on her foot without a shoelace to hold it in place. She kicked off the offending footwear and laid her forehead against the steering wheel.

Oh, Lord. I don't know what to do, and even if I did, I don't have the strength or the money to do anything. I'm going to lose the farm I've tried so—

"Lily? Are you okay?"

A tap on the window interrupted the closest thing to a prayer she'd allowed past her lips for ever so long. She rolled the window down and met Joe Kendall's furrowed brow above eyes so full of questions and concern that all the pent-up emotion of the past spilled down her cheeks and through her lips. "No, I'm not okay, Mr. Kendall. I…broke my shoelace and…and Florence Bower noticed and sneered at me and…and…did you know Neal Murphy is now at the bank and not his father? Did you? It doesn't make any difference anyway. He didn't pay me for the cream and eggs and the car is out of gas and I barely made it into this parking space and I have no money to buy more gas or groceries and I'm mad at you and Neal Murphy and mostly at my papa for dying and—" She used both hands to shove Joe to one side. "Where's Mama? What have you done with my mother?" Bending to one side, she retrieved the discarded shoe. "So help me, Joe Kendall, if anything has happened to Mama—" She drew her arm back, the heel of the shoe aimed at his forehead.

He grabbed her arms. "You're going to what, Lily? Conk me with your shoe?" He wrenched the shoe away from her. "Your mama is in my car, right next to this one. See? She's fine except—"

"Except what?" Try as she might, she couldn't loosen his grip on her arms. "Tell me. Except? What?"

"SHH." JOE UNDERSTOOD all too well what had happened with Mrs. Archer, but he didn't know quite how to tell Lily without embarrassing her. He took a deep breath. There were only so many ways to get through this, and all of them included using words. "I didn't realize soon enough that your mama needed to go to the bathroom."

Her face flushed. "Oh, please. Don't tell me she…where were you? Who saw her?"

Fresh tears filled Lily's eyes and he struggled with the urge to open the car door and pull her to him. "Don't cry. Please. We were completely alone on the street and I don't think a single person saw us. I didn't want to bring her into the bank, but I wasn't sure which car belonged to you."

"I need to get her home. It's my fault. I hurried her this morning because I wanted to be the first customer at the bank. This has never happened. I didn't bring clean clothes, but I don't know how I'm—"

"She's already in my car but she thinks it belongs to Bruce. You can drive it home, so it doesn't upset her more. I'll bring your car to you later."

She yanked her hands from his grip and pounded on the steering wheel. "Were you listening to me at all? My car is out of gas and I'm out of money. I have nothing left, Joe Kendall, nothing."

"I heard every word, Lily, and you're wrong. You have me."

"You?" She leaned her head against the back of the seat and covered her eyes with her hands. "I have you? And you want to buy my farm, so it's *be kind to poor Lily Archer and her mother*, isn't it?"

Joe clenched his jaw. "Stop it, Lily." Did this girl have any idea what effect she had on him? One minute he wanted to hold her so close she couldn't breathe, the next moment he wanted to turn her over his knee and give her a good spanking. "I heard every word, and I kept my mouth shut while you were spewing them all at me. Now it's my turn. What I am offering you is not pity or some harebrained plan to take your farm away from you. I am hoping you will accept my friendship. Nothing more."

"Nothing more?" she squeaked. "Ha!"

He shook his head. "Nothing more." It wasn't exactly a lie. He was offering his friendship, but what he *hoped* for was much deeper than that. For now, friendship would have to do.

She shrugged. "I can't repay you for the gas it will take to get my car home."

He cocked one eye her direction. "Did I ask you to pay me?"

"No, but—"

He opened the car door and gave her his keys. "No buts. Haven't you ever had a good friend, Lily? One who would do anything for you without asking for or expecting anything in return?" If she uttered Neal Murphy's name, he wasn't at all sure he could stay calm. He couldn't imagine that guy not wanting something in return. He rubbed his hand over his forehead. Lily's prior relationships were none of his business.

She turned sideways and dug in her purse, then turned dull, puppy-dog eyes to him and handed him the keys to her car. "I've had friends, Mr. Kendall. But they've all wanted something—either the attention of my brother, or a commitment I couldn't make. I'll believe you have no ulterior motive when you prove it to me. Not before. For now, I have no choice but to take Mama home and get her into some clean clothes." She pointed to her bare foot. "And this is all I have left of any vanity I might have at one time possessed."

JOE WAITED UNTIL his car turned the corner and headed out of town, then his cheeks puffed with a long exhalation. It had never been his intention to have any personal involvement in this project. He was to secure the land necessary to accomplish the goal, oversee the building of the lake, then move on to the next job. Pure and simple. At least it started out that way. Who could have predicted a force like Lily Archer? And who would have believed one tiny female could punch such a huge hole in his reservoir of memories?

He turned to go into the bank and noticed Miss Bower at the window. Had she witnessed his meeting with Lily and her leaving in his car? So be it. He stepped into the lobby and watched with amusement as she scurried back to her desk. "I've changed my mind, Miss Bower. I don't need to see Mr. Murphy today after all. Please give him my gratitude for seeing Miss Archer first and assure him that I'll come back another time."

Blotches of red polka-dotted her face. "Oh, but…but…yes, yes, of course, I'll give him the message." She lifted a pencil and jammed it into the sharpener mounted on the edge of her desk and began to crank as if her life depended on a sharp lead point. "Do you…would you perhaps care to make an appointment perhaps for later today, perhaps?" She cranked away.

He surveyed the empty lobby. "Thank you, Miss Bower, but I really don't think an appointment will be necessary." He arched his eyebrows as the sharpener appeared to swallow the yellow pencil. "Do you?" He raised his voice above the furious grinding of the writing tool.

"Do I, what?" Now she added a bounce with each crank of the handle.

Joe braced the palms of his hands on her desk. "Do you think an appointment is necessary?" He tapped his finger on the empty pages of her open appointment book. "*Perhaps* I'll take a chance he won't be too busy to see me another day."

He didn't wait for an answer but walked out the door without looking back. He couldn't, however, resist the urge to peek in the window as he walked past. Poor Miss Bower sat with her elbows propped on her desk, holding the stub of a pencil in both hands as if offering it as a sacrifice. And *perhaps* it was.

He was not, by nature, a vindictive person. Was this another manifestation of the influence Lily Archer now yielded over him? He stuffed his hands in his pockets and made his way toward Milly's Diner. If anyone had witnessed Lily leave in his vehicle, he didn't want to appear in a hurry to follow after her. Although the diner wasn't the place to go to avoid gossip, it was a place to loiter over a cup of coffee without arousing suspicion.

The usual long table of the old-men coffee crowd was empty when he entered Milly's. He slid into the first booth.

"You wantin' breakfast, handsome?" Milly sashayed from behind the counter with a cup in one hand and a pot of coffee in the other.

Joe swept his hand toward the empty table. "Looks like I'm too late for that."

"Nah." She plunked the cup in front of him and filled it with the steaming beverage. "This is Wednesday. They meet down at the Methodist church on Wednesday mornings for their weekly Four-G meeting."

"Four-G?" He took a cautious sip of the hot coffee. "Never heard of that."

Milly laughed. "Don't reckon you have, and don't you go tellin' anybody you heard about it here. When they're all sittin' at that long table in here, it's only three Gs—guzzling, gossiping, and growling. Down at the church they add the fourth G—God." She pulled her order pad from the pocket of her apron. "Ain't nobody can squawk as loud about everything and nothing all the same time as a bunch of old men around a table. Half of them can't hear what's going on and the other half don't have anything worthwhile listenin' to anyway. Kinda have to wonder how adding God to the mix helps but Gladys Finley has made them her sour cream coffeecake every Wednesday for as long as I've been in Anderson, and I was born here so—Oh! My! Everlasting! Stars!" She used her hip to scoot Joe so she could sit next to him, laughing so hard tears ran down her face.

"What's so funny?" He scooted closer to the wall so she wouldn't fall off the seat while giggling.

"Don't you see it?" She wiped her eyes with the hem of her apron. "I dubbed the fourth G for God because it was at the church and all this time those ornery old men are gettin' religion one day a week because of Gladys Finley. G for *Gladys*."

He took another sip of his coffee. "She must be quite the looker to keep every old man in Anderson interested."

Milly sobered. "Hear tell she was in her day. She's plump as a feather tick now, rosy cheeks, snow-white hair, and every bit as sweet as she looks."

"Is she a widow?"

Milly brushed an imaginary crumb from the table. "Never married. She and her brother, Benton is his name, live in the same big ole farmhouse they were born in, and their parents before them. She stayed on to take care of their mother after ole man Finley died, and people say Benton stayed to take care of Gladys. Now I'm not sure who takes care of who, but Frank Scott farms their land, what's left of it. I'm pretty sure that church will fall down once they're gone. Benton mows the yard, whitewashes the privies, and fixes anything that's broke. Gladys keeps the inside shining like the crown she'll one day wear if what they say about Heaven is true. You can always tell who's been to church on Sunday because they come in here on Monday smelling like whatever Gladys used to clean that week. Benton stands at the front door greetin' people every Sabbath morning, while she pumps away at the organ. Doubt they've ever missed a Sunday."

He pushed his cup toward her for a refill. "So why do you think Gladys is the other G? Aren't most of the old men who meet here married?"

Milly stood and gathered the order ticket that had flown out of her hands in her fit of laughter. "Nah. Most of them are widowers. The rest of them wish they were. But the Finleys have the love and respect of every one of them. Now, we've been jawin' long enough. What can I get ya? I took two apple pies out of the oven right before you walked in. And I have fresh sweet cream to pour over it. You interested?" She filled his empty cup.

"Sweet cream and apple pie. Who can resist that? I'd have asked for cream for my coffee if I'd known it was available."

She stuffed the ticket pad back into her apron pocket. "Don't usually have it. Florence Bower brought it in yesterday. Said some customer left it at the bank but she didn't have any way to keep it cold and in this heat it wouldn't have lasted long sittin' on her desk."

The hair on Joe's arms bristled. "Did she say what customer left the cream?"

Milly sat back down in the booth across from Joe. "Look, Joe. You're new in town and most likely you think I'm a big gossip. But allow me to let you in on a secret. I don't like busybodies."

Joe crossed his arms on the top of the table and leaned toward her. "That didn't answer my question, Milly."

She patted his hands. "Fair enough. All I'm gonna say is, I know and you know who brought that cream. Question is…now what are you going to do about it?"

"Did you pay Florence for the cream? And what about the eggs?"

Milly's forehead crinkled. "Eggs? I don't know a thing about any eggs. But no, I didn't pay her. I tried, but she said there was no need. Said it would go to waste if she didn't donate it to me." She slid out of the booth. "You wait right here. Don't move."

Milly went to the cash register and returned shortly with two dollar bills. "Here. I'm paying for the cream, and you tell Lily that I'll take as much cream as she can spare every week. Be interested in eggs, too, if she has any to spare. Now, you go put gas in that girl's car."

Joe rubbed the back of his neck. "How did you—"

She stood and cupped his face in her hands. "I see things and I know things. Don't mean I tell things. Get out of here before young Murphy suspects something and beats you to it."

Joe took Milly's hands and kissed each one. "If you weren't so old and ugly, I'd marry you. You know that?"

"Yeah. Yeah. You think you're the first one to make me that promise?" She tweaked his nose. "If you aren't married by the time that lake gets water in it, I might consider your offer. Now, get."

He stood to leave but she grabbed his arm. "Wait. Come around back. I got a gas can you can take to Ernie's. Oh, and you buy that girl some shoelaces."

"Wha—"

She shooed him away. "I got me a front window. Done told ya I see things, and right now I see that big ole heart of yours a-hangin' on your sleeve. Shoo!"

Joe took a couple of steps, then stopped and turned around. "You sure you're done giving orders?" He laughed, ducking as Milly's order pad flew toward him.

Nine

THE UNMISTAKABLE RATTLE of the Archer family car came to a clattering stop at the front gate as Lily flopped Mama's wet underwear over the fence to dry. *If this day could get any worse, it just did. I knew Joe Kendall would return my car at some point, but I sure didn't think it would be so soon.* She'd tried, in vain, to explain to her mama why she needed a bath and change of clothes all before noon. A child would know why, but Mama wasn't a child and no matter how hard she tried, Lily couldn't get her to understand. Now they were both exhausted from the ensuing struggle to disrobe her in broad daylight, get her to sit in the washtub long enough for Lily to bathe her, and then get her redressed in a housedress rather than a nightgown.

If only she'd taken the time to change her clothes before trying to get Mama situated. Here she stood, barefoot, her one good dress soaked and clinging to her like flies on a jam jar, her hair no longer in the tidy bun at the nape of her neck but hanging loose around her face, while she hung Mama's clean but wet clothing over the fence like a washerwoman. Well, so be it. Joe Kendall had already seen her at her worst so he shouldn't be surprised at the sodden, unkempt person he'd encounter once he stepped from the vehicle.

He opened the door and slid from the seat, his head towering above the roof of the car. And to add to Lily's humiliation, her heart thrummed an extra beat at the sight of him. At least that added thump couldn't be seen by the very person who caused it.

"I left the keys in your car."

Please, please don't come through that gate.

Joe opened the gate and stooped to scratch behind Dog's ears. "Hey there, Dog. Can't you find a shady spot?" He grinned up at Lily. "I don't suppose you would have a cool glass of water to offer a weary traveler. It's hot as Grandma's fryin' pan."

A smile pushed at Lily's cheeks. He'd most likely gotten that line from Ernie, but she'd pretend not to notice. She didn't want him to come into the house, but good manners forbade her to deny him a glass of water. "I don't have ice, but our well water is fairly cold." She didn't need to look to know he followed her up the steps, the fragrance of Old Spice wafted from him. Papa had never been given to anything sweeter smelling than new-mown hay and sunshine, but last time she was at the apothecary, Daisy Miller was all a-flutter about the new fragrance for men. '*Can you imagine any man from Anderson buying this stuff,*' she'd squeaked.

Lily had agreed, mainly because she didn't know any man who'd want to smell all spicy, except maybe Neal Murphy, but at the time he was nowhere around, and she wouldn't allow herself to linger on what might have been. But now here was Joe Kendall, tall, rugged, and bigger than life, who didn't seem to mind smelling like Grandma Archer's kitchen at Christmastime. She tried not to take in a big sniff of air. She'd have to tell Daisy what it was like to have a man actually wear the stuff. A wave of heat tingled across her cheeks and she scolded herself for such a thought.

Stepping into the kitchen did nothing to relieve Lily's angst. Mama sat at the table, clad only in her petticoat and one sock, her dress draped across the chair next to her. Who knew where the other sock might be? There was no way to hide her, and Mama, oblivious to her improper appearance, clapped her hands at the sight of Joe.

"Bruce. You came home again."

Joe bent and kissed her forehead. "I came home." He lifted her dress from the chair. "Let's get you dressed, Mama. You look so pretty in green." He slipped the garment over her head and buttoned it without her making so much as a wiggle. "There you go." He patted her hand and seated himself beside her. "Lily's going to get me a cool glass of water. Would you like one, too?"

Mama tilted her head. "Lily's here? Did she come with you?"

Lily held her breath.

"Yes, she's here with me." He beckoned Lily to come stand beside him. "She's missed you, but she's going to stay here with you for a while, if that's okay."

Mama peered at her through squinted eyes, then leaned toward Joe. "That's not Lily. That's the girl. But she can stay if she wants."

Hope deferred...Lily's heart dropped. Did she exist at all in Mama's befuddled mind?

A small crinkle of his forehead accompanied a slight shake of the head as he leaned closer to Mama. "That girl's name is Lily. Did you forget?"

A smile lit Mama's face. "Oh, yes. Yes. I think I forgot." She giggled. "I think I forget a lot of things." She pushed away from the table. "I think I'll take a nap now. I'm tired after swimming." She stood and linked his arm through her elbow.

Lily rubbed her hands across her face. "I...there's a mattress on the living room floor. It's cooler down here and—"

Joe put his finger over his lips and shook his head. "You needn't explain. If you'll fetch me that glass of water, I have an idea to suggest to you when I return."

She didn't want to hear his idea. She didn't want him to stay, but neither did she want him to leave. Dog liked him. Mama was obviously infatuated with him. Why, then, did his presence cause her such a turmoil of emotions? He'd seen her angry, had withstood her outrage, and witnessed her tears. Yet, nothing seemed to faze him. Who was Joe Kendall?

Oh, yes. How could she forget? He was the man whose job was to purchase land for the new lake. Her land...land she would never sell.

BY THE TIME Joe returned to the table, any coolness the water might have held was now puddled onto the table, not unlike the tears pooled in Lily's brown-velvet eyes. He longed to reach out to her, but the set of her shoulders signaled she'd retreated behind the safety of her ever-present wall. However, he was an engineer. He could construct barriers and he could bring them down. This one was coming down. He reached into his shirt pocket, retrieved a pair of shoestrings and the money Milly had given him for the cream, and laid them on the table. He'd paid for the gas himself, but no one needed to know that, and he knew Ernie would never tell.

"You want to know my idea, Lily?"

Her shoulders drooped. "Please tell me there is a least one thing in my life for which I have a choice." She fingered the shoelaces. "I will repay you for these, but I won't take your money."

He folded his arms atop the table. "It's not my money, Lily, it's yours."

Doubt frosted her gaze. "How many times do you need to hear me say I. Have. *No.* Money."

"I hear you loud and clear, Lily. During your rant at me earlier today, I also heard that Mr. Murphy had not paid you for the cream and eggs you delivered to his office."

"And he paid *you*? Why?"

"No, he didn't pay me. Someone delivered the cream to Milly at the diner and she paid me. She also asked me to tell you she would take all the cream and eggs you could spare in the future."

Lily leaned back in her chair and crossed her arms. "Did she say who delivered the cream? Was it Neal? No. Wait." She shot straight up and slapped her hand against the table. "Florence Bower. It was Florence wasn't it? I bet she never even told Neal that I—"

Was her aversion to Florence Bower because of the shoestring incident, or did Neal Murphy play a role? "Does it matter, Lily? What matters now is that you have a new customer, and you have money to buy groceries. Now, do you want to hear my idea?"

She slumped back into her chair. "I don't particularly want to hear it, but I'll listen."

He laughed. "I'll believe that when you let me say a full sentence without interrupting. Okay, this is my idea—I'll stay here with your mama while you go back into town to—"

She jumped to her feet and slammed her hands on her hips. "Really? Really? Take a good long look at me, Joe Kendall. Do you think for one minute I can go back into town looking like this?"

"I knew you couldn't do it."

"Do what?" Her lips barely moved.

"You couldn't let me finish one full sentence without interrupting." He winked at her, then tilted his head to one side and let his eyes slowly travel along her disheveled form from the tip of her upturned nose to the clenched hands on her hips.

"Wait!" Her eyes widened as she folded her arms across her body. "What are you doing?"

His answer would get him in a whole lot of trouble, but he couldn't resist the opportunity. "I'm following orders, m'lady." He grinned.

She stomped her foot. "Orders? What orders?"

He sobered. "Did you, or did you not, tell me to take a good long look at you?"

She blushed. "Don't tease me, Joe Kendall."

"Never. I was wrong, though, to suggest you go back into town."

"Because that good long look revealed I'm a mess? Thank you very much."

He clamped his top lip between his teeth. If only she knew what that long look did to his heart. "No, because that good long look revealed a beautiful woman who is angry, frightened, and exhausted. Make me a list, Lily, and I'll go get groceries for you. It's not charity. I'll use the money you earned from the sale of your cream. No one need know they are for you. In the meantime, you go to the coolest place you can find in this house, put your feet up, close your eyes, and don't move until I get back." He bent to look her in the eye. "Understand?"

She slowly sank onto the nearest chair. "Why are you doing this when you know that I'll never voluntarily sell you this land? Ever."

"You want the long version or the short one?"

Her eyebrows arched. "I have a choice?"

He studied her weary countenance and prayed for a way to break through the hopelessness that was etched there. "You always have a choice, Lily, but for now I'll spare you the long tale. You see, my mama died when I was ten years old, but her death came after two very long years in a TB sanitorium miles from our home. Her sister, Aunt Hazel, was the only relative and thus this dear lady became my mother. The short, short version is—"

Lily leaned back on her chair and squeezed her eyes shut. "The short version is that your Aunt Hazel is, or was, like Mama, isn't it?"

He nodded, aware she couldn't see him with her eyes closed but hoping the silence would answer her question.

"How long?"

"Too long." He took a deep breath. "Not nearly long enough."

She sat up and met his gaze. "How can it be both?

"Too long to watch her fade away by inches. Not nearly long enough for me to tell her all the things I wish I would have said in the years before she no longer knew me."

Her face contorted. "Did she understand? I try…I want to talk to Mama but…"

"But she's not there. Right?" He knuckled away a tear that rolled down Lily's cheek. "I know. That's why I allow her to think I'm Bruce. Somewhere, way down deep, past this terrible thing that is happening to her, your mama is still there and so are you. For now, Bruce is closer to the surface. I can talk to her for you, Lily. I can tell her all the things you want her to know because—"

"Because then you can persuade her to sell this farm."

"Oh, Lily." He fought to keep his voice calm and void of the frustration this girl always seemed to produce in him. "What do I have to do to prove to you that I want to be your friend? Please make the list and allow me to go to town for you, then I'll go away and leave you alone. Any further dealings that include you and this farm can be handled by Neal Murphy and the bank, if that's what you prefer."

Joe held his breath while Lily's eyes widened and her mouth opened and closed like a baby bird waiting to be fed. He was not the mother bird, and he had nothing more than his already promised friendship to offer. Neal Murphy and the bank ultimately held the prized worm in his hands, while all Joe could do was perch on the edge of the nest and hope.

LILY'S CHEST TIGHTENED. Hadn't she voiced her annoyance at not having choices at least twice during this visit with Joe Kendall? Now here he was, freely offering her a choice, and he might as well have asked her which tooth of the saw she wanted to make the first cut. If they were going to eat this week, they needed groceries, but to go to town looking like a charwoman wasn't an option. It would take too long to get bathed, dressed, and ready—something she couldn't do with Joe Kendall present. The bank owned the farm and it made little difference who was at the helm…the ultimate outcome was obvious even to a casual observer. If Joe Kendall kept his word to never bother her again, what would become of Mama? And if…she wouldn't allow herself to think about anything future with Neal Murphy. The bottom line—she had no choice.

She raised her arms in defeat. "I'll make the list."

Ten

NEAL SHRUGGED INTO his jacket but didn't bother buttoning his shirt or tightening the tie. What would it matter? He was only going to Milly's for a quick lunch. He was not in any mood to visit with anyone, but sitting in his office mulling over his early-morning encounter with Lily yielded nothing but a deep sense of foreboding.

He couldn't help but notice Lily's broken shoelace after Florence so rudely called it to everyone's attention. He should never have allowed her to leave the bank. Why hadn't he gone after her? Was it because the townspeople had already witnessed him galloping down the street yelling her name the previous day? Or could it be fear of being rejected one more time? He'd suffered very few rejections in his life. Though it didn't surprise him that the townspeople hadn't thrown him a homecoming parade—one more reminder that he was no longer the high school hero—it did make a big dent in his pride to have Lily, of all people, show so little interest in his return to Anderson.

He pulled his office door shut behind him and took a long, deep breath of resolution. He'd put off talking with Florence after Lily's departure under such unfortunate circumstances. His secretary's attraction to him was nothing new. He'd been fully aware of her fascination with him all through high school, even though his relationship with Lily was a well-known fact among everyone in the community. He should have known better than to ask her to work late on so many evenings without explaining his reasoning. It was imperative that he set the record straight. So why hadn't he? If he were honest with himself, he found Flo's open flirtation quite appealing. But he'd had a wife. That should have been his first clue that a woman's mind worked in perceived intent before reality.

Stepping to her desk only confirmed the need for another gulp of air. The too-casual toss of Flo's hair over her shoulder didn't mask the red eyes, splotchy face, or the dagger-filled glare. He didn't have time for a discussion now, but he would certainly have to make time before the day was over. "When Mr. Kendall returns, please let him know I went to Milly's for lunch."

She jutted her chin. "Mr. Kendall won't be returning today."

Though somewhat of a relief because he wasn't ready to address the issue of Lily's absent name on the deed to the Archer farm, he did wonder what made Kendall change his mind. "Oh? Did he leave a message or say when he might return?" By the squared shoulders and ramrod-stiff back, he knew he'd asked a loaded question and braced himself for the answer.

She extended her arm and studied her bright red polished fingernails. "I think Lily Archer might best answer your question."

Unless he was mistaken, Florence Bower was waiting for him to pull the trigger on the second barrel. Well, he wouldn't give her the satisfaction, though he'd admit she had his curiosity aroused beyond comfort level. Why would Lily know Kendall's plans? And why must this response plague him in the middle of the day? It wasn't like he could close the bank and drive to the Archer farm to satisfy his interest.

He gave her what he hoped she'd interpret as a nonchalant smile.

"I guess that opens my afternoon then. At any rate, I'll be back by one o'clock should anyone need me."

The streets were eerily empty as he made his way to Milly's Diner. What happened to the usual hustle and bustle of townspeople that he remembered growing up in this place? Had he made a mistake coming back to raise his daughter in this sad little town?

Neal stepped into the diner and all chatter came to an ominous hush. Milly acknowledged his presence by pointing to an empty stool at the end of the counter. He preferred a booth, but all were occupied by the same aged faces he'd considered old before he left Anderson. Though some old-timers nodded his direction as he passed them, most averted their eyes, but not before he observed…what? What would you call a mixture of anger, pain, and suspicion? These were the same people who stood and chanted his name when he'd made a touchdown, hit the winning basket, or cleared all the hurdles before being first to break the string at the finish line. They were parents and grandparents of his friends. He'd stayed in their homes, eaten at their tables, and been made to feel a part of their families. Why the difference now? Was it because he was no longer the banker's son, but now the banker? The one who knew how much they did, or didn't have, in their accounts?

He slid onto the stool, and as soon as he turned his back the low hum of conversation began again. Not the happy chatter he'd heard when he first stepped into the establishment, but a low, hushed, secretive kind of murmuring one might hear before the start of church…or a funeral.

Milly plunked a cup in front of him. "Looks like you could use something strong, but coffee is all I serve." She poured the steaming beverage into the cup.

"That obvious, huh?" He pulled the menu from between the salt and pepper shakers. "What's the special?"

She pointed to the chalkboard mounted on the wall above the coffee maker. "Same as always on Wednesday, Neal. Meatloaf or a roast beef sandwich with gravy. Both with a side of mashed taters and your choice of salad or corn."

Neal thrummed his fingers on the counter. He'd take the roast beef, but last week it was as tough as shoe leather, and no doubt his mother would have her usual meatloaf for tonight's quick supper before prayer meeting. He shoved the menu to one side. "I'll take a salad and whatever pie you have today."

Milly slid the menu between the salt and pepper shakers. "Whatever you say. Apple pie today, but I have cream for it…that is, if you're interested in fresh sweet cream."

"Cream? I thought you told me you didn't have a supplier for cream after Franklin's Dairy went under."

Milly's eyes held a mysterious gleam. "Thanks to Florence Bower, I've found a new supplier. And this one can even deliver fresh eggs. Now, do you want cream with your pie?"

Florence? Cream and eggs? Something niggled at the back of his mind, but he couldn't decipher the message. He nodded. "Yes, please, cream with the pie and some for my coffee, too, if you can spare it."

Was he mistaken, or did Milly set the small blue-and-white pitcher of cream in front of him with an extra thud?

NEAL PUSHED HIS empty pie plate away from him and slid off his stool. Except for Benton and Gladys Finley, he was the only customer left in the diner. Not wanting to sit through another lecture about being a negligent parent, he'd chosen to eat lunch at Milly's. In retrospect, listening to his mother's scolding would have been less painful than the rebuke of silence he'd received from the townspeople.

Milly tore his receipt from her order pad and handed it to him. "Don't know how a big man like you is going to make it through the day on a puny salad and a slice of pie."

"The pie alone would keep me going for a good long time." He glanced at the ticket, then pulled his wallet from his pocket and handed her a five-dollar bill. "Take this for the Finleys, too, and keep the change." He smiled at Milly.

She folded her arms on the counter. "That's good of you, Neal, but I hope you know you can't buy your way back into the life of this community."

He plopped back down onto the stool. "What have I done, Milly? I didn't cause the drought. I haven't foreclosed on anyone. I came back here so my little girl would have the advantage of being raised in a small town...a town that I thought would embrace her as it did me."

She straightened and braced her hip against the counter. "You ever hug someone who turned their back and kept their arms locked to their sides?"

He shrugged. "What does that have to do with how I was received in here today?"

Milly tapped him on his chin. "You admit this town embraced you. And they did. But they see you leaving as you turning your back."

"I went to college, Milly. I didn't leave anybody." He rubbed the back of his neck. He did go to college, that part was true. The part about not leaving anybody was a lie, and, by the look on Milly's face, he was about to get called on it.

Milly gave a quick glance toward the Finleys and then leaned across the counter. "You and I both know that's only partially true, Neal Murphy. You went to college for two years. You've been gone from Anderson for eight. If Lily Archer had accepted your proposal, you'd have returned every weekend of those two years, and come back here to stay six years ago."

"But she didn't—"

"I'm not done." Milly slapped both hands on the counter. "That little gal is probably the first person who ever dared to say *no* to you, and you tucked your tail between your legs and slunk away like a whipped pup. In the meantime, hard times fell on these parts. Real hard times. But the good people around here stayed, and they stayed some more and now—"

"I…I got married."

She thumped him on the nose. "Will you quit interrupting me? I don't want to hear your lame excuses. Yes, you got married, and not one person from this town or for miles around this community was invited to the wedding. You never brought your wife to Anderson. We only learned of her through the picture sitting on your father's desk when we had to go in and beg for his mercy to extend our loans."

"She…she didn't like…her family was…" Neal braced his elbows on the counter and covered his ears with his hands. He didn't want to hear more, but he knew Milly well enough to know that she'd only gotten a running start.

Milly grabbed his hands and pulled them away from his ears. "Don't you dare try to blame that on your dead wife. You're a grown man, or at least you want us to think you are. Sometime in the past eight years you could have stiffened your spine enough to bring her home, introduced us to her so we could have known her name before reading it in the obituary. Do you have any idea how many people in this community would jump at the chance to love on your little girl?"

"I—"

"Uh, uh, uh." She held her hand over his mouth. "You not only turned your back, Neal, but you locked your arms to your side and refused the embrace this town would have given you with their hearts wide open. That's your doing, not your wife's."

He hung his head. His chest hurt and heat flowed like hot water through his body. Though Lily was indeed the first person who'd ever refused an offer of any kind from him, Milly was the only townsperson bold enough to skin him and salt him down. He wiped his hands down his face. "So how do I fix it, Milly?"

She straightened, crossed her arms, and huffed out a sigh. "The *it* you want to fix isn't only one thing, my boy. There's been a whole chain of events tied together, and now you're the only one who can figure out what they are and how to undo the tangle."

Benton Finley approached the counter before Neal could answer. "I certainly do thank you, Milly. Me and Gladys sure enjoy our Wednesday dinners. Bless her heart, Gladys tries but she never has made a good meatloaf." He nodded to Neal. "You visiting, are you?"

Neal cleared his throat. "No, Mr. Finley. I...I've come home to stay."

"I see. Are you working at the bank now?"

"Yes, as a matter of fact, I am. Dad is ready to retire and, well, I—"

The older man's forehead wrinkled. "Hmm. I was in earlier, but Florence said the procedures had changed and I now needed an appointment to see Mr. Murphy. She didn't say you were the Mr. Murphy who changed the way things have always worked."

If his chest got any tighter, he'd be unable to breathe. "I have time right now, Mr. Finley, if you care to accompany me back to the bank."

Sad eyes matched the older man's smile. "No. No. It can wait. No money will grow on our bushes between now and next week." He leaned closer. "I don't like to worry Gladys so I try to do my banking business when she's busy serving her coffeecake to the gentlemen for Wednesday morning prayer breakfast. We both need a good long nap by afternoon so we can make it back in for evening services." He nodded at Milly. "Are you sure you won't let me pay you, dear?"

Milly bustled around the end of the counter and kissed the older man on the cheek. "Not on your life, Benton. You've helped me and many others out of a bind so many times we can never repay you."

Tears filled the man's faded blue eyes. "Never did it to be repaid. Did it, when I could, because what is ours belongs to God anyway. Don't keeps us from being grateful, though." He turned to Neal. "I'll stop by the bank and make an appointment for next week."

Neal stood and put his arm around Mr. Finley's shoulders. "No appointment necessary. I'll see to that."

Milly turned to Neal as soon as the Finleys departed. "Now that you know I never make the Finleys pay for their meals, you want some money back?"

He shook his head. "No, Milly. Maybe you know of someone else who needs it worse than I do."

"Every person you saw in this diner today needs it worse than you do, Neal Murphy. You'll find that out soon enough."

"I'm not so sure of that. I seem to be a slow learner." He didn't wait for a reply, but no doubt the woman agreed with him.

Eleven

JOE SMILED AT the young woman at the grocery store register. Her copper pigtails tied with green bows and the sprinkle of freckles across her upturned nose gave her the appearance of a schoolgirl. He'd not even attempt to guess her age, but she always had a smile, and in this town such a treat was hard to come by. "I see you're pulling double duty again today, Daisy." He lifted items from the cart onto the counter.

Daisy blushed. "Yes, sir. I work at the drugstore of a morning and here of an afternoon." She leaned across the counter and motioned for him to come closer. "They can't neither business afford to pay me full time, you know." She closed her eyes and took a long breath. "Oh, my! That Old Spice you bought this morning surely does smell good." She tilted her head and pointed at the various items he'd placed to be rung up, then peered at him over the top of her horn-rimmed glasses. "Mr. Kendall, are you buying groceries for L.A.?"

"Who?" Heat burned his cheeks. How did this girl know these weren't for him?

She gave a furtive glance toward the door, then motioned for him to lean closer. "These aisles have ears. Think really hard. L.A. L, like

93

in Lil—"

He put a finger of his lips. "Shh. How did you know?" While he didn't see another person in the store, he'd take her word that the aisles had ears, a unique gift, he'd discovered, in small towns.

Daisy held up two bananas. "She buys the same thing every time she has money to spend. Bananas are for her mama, you know. Only luxury she allows. Nothing ever for herself."

"Nothing for herself? Ever?" Well, he could change that. "How well do you know her?"

"Oh, we've been friends since we were born, I suppose you could say. I know lots of stuff I won't ever tell."

Joe leaned his elbows on the counter. "Okay. Are you allowed to tell me one thing I could purchase in this store that would be a surprise? Something she would really like?"

Another customer stepped into the store and Daisy squared her shoulders. "Aisle three, top shelf, green can, Mr. Kendall. I believe that's where you'll find the canned salmon." She greeted the new arrival with a smile and a nervous giggle. "Mr. Kendall here hasn't learned his way around the store yet. Couldn't find the salmon." She turned her attention back to Joe. "You might want to get two cans. They're on special. Oh, and you inquired about a lace-edged handkerchief. I'm sorry, we don't carry anything like that here, but you'll find them over at the apothecary. In fact, we got a new shipment in this morning. Your *mama* will love the pink ones, I'm sure. You run get the salmon you asked for, and I'll finish ringing these up for you." Her lips tipped into a mischievous grin.

Joe rolled his lips to keep from smiling on his way to aisle three. Daisy was quite the girl. He'd not even come close to inquiring about a lace-edged handkerchief, but, bless her heart, he got the message loud and clear. He'd hug her if it wouldn't appear so inappropriate. He grabbed two cans of salmon from the top shelf and hurried back to the register.

Daisy had the other items sacked when he returned. After a furtive glance around the store, she motioned for him to lean forward again. "You'll find a bag of peanuts in one of the bags, and if you stop at Ernie's on the way out of town and get a couple bottles of orange sodas, you'll…well, you'll see what happens. Oh, and I'm glad you purchased that good-smelling stuff before N.M. knows we carry such a thing."

"N.M.?" Why did this girl insist on speaking in abbreviations? And what was with the bag of peanuts and orange soda? He'd tried the soda and failed miserably. Was the bag of peanuts a special potion of some kind? *Guess it wouldn't hurt to try again.* "Who is N.M.?"

"You'll figure it out, only please don't tell L.A. what I said." She straightened and rang up his latest find, then situated the cans of salmon on top of the other things in the sack. "Do come again, Mr. Kendall. Always a pleasure to serve you."

He winked at her. "I'll do that, Miss Miller. You say my mama would like the pink handkerchief the best?"

She pushed her glasses up on her nose. "Oh, yes. Pink. For sure."

He lifted the groceries from the counter. "Thank you so much for your help."

"Any time, Mr. Kendall. Oh, wait! You have your arms full. Let me help." She rushed around him to open the door.

"Well, now, this is real service." He nodded his appreciation.

She flipped one shiny braid over her shoulder. "Like I said, any time."

Joe stepped out of the store, pleased that he seemed to have gained a friend and perhaps a very helpful confidant. But his pleasure was short-lived when he bumped against someone, sending a can of the salmon crashing to the sidewalk. "I'm sorry." He lowered the sacks and met the annoyed countenance of Neal Murphy. *N.M. Of course!*

The frown on Murphy's face quickly faded. "You couldn't see me. I should have warned you somehow." He retrieved the can from the sidewalk and placed it back in one of the sacks. "I'd shake your hand, but it appears that would be difficult. I am sorry about this morning, however. If you have time, perhaps we could have our meeting after all. I'm headed back to the office right now. Unless you'd rather take your groceries home first, of course."

Well, this is awkward, Joe. You better think fast. He used his knee to hoist one of the bags further up into his arms. "I do thank you, but I'm afraid I'll have to make it another day. I have one more stop and then I'll be out of town until later this evening. Perhaps Miss Bower could pencil me in for first thing in the morning."

Murphy rubbed his hand over his chin. "Ah, yes, Miss Bower and her famous appointment book. I can't believe I thought it a good idea. Strange how quickly one forgets how small a small town becomes in a few short years after leaving home."

"Or how long a year becomes to those who have no choice but to stay and call it home."

Murphy's eyes darkened. "Yes, there's that, too." He gave a mock salute. "I'll make sure my heavy schedule has room for you whenever you decide to keep our previous appointment. Though I must say, I'm not looking forward to what I'm sure will be a most touchy situation. Do you drink anything stronger than black coffee?"

"Never. But have you ever had a cup of Milly's coffee after it's been on the burner for a few hours? It will curl nails."

Murphy laughed. "Dear Milly. That's something that hasn't changed in this place. I'll quit talking so you don't drop that armload of groceries. You needn't worry about being penciled in." He stepped past Joe with a wave of his hand. "See ya tomorrow."

Joe wrestled the sacks into the back seat of the car, then made a dash across the street to the drugstore. How did Daisy Miller know…He stopped and slapped his forehead with the heel of his hand. While he'd been busy smiling and nodding at the inquisitive shopkeepers on his walk with Mrs. Archer this morning, they'd all been busy putting two-and-two together to come up with solutions to satisfy their own curiosities. Not only did the aisles of the grocery store have ears, but the entire main street had eyes, and each business had a telephone. Party lines could spread news faster than ticker tape. He'd have to remember that the next time he so blithely walked hand-in-hand with someone along the sidewalks of Anderson.

Joe stepped into the apothecary and was greeted by the druggist before he could take ten steps. "Got it ready for you, Mr. Kendall. And got a message, too."

The druggist glanced around the premise, then leaned closer to Joe's ear, though there wasn't another soul in the place. "Can't be too careful, you know. Daisy said to remind you to get three bottles of orange soda, not two. Guess she doesn't want Ruth Archer to have to go without." He took a step back and handed Joe a small sack and winked at him. "That'll be fifty cents. Well, fifty cents for the…for what's in the sack. Unless…" He cleared his throat, then whispered, "If you're needing more of my special sleeping potion, it'll be seventy-five cents. No need for the whole town to know you can't sleep at night. Most would likely think it's because of your job, talking people out of their homes, you know. But you and I know the real reason, don't we?" He winked at Joe, then leaned his head back. "La, la, la, la, la, la," he sang. "See, it even makes a little tune." The druggist's bald head turned as pink as the man's face.

"It…It isn't what you think, Mr. Jackson." Joe dug two quarters from the pocket of his britches.

"It never is, my boy. But that bag of peanuts Daisy sneaked into your sack of groceries will tell the real story. Yes siree, the real story." He took the money and padded to the cash register. "You need a receipt? Now, if pink won't do, we got yellow, blue, or green and will exchange with no questions asked *if* you have a receipt."

Joe chuckled. "I'll tell you what, I'm going to take Miss Miller's word that pink will be just fine."

The druggist's *la, la, la, la, la, la* followed Joe all the way to his car and was still ringing his ears when he drove up to the gas station, only to find Ernie standing in the doorway holding three bottles of orange soda.

"What took ya so long?" Ernie's gold tooth shone as if it had been polished. "Daisy saw you leave the drugstore three minutes ago." He cackled as he approached the car. "No need gettin' out if ya can dig fifteen cents on ya somewhere."

Joe pulled the change from the pocket of his britches. "Wait, Ernie. I also have a question."

Ernie set the sodas on the fender. "Now then, you know I don't chinwag."

"I know." Joe handed him a nickel and a dime. "This isn't gossip. At least I don't think it is. What kind of magic is in a package of peanuts?"

Ernie bent at the waist and slapped his knees with both hands, laughing so hard he wheezed. "It ain't gossip and that's a fact. It's a game...the peanut game." He pulled his dirty red shop rag from the pocket of his grimy overalls and swiped it across his face. "Lands to Betsy. I can't believe a big important fella like you ain't ever took a bag of peanuts with you when you went a-courtin'. Ya wait right here and I'll show ya." He hurried into the station and returned with a bag of peanuts. "Now, ya pay close attention." Ernie tore the top off of the cellophane bag with his teeth. "Hold out your hand."

Joe switched off the engine and stuck his hand out of the window. Evidently this was something that couldn't be explained without a demonstration.

"No, no. Palm up." Ernie poured about half the sack of peanuts into Joe's open hand. "Now, I'll go first." He popped a peanut into his mouth. "You love me. Now it's your turn."

Joe frowned. "My turn to do what?"

Ernie looked at him cockeyed. "Your turn to pop a peanut into your mouth and say, 'I love you not'."

98

This is crazy. Joe placed the peanut in his mouth and said the prescribed words. "Now what?"

"You love me." Ernie popped another peanut into his mouth. "And then it's your turn again. We keep this up until the peanuts are all gone."

"A game with no winner? What's the sense in this?" Joe placed a peanut in his mouth and chewed but didn't repeat the phrase.

"Well, now, if I was the one what ended up with the last peanut, I'd be sayin' you love me and you'd be givin' me a kiss, right here." He pooched out his lips. "Can't get no more winnin' than that."

Joe chuckled. "I can't argue with that, but what happens if I end up with the last peanut?"

Ernie huffed and shook his head as if he'd encountered the dumbest creature ever made. "Well, boy, if you was the one with the last one, you'd be declarin' 'I love you not' and there'd be no smoochin'. Some folks say it's gamblin' and don't like their young'uns playin' it."

Joe nodded. "It is a gamble, all right. But why the orange soda?"

Ernie stuck another peanut in his mouth, chewed, swallowed, and then wiped his mouth with the back of his hand. "Half a bag of peanuts gets right down dry. Don't have to be orange soda, but it happens to be Lily's favorite. I reckoned ya knowed that since you got three of them the other day."

"I didn't know. You were drinking one when I drove up and I thought it looked good. That's all. Besides that, how did you—"

"Nope. Don't be askin' how I knowed what I know 'cuz that's gettin' real close to chinwaggin'."

Joe started the car. "It's not at all what you think, Ernie. Not even close."

Ernie reached through the open window and gave Joe's shoulder a shove. "Never is, you know. Never is."

One last glance in the rearview mirror as he drove away revealed Ernie waving his shop rag. Even from the lengthening distance, Joe could see the grin on the man's face.

He doubted Lily would find it at all amusing. But...he was not above gambling.

LILY CLUTCHED THE cans of salmon to her chest. "How did—"

Joe shrugged. "Before you scold me, D.M asked if I was buying groceries for L.A., and once I figured out her abbreviated message, I asked questions. Please, don't be angry with either of us."

"D.M.?" She giggled. How long had it been since she and Daisy had communicated with only the use of initials? "And I suppose D.M. also advised you to purchase the peanuts and orange soda?"

"Well, Daisy put the peanuts in the sack herself and advised me to go to the drugstore and purchase the lace-edged handkerchief in pink for *my* mama. The druggist had it ready for me, and Ernie gave me the lesson on peanuts. I don't suppose you'd be interested in playing the peanut game. We could make it D or N."

"D or N?" She was familiar with the game but had no idea what he meant with the letters.

His lopsided smile signaled mischief. "Oh, that's simple. Double or nothing." He wiggled his eyebrows, but the gaze below them communicated much more. If only his eyes weren't so blue, his voice so gentle, and her heart so tempted. But she'd played this game before and vowed she'd never do it again. She couldn't afford to lose.

"No, Joe." She turned and walked to the sink so she wouldn't have to look at him. If Neal Murphy was a magnet, Joe Kendall was the force behind magnetism. "The last time I played that game, I got nothing."

"Neal Murphy?" Joe's breath was hot on her neck. "I was told you turned him down."

"I thought you didn't discuss me in your meeting."

He took her by the shoulders and turned her to face him. "We've never had a meeting, nor have we ever discussed you or anything pertaining to you, Lily. I was warned, or advised, or whatever name you want to put to it, by more than one person in this town, that the two of you were once sweethearts and that he left when you didn't accept his proposal. I don't know any more than that and I'm not asking you to explain."

He didn't expect an explanation, so why did she want to give him one? Why was it important for him to understand when she had every intention of sending him away? "I had to choose to keep a promise I made to my papa or make a promise to Neal. I couldn't do both. He told me I broke his heart, but the truth is, he didn't stick around long enough to hear mine shatter as he walked away. You know how they say it is better to have loved and lost than never to have loved at all? It's a lie. I loved. And I lost because I loved. So...no more games."

The intensity of his gaze burned into hers and she was powerless to look away. He stroked her cheek. "What if I were to tell you that what I feel for you is not a game?"

For a split second, she was tempted to walk into the embrace she knew would enfold her...but only for a split second. "You told me that if I made a list you would go away and leave me alone. I made the list. Now please, go away." *No, please, please stay. Don't leave me. Don't go.*

Joe's face blurred, but not before she saw pain etch itself across his countenance. He raised his arms in surrender. "I'll go, but only because I promised. Any further dealings that involve this farm can be handled through Neal Murphy at the bank." The muscle in his jaw rippled. "I gambled. I lost."

"Bruce?"

Lily startled. How long had Mama been standing in the doorway? How much of the conversation did she hear, or understand?

Joe's shoulders drooped. "May I have permission to give her the handkerchief?"

Lily nodded, not sure words would make it past the lump in her throat.

Joe turned from Lily and lifted the handkerchief from the table. "I bought you something, Mama. Someone told me you liked pink."

Mama smiled, took the handkerchief from him, and held it against her cheek. "Pink. I like pink. Lily has a pink dress." She fingered the lace edging. "What a good boy you are, Bruce."

Lily pressed her fist against her mouth. Mama remembered Lily yet didn't recognize her.

Joe took Mama's hands and kissed them. "You're good, too, Mama. But I have to leave now."

"Leave?" A single tear made its way down Mama's cheek. "I wish you didn't always go away." She swiped at her cheek with the handkerchief, then wound it around her hands. "Everybody always leaves me, you know. First…first…" Her brow furrowed and she looked at Lily. "Girl, who was that man who left a long time ago?"

Lily swallowed. "You mean Papa?" *She can't remember the man she married but she can't seem to forget her one and only son.*

"Oh, yes. Papa. First my papa left. Then Lily left. Now you're leaving." She stood on tiptoe and kissed Joe's cheek. "Be a good boy and come right home after school."

Pain clouded Joe's eyes. "I can't tell her goodbye, Lily. I can't. I've had to say goodbye to too many people that I love. I can't and won't do it again." He put his hand against the cheek that held Mama's kiss. "I'm keeping my promise to leave, but I won't say goodbye because the truth is…I'm not going anywhere."

The click of the screen door and the sound of his footsteps moving away from her resounded against Lily's head like the death toll that rang the day of Papa's funeral. She couldn't bring Papa back. She didn't know how to reach Bruce. She couldn't make Mama well again. But all it would've taken to stop Joe Kendall from driving away were two simple words she couldn't get past her lips…*Don't go.*

Twelve

"WHERE WE GOING, Daddy?"

Neal smiled at his little daughter as she bounced on her knees beside him. "For a ride, Rosebud. It's a surprise."

Rosie hung her head out the open window and squinted her eyes against the wind and dust as it pummeled her cheeks. "If I do this," she opened and closed her mouth while going *aah-ooh-aah-ooh*, "it makes a funny noise, like a fire engine. Can you hear me?"

Neal grabbed the hem of her dress. "I hear you, but get your head back into this car before a bug flies into your mouth. Next time you open that window you're going to be in big trouble. Your hair is a mess and you let all the dirt blow inside."

"Ewww!" She plopped onto her bottom and scrubbed at her mouth with her hands. "When will we get there? Will I like the surprise?" She hopped to her knees again and hung over the back of the seat. "Can we get ice cream after our surprise?"

Neal grabbed her dress and pulled her back to down onto the seat again. "If you don't stay sitting, I'm going to turn this car around and go right back home. You're going to end up hurting both of us if I have to keep taking my eyes off the road to make you sit still."

Rosie folded her arms over her chest with a huff. "I can't see when I sit like this, Daddy. It makes my tummy feel sick when I can't see where we're going, and it's too hot in here with the window closed."

Neal pulled to the side of the road, pulled the keys from the ignition, and opened his door. "You stay in here and I'll see if I can fix something so you can see." Helen had always insisted they carry extra blankets with them while traveling in case of an emergency. With any luck at all, there would be at least one in the trunk. But then, the way his day had gone so far, *luck* would not be included in the events to be remembered.

Florence Bower had cried and threatened to quit when he told her she didn't need the appointment book—or maybe it was because he also informed her that while he valued her as a friend and employee, he had no romantic interest or intentions whatsoever.

Then his mother had whipped up her usual Wednesday meatloaf along with a great big dish of guilt because he rejected her offer to accompany them to prayer meeting. She did seem rather pleased and even kissed him on the cheek when he told her of his plans to spend the entire evening with Rosie, though she made sure he knew her bedtime was eight o'clock. It didn't take away the guilt—his plan to spend the evening with Rosie was a last-minute ploy to avoid further argument from his father about his reluctance to attend church with them. His original plan was to visit the Archer farm and plead once more for Lily's affection. However, having Rosie with him could well serve a much better purpose and hopefully result in a much better end. Lily loved little kids. And Ruth Archer had headed the children's department at church for as long as he could remember so she would not be home tonight.

He fumbled with the lock on the trunk, then heaved a huge sigh of relief when it opened and revealed not one but two large comforters. He'd thank God, but it was Helen who'd stuck them in there. He slammed the trunk and went around to Rosie's side of the car, only to find his daughter's nose flattened against the window, a smile as big as her little pudgy face would allow, and the door locked.

He scooted around to the other side, but she beat him to it and pushed the lock before he could grab the door handle. "Rosie, roll down the window." If only he'd listened to Helen and purchased a four-door vehicle to begin with.

She shook her head. "You told me I'd be in big trouble if I rolled the window down," she yelled through the glass, then plopped back down on her bottom, the top of her head barely visible.

He knocked on the window. "Rosie. Open this window."

What he could see of her head shook from side to side, a sure sign she was through using words. "Okay, then. See that little black knob you pushed down? Pull it up again, sweetheart. I can't show you your surprise if you won't let me back into the car."

Up came the chubby cheeks. "Am I in trouble?"

"Not yet, but I want you to pull up on that little black thing."

Pudgy fingers grasped the lock and pulled, but nothing happened. "It's too hard, Daddy. It won't come up."

"Then try the other one."

She bounced on her knees to the driver's side and pulled and pulled, but it proved to be as stubborn as the other one. "It won't come up, either." Tears now rolled down the already pink cheeks. "It's too hot in here." She swiped at her face.

"Rose Anna Helen Murphy, you roll down that window right now." Helen would never have raised her voice, but she'd never been locked out of the car by a four-year-old, either.

Curls bounced as Rosie shook her head in defiance. "You're crabby and I'm always in trouble when you're crabby." She threw herself onto the seat, face down, her sobs resonating loud and clear.

He should have taken his mother's offer. He could certainly use a prayer meeting.

A cloud of dust fast approached from the west and he stepped from the road to wait for the car to pass. He groaned when the motor slowed. Gravel rolled and dust and grit enveloped him as the vehicle pulled to a stop beside his. *Great. Of all people to find me like this, it has to be him.*

"Got trouble?"

Neal sighed and brushed at the dust. "Joe Kendall. What are you doing out this way? I thought you had business out of town."

Joe grinned and swept his arm in an arc. "I *am* out of town, Neal. Had some landowners to see, papers to sign…all in a day's work but it did take me away. I'm headed back in now, but it looks like you might need a ride. What seems to be the trouble?"

Neal braced one foot on the running board of Joe's car. "My trouble comes in a blonde-headed, four-year-old package by the name of Rosie. If you listen closely enough, you can hear her. She's locked the doors and refuses to roll down a window."

Joe laughed. "You have an armful of blankets. Are you thinking you might have to spend the night?"

"No, I was going to fold them so she could sit higher on the seat. It sounded like a good idea."

"Hmm. Where'd you get the blankets?"

"My late wife insisted we always carry extra blankets in case of an emergency. Thank goodness they were still in the trunk."

"I see." Joe's face broke into a smile. "And may I assume the doors were locked *after* you exited the car and opened the trunk?"

Neal's cheeks puffed. "Obvious, don't you think, Kendall?"

"And how did you *open* the trunk?"

Neal hung his head and slowly withdrew one hand from beneath the stack of blankets. The hand that still held the keys to the car. He groaned and dangled the keys in the air. "Do you have any idea how stupid I feel right now?"

Joe's face turned red with laughter. "The banker outsmarted by a four-year-old. You pay me big bucks and I promise to keep quiet about this when I get back to town."

Neal joined in the laughter. "I tell you what, Kendall. You ask *anything* and you shall receive. And I mean anything."

Joe sobered. "Are you serious, Murphy? As I recall, we have a meeting in the morning. Give me tonight to think it through, but I intend to take you up on your offer of *anything* if you really mean it."

"Wait a minute." Neal turned, unlocked the car door, and lifted his hot and sobbing daughter from the seat. "You can stop crying now, little one. You're not in trouble. Daddy had the keys all along."

She snuggled her face between his neck and shoulder. "Do I still get a surprise?"

"Yep. Sure do. As soon as I finish talking to this nice man." He wiped her face with his hand, then settled her on his hip. "See, this is Mr. Kendall. He's our friend. And Kendall, this is Rose Anna Helen Murphy. My four-year-old bundle of trouble."

Joe gave a mock salute. "Hello there, Miss Rose Anna Helen Murphy. I'm very glad to meet you. I've seen your picture on your grandpa's desk, and you know what?"

She shook her head. "No. What?"

"I don't think you look like a bundle of trouble at all. I think you are a very pretty little girl."

She giggled. "Can we go now, Daddy?" She looked at Joe. "My daddy has a surprise for me."

Joe dropped his chin and widened his eyes. "A surprise? Well now, that sounds like fun. I better let you get on the way. See you tomorrow morning, Neal? If you don't mean *anything,* you better tell me now before I have an entire night to think on it."

Neal pursed his lips and shrugged. "Anything within reason, Joe. The truth is, it might not hurt for the townspeople to see me as the fool I feel, but for now I'll grant you one big *anything.*"

"I'll let you get on with your mission, then. Can't imagine what kind of a surprise you have way out here, but I'll take your word for it."

"Rosie's never been this far outside of city limits. I was hoping to sit beside her on the banks of Willow Creek, but if I don't hurry it's going to be too late. I do happen to know a place so special I could get there with my eyes closed, however." He winked. "Not easy starting all over again, Kendall. If you've never been in love, or married, you won't understand. Thanks again for your help. I'll look forward to our meeting in the morning."

Neal waved as Joe drove away. Something had happened between introducing Kendall to Rosie and offering the last little hint of the surprise for his little girl. Was it his remark about starting over, being in love, married? Had he hit a sore spot on the man? *Wait!* A new thought smacked against his mind. The guy wasn't jealous, was he? He didn't have time to worry about it this evening, but it was for sure something he'd consider later. He'd never had to compete for Lily's attention in the past and he didn't like the idea of doing so now, especially not with someone like Joe Kendall.

He put Rosie back into the car. "You know what, sweetie? You stand here right beside me so you can see while we drive. You keep watching. Maybe you'll see some cows."

JOE'S GUT TWISTED as he drove away from Murphy. He was tempted to leave him in a cloud of dust, but he couldn't afford to lose the opportunity to plead for Lily's land.

As sure as his name was Joe Kendall, Neal Murphy was headed for the Archer farm…and Lily. Little Rosie was a ploy, but a good one. What kind of a person could turn away a pudgy, pink-cheeked, curly-headed girl like that? Lily loved an ugly mutt named Dog. She'd adore Neal's child, and the thought made him sick to his stomach.

He drove to the end of the mile, then pulled to the side and switched off the ignition. After leaving the Archers' earlier, he'd spent the rest of the day driving around. Until meeting Lily, the names on the mailboxes along the road had only been faded lettering on the sides of dented, leaning boxes beside rutted lanes leading to rundown farmsteads.

Now, however, he could put faces to the names. Sad but proud faces of both men and women who'd spent their lives making homes that were more than houses in need of paint or barns that leaned away from the wind.

He'd sat in those homes and observed numerous family pictures— mothers and daughters, fathers and sons—all in a row lined atop the tall piano that sat as a prized possession in the living room of nearly every home he visited. Photographs taken by a traveling photographer who set up his equipment in the church basement. Black-and-white images of men in suit coats that strained against the buttons, their wives in dark dresses with white collars, and children attired in matching outfits cut from printed flour sacks, seams carefully ripped open, washed, and saved until there was enough fabric to make the prized picture-taking clothing.

Until the Archer farm. Oh, there was the piano in the living room, adorned with the predictable crocheted-edged topper. But only two photographs, one of whom he presumed to be Paul and Ruth Archer, and the other of Lily and Bruce.

He pounded the steering wheel with his fists. If he hadn't used nearly all the gas in his car to roam the countryside this afternoon, he'd follow Murphy now. But having the banker find him along the road, out of gas, would be every bit as embarrassing as finding the banker locked out of his car while holding the keys. He started the car and pulled back onto the road. He had tonight to figure out a way to make sure Lily and her mother would be cared for, though there was nothing he could do to preserve their farm. *Anything.* That's what

Neal Murphy promised, though it rankled him to know that the slick, hometown boy was, most likely, sitting right now in the presence of Lily Archer, introducing her to his little princess. And there wasn't a single thing he could do about it.

Thirteen

NEAL CLENCHED HIS teeth as he turned down the lane leading to the Archer farm. What was he doing? The plan that seemed so right, though very last minute in order to keep him from sitting through another lecture from his father, now seemed foolhardy. How many times did he have to be told *no* before he understood the meaning? Bringing Rosie along bordered on pandering in so many ways. Helen would never have allowed their daughter to be used in such a ruse. What if Lily was at prayer meeting with Ruth? How would he explain that to Rosie, who was expecting some kind of grand surprise at the end of this venture? For that matter, what was the surprise? Cows they didn't see? A creek they didn't stick their feet in? Or perhaps a dog that wouldn't let him beyond the gate unless someone was there to call it off.

Rosie leaned across his shoulder and peered through the windshield. "Is that house my surprise?"

Well, Neal. You should have turned around when you thought about it. "Not the house, sweetie. But someone very nice lives there and I want you to meet her."

She bent and cranked her neck to look at his face. "How do you know she's nice?"

"Well, first of all, she has a flower name like you."

Rosie clapped her hands. "Her name is Rose Anna Helen Murphy?"

"No. No. I mean like your name is Rose, like a flower. Her name is Lily, like a flower."

"Oh." She scrunched her nose. "You mean Lily Like A Flower means she's nice? Why are we stopping? I don't think I want to live here."

They'd reached the gate and were greeted by Dog standing on guard, crouching with teeth bared as if he would attack at the slightest provocation. At this point, he'd rather face Dog than try to answer his daughter's questions. He leaned across Rosie to peer at the house. "We're not going to live here, Rosie. Just visit."

"Oh." She scooted from behind his shoulder and plopped to her bottom on the seat. "Does the lady know we are visiting?"

Lily stepped from the house, hands on her hips.

He'd seen that stance too many times and it wasn't one of welcome. "She does now." Did he dare open the car door? He reached across Rosie and rolled down her window a few inches. "Is it safe?"

Lily shrugged. "What are you doing here, Neal? I thought—"

Rosie rose to her knees and did her best to get her head out the window. "Hi. My name is Rose Anna Helen Murphy but mostly it's Rosie. My daddy says you're nice because your name is Lily Like A Flower, but we're not going to live here. May I have a drink, please?"

SO, THIS WAS the new game Neal chose to play? *If at first my appearance doesn't win you over, try my little girl.* Lily pinched her hands against her hips. She had a weak spot for little ones, and he knew it. How could she refuse the child a drink? It was an unspoken rite of country hospitality—you never refused a cup of cold water, even to a stranger. Lily sighed. She was sure if she dug deep enough, she'd remember a Bible verse that went along with that thought but she had neither the inclination nor time to worry about it. Right now, Neal Murphy was her concern. If it weren't for his thirsty little girl, she'd go back inside and let growling Dog handle the intrusion.

"Dog. Stop." Lily walked to the gate and smiled at the little girl hanging her head out the window. "Well hello there, Miss Rose Anna Helen Murphy, mostly Rosie. What would you like to drink? I have water or milk."

"Are you inviting us in, Lily?" Neal lifted his daughter from the car. "Are you alone?"

"You knew I would, Neal." She nodded her head toward the little girl in his arms. "You brought the winning ticket." She turned and made her way up the steps to the kitchen door, then swiveled to face him. "By the way, to answer your other question…I'm not alone. Mama is here." The corners of his mouth turned down in a pout. Did he think he'd find her alone waiting for him? Those days were long past. "We're finishing supper. Have you eaten?"

Neal nodded. "Wednesday, night. Mother's meatloaf. I…I supposed your mama would be at church."

She made sure he was looking at her before she addressed his supposition. "I was asked two years ago to not bring my mother back to church." She didn't try to keep the anger from her voice.

His eyes widened. "You were…? Why? Who would—"

Why did it give her so much satisfaction to see him struggle for a response? Neal Murphy, who never lacked for words. "Ask your parents, Neal." Lily stood to one side as he sidled past her into the kitchen, then waited for the deep breath or scowl he was sure to offer when he focused on Mama. Perhaps his unfinished questions would be answered. She slid past him and sat beside Mama. "Look who's here, Mama. It's Neal. Do you remember him?"

"Why wouldn't she remember me?" Neal reached for her mama's hand. "How are you, Ruth? It's been a long time, hasn't it?"

Mama ignored his hand, her eyes resting on Rosie. "Lily! You came back." She reached for the little girl.

Neal's eyes widened full of questions as he turned to Lily with a scowl. "What's wrong with her?"

Mama turned sideways on her chair. "Come, Lily." She beckoned to Rosie. "Come to Mama. Where have you been? I thought you went away."

ROSIE SLIPPED FROM Neal's arms and made her way to the arms of Ruth Archer before he could stop her. "Hi. My name isn't Lily, but I have a flower name, too. It's Rosie. What's your name?" She wiggled onto the older woman's lap and lifted a glass from the table. "Did you have milk with your supper?" She turned to Lily. "I'll have milk, please."

Neal was close on Lily's heels as she went to the cupboard. "Would you mind telling me what is going on?"

Lily tilted her head. "I'm getting your daughter a glass of milk. That should be obvious, even for a city boy."

"Stop, Lily." He stood between her and the icebox. "You know that's not what I'm asking. Besides that, don't give Rosie milk. She's never had cow's milk before."

A smirk greeted him. "Really? Oh, let me guess. You buy your milk from the store, so of course it wouldn't come from a cow. And the milkman has the night off?"

"Why are you being so sarcastic?" he hissed, not wanting Rose to hear them argue. "Helen…Helen never allowed her to have anything but pasteurized milk. It's dangerous. A child can get all kinds of—"

Lily slammed the glass down on the cupboard, her face within inches of his. "Look at me, Neal Murphy. I am *not* Helen. The milk I serve, the milk I have freely drunk my twenty-six years, comes straight from this farm, our cow, and so far, no child has gotten anything from it except strong bones and pink cheeks. You brought her here. Exactly what did you expect? What is it you *really* want from me? It's more than something to satisfy your daughter's thirst, isn't it?"

He glanced over his shoulder at Rosie chattering away at Ruth, who seemed to be content to nod her head and smile. "What is wrong with your mother? You were standing right there. She thinks Rosie is you. Has she—"

Lily cocked her head to one side. "Lost her mind? Well, it would appear so, wouldn't it? That's not a question I can answer. You, on the other hand, have yet to answer mine. Why are you here? What is it you really want?" She leaned her back against the cupboard and crossed her arms. "Go home, Neal. There's nothing and *no one* here for you."

Years of knowing Lily Archer gave him the nerve to take her face in his hands. "I'm here for you, Lily." He bent to kiss her—she'd never been able to refuse this show of affection—but she pushed his hands from her face and gave him a shove. As he stumbled backwards, his eye caught an empty salmon can on the counter, next to a bag of peanuts and three bottles of orange soda.

He lifted the empty can from the counter. "I thought something was fishy." He slammed it back down. "Joe Kendall? Really, Lily?"

"It's not what you think, Neal. But even if it were, you have no say over my life. You relinquished that right a long time ago." She opened the cupboard and reached for a glass.

He fisted his hands at his side. This was not at all the evening he'd envisioned. "If it's not Joe Kendall, then what, or *who*, is it?"

She slammed the cupboard door shut and turned, her face red and her hands clenched. This was a side of Lily he didn't know…a side that wasn't afraid to charge him head-on.

"What is it? Who is it? I owe you no explanation, Neal. Not now.

Not ever. But I know you. You won't be satisfied until you get the answer *you* want to hear, not the truth. Well, guess what? You're going to hear the honest-to-goodness truth, then you're going to take your little girl and leave and you're not coming back. Ever."

"Never?" He took a step toward her but stopped when her eyes shot arrows of warning. "You can't mean that, Lily. Never is a long time."

"You think I don't know that?" Lily's eyes welled with tears, but she raised her chin as if to refuse to let them fall. "My papa is *never* coming back. Mama will *never* be well again. And no matter how hard I try, no matter how much I *have* tried, I will *never* be able to keep this farm. Yes, Neal. I do realize that never is a long time."

"Then—"

"No! You listen. *I'll* talk."

By the time Lily had unleashed eight years of anger and anguish, Neal felt as though he'd been tackled and dogpiled. Only there was no referee's whistle to disengage the weight that now had him pinned. To say that he'd fumbled the ball was an understatement. And to be informed that Joe Kendall had recovered the fumble and was well on his way to score big time only added to his angst.

Without a word—because he had none—he lifted Rosie from Ruth Archer's lap and limped his bruised and battered ego out the door. Even Dog seemed to sense his defeat, although a nip at his heel would hurt less than the pain in every word Lily had unleashed. There was nothing to do now but tuck tail and retreat—once again.

The trip home was a nightmare. Between replaying Lily's words and trying to answer Rosie's questions, his mind was in such a muddle he couldn't even give his correct name if asked.

He gave a long sigh of relief when a dark house greeted his return. With his parents still at church, he could get Rosie settled for the night before she added any information to the conversation that was sure to come.

ROSIE'S BARE FEET pattered across the hardwood floor as she came from the bathroom and hopped into bed. Her face was still pink from the warm bath and she smelled as sweet as the flower for which she was named. "Night, Daddy." She flopped to her back and snuggled down on her pillow.

He smiled at his little girl. She looked so much like her mama, and for a fleeting moment guilt added to his already tangled nerves. "Goodnight, sweetheart." He bent to kiss her.

"Daddy, are you mad?"

He sat on the edge of her bed and pushed a damp curl from her forehead. "No, I'm not mad. Why do you ask?"

"That lady at our surprise sounded mad, not the grandma one, the other one who has a flower name. I forget what flower. Then you got all red and pouty on the way home."

He smiled at his daughter. *Pouty* was a mild word to use for his reaction to Lily's tirade. In reality, he was embarrassed. No, it was much more than mere embarrassment. He was mortified and humiliated and if there were stronger words, he couldn't think of them. The worst part, he deserved every syllable.

"Sometimes when grownups talk, they use loud voices." He folded his hands over hers. "Besides, I'm not mad at you, so you go to sleep and have sweet dreams." He reached to her side table and turned on the fan. "You want me to leave the light on until I go to bed?"

Her blonde hair bounced against the pillow. "No, but aren't you going to listen to my prayers? Grandma Murphy always listens."

Another wave of shame splashed over him. He should have been the one listening to her prayers all along. Helen did. It was Helen who taught her to pray in the first place, something he argued she was much too young to understand. How long had it been since he tucked this little girl into bed? Or said a prayer of his own, for that matter. "Of course, sweetie. I'll listen to your prayers."

Rosie pulled her hands from his and folded them under her chin.

"You have to close your eyes, Daddy."

"Oh, I forgot." He winked one eye shut. "Will one eye do?"

"No, silly." She giggled. "Both of thems."

He closed his eyes. "Okay. Now I'm listening."

"Dear Jesus. Thank you that Mommy lives with you in Heaven and isn't hurted in the bad car crash any more. Thank you for Daddy, only could you please help him not to work so hard so he has time to play with me? Thank you for Grandma and Grandpa Murphy. Thank you for the surprise grandma who talks funny and calls me Lil—" She poked Neal's arm. "Open your eyes, Daddy. I 'membered the lady's name. It's Lily Like A Flower, only Surprise Grandma called *me* Lily, didn't she?"

He tweaked her nose. "Yes, she did, sweetie. Are you through praying now?"

"Oh, no." She squeezed her eyes shut again. "Thank you for Surprise Grandma and thank you for dying on the cross. Amen." She opened her eyes. "You can turn the light off. Grandma Murphy says I'm a big girl and Jesus has angels who look after me." She flipped to her side and tucked one hand under her cheek. "Night, Daddy."

Neal ran his hand along the bannister as he descended the steps in the dark. How much disgrace could one man handle in a night? He'd come back to Anderson strutting like a bantam rooster, a real cock of the barnyard. Tonight he'd been scalded and plucked by Lily and was now singed of any remaining fine hairs of pride by the prayers of a four-year-old.

He shuffled to the kitchen and turned on the light. The coffee would be cold by now, but it was the strongest thing he'd ever find in the Ed Murphy household, and he did need something strong.

He poured himself a cup of coffee, turned off the light, and made his way to the living room. He'd wait for his parents. It was high time he acted like the man he thought himself to be—until tonight's reckoning of the dismal truth.

Fourteen

NEAL SQUINTED AGAINST the sudden burst of light as his parents entered the house and flipped on the overhead fixtures.

"My goodness, Neal. Why are you sitting in the dark?" His mother unpinned her hat and laid it on the table beside her chair. "Is something wrong?" She wrung her hands. "Oh, dear. Don't tell me Rosie is sick."

"Rosie is fine, Mother." Neal crossed his legs and ran his fingers down the crease of his trousers. "How was prayer meeting?"

"Wouldn't hurt you to come along and find out for yourself, son." Father took off his suit coat and hung it on the stair rail. "People ask about you all the time."

Neal wasn't going to allow this conversation to center on the fact he was considered backslidden. "Was Ruth Archer there? Or Lily?"

"Oh, my." Mother settled into her chair. "I can't even remember the last time Ruth was there. Can you, Ed?"

Father leaned back in his chair and tented his fingers. "I don't think Ruth's presence at prayer meeting is what Neal is wanting to discuss, Mildred." He nodded to Neal. "Am I right?"

Neal braced his forearms on his thighs. "I visited the Archers—"

"Oh, Neal, you didn't take Rosie with you, did you?" Mother held her Bible to her breast. "That dear woman is—"

"What, Mother? Not all there? Sick in the head? Have you or anyone else from church visited with Lily to see if she needs help? Does anyone really know what is wrong with Ruth, or if she could be helped in any way?"

"Well…" She placed the Bible in her lap, her fingers tapping on it as if she might be able to coax words or music from its binding. "We took a care basket out at Christmas maybe two years ago now. Lily, however, returned it the next day."

"A care basket?" His voice broke as if he were going through puberty. "So, did you or anyone else load that basket up and take it right back out there, along with an extra good full measure of real concern, Mother?"

Mother raised her chin and sniffed. "It seemed a bit…a bit ungrateful to have it returned, Neal."

"Ungrateful?" Neal jumped to his feet, then sat down again. If he were to make any kind of point, he had to remain calm. "Oh, Mother. How many years did Ruth Archer help you put together those so-called care baskets? You don't think Lily knew how the people who received them were labeled? Poor? Old? Homebound? Unchurched? Was Ruth any of those?"

"Exactly what is it you want us to say, son?" Father lifted the newspaper from the floor beside his chair. "Or maybe you have something you would like to address. Obviously while you were gone, we've not acted or done anything in a manner which pleases you." He folded the paper in half.

So help me, if he rolls that paper… "I'll be the first to admit, I've not acted in any way that would convey to anyone observing that I am a Christian. No way." He scrubbed his hands down his face. "That was driven home to me tonight in a manner that I'll not soon forget."

"By whom?" Mother's voice shook.

"By Lily, Mother. And all the while she was saying what I should have heard years ago, Rosie was sitting on Ruth's lap chatting like they were two lost friends. Only Ruth thought Rosie was Lily."

Mother clutched her neck. "Oh, Neal, you didn't let—"

"Is that why Lily was asked not to bring her mother back to church?"

Father rolled the paper. "There are things you—"

"I can't believe you two." Neal stood. If he was going to get a lecture, he'd meet it head-on. "Are you still chairman of the deacon board, Dad?"

Father nodded. "Only because no one else will take the responsibility."

"Why, then, when the main focus of every meeting you've ever chaired was how to get more people inside the four walls of your tidy little church, would you ask someone who has been as faithful as a sunrise to not come back?"

Father's face turned red and he threw the paper to the floor. "Ruth Archer hasn't been…isn't…she's not—"

Neal stood and paced between his chair and the stairs. "She's sick, Dad. The doctor doesn't even know what is wrong with her. She can't help her actions, and neither can Lily."

Mother hugged her Bible to her breast again, as if it were a shield. "Some of the children were…well, we had some parents who were concerned. Children ask questions, you know, and…and—"

Neal stepped in front of his mother. "And because you good, God-fearing people couldn't come up with Bible verse to satisfy a child's natural curiosity, you thought it best to *cleanse* the church. Get rid of the question and you don't need an answer. Right? You do realize that what is wrong with Ruth isn't contagious, don't you?"

"There's no need for rudeness, Neal." Father thrummed his fingers on the arm of his chair. "It's a difficult situation, and I'll admit it might have been handled with more forethought. However, I have extended Lily's loan several times over the past years. And—"

He shook his head. Of course, money was always the solution. "But you never extended a hand, did you? Did anyone? Why is it if a person doesn't know what to say, they seem to lose their power to *do*?"

He turned to his mother. He'd never talked down to her, but this had to be said. He'd deal with the consequences later. "You might not want to hear this, Mother, but tonight when Rosie prayed, she thanked God for the *surprise grandma.* Ruth Archer, no less. And one more little tidbit that might interest you both—while the church was busy trying to figure out how to get people to join them, and preparing care baskets, and praying for the foreign missionaries, a stranger came to town. A stranger who allows Ruth to think he's her prodigal son and has done more for Lily in the few days since he's known her than those of you who've lived here your entire lives."

Mother gasped. "A stranger? Lily let a stranger—why, son, we made sure that Lily knows she can call on any of us at any time if she has needs. I distinctly remember telling her myself to let the church know…a stranger? Does she know how dangerous that—"

Neal sat back onto his chair and ran his hands through his hair. "The stranger is Joe Kendall, Mother. The man in charge of building the new lake."

Father raised his eyebrows. "Kendall? You think he doesn't have an ulterior motive for what you call his *doing*? I'm sure he's well aware how vital the purchase of the Archer property is to the whole lake project."

"Ulterior motive or not, Dad, at least he did *something.* And guess what? He didn't even call a committee meeting first.*"

Father pounded his fists on the arm of his chair. "That's quite enough."

Neal jumped to his feet and faced his father. "No, it's not nearly enough. Do you know that when I saw Lily at the bank this morning, she was wearing—" He swallowed past the lump in his throat. "She was wearing the same dress that she wore the night I proposed." He swiveled to look at his mother. "Eight years, Mother. When was the last time you wore a dress eight years old?"

Mother gave a small shake of her shoulders. "Well, I wish she would have called someone."

"Called someone? Who, Mother? You? Were you listening at all? Do you think for one minute that Lily would call on anyone? Would you?" He dropped his arms to his side. "Are you even aware that the Archer farm still has neither a telephone nor electricity?"

Mother gasped. "Why, for pity sakes?"

He shrugged. "I didn't ask, Mother, but I would imagine money, rather the lack thereof, is a big factor. Things that you take for granted don't come without a price tag."

"And still you think that this Joe Kendall doesn't have a price tag attached to his good deeds." Father flicked his hand as if shooing a mosquito. "Don't be foolish, my boy. There are no free lunches these days."

Neal sank slowly back into his chair and massaged his temples. "I very much would like to think badly of the guy, Dad. You have no idea how my gut wrenches at the thought of him doing for Lily what I can only sit back and watch because my pride wouldn't allow me to accept her refusal of my proposal. I tucked tail, as Milly so painfully put it, and ran away rather than stay to fight for her."

"Oh, Neal. *Gut* is such a…a coarse word." His mother shut her eyes as if she could see the actual anatomy.

He slammed the heels of both hands against his forehead. "You don't get it, do you, Mother? Let me put it in perhaps a more refined manner. I'm jealous of the man, and I've never before had reason to be jealous of anyone. I was Neal Murphy, after all. I came back to Anderson wearing my high school crown of laurel and riding in my bright red steed. I was to be the new banker, make new rules, whip this sorry little town into shipshape with my appointment book and my twenty-six-year-old, still-wet-behind-the ears, suave persona. Then today happened."

"Today?" His parents donned matching frowns.

Neal recounted the entire day's events, from Kendall relinquishing his appointment to Lily, Florence's intentional embarrassment of Lily, his awkward lunch at Milly's and even more awkward conversation with Florence Bower, to his ploy to *surprise* Rosie and finding evidence that Joe Kendall had not waited to be asked, but rather took it upon himself to make sure Lily and her mother had food in the house.

Father scoffed. "If you think buying the girl groceries isn't putting a price tag on his *doing,* then you aren't using your head."

Neal clenched his fists. "And if all you've gotten from this conversation is that Joe Kendall is a conniving rascal, then you're not using your heart."

Father scooted to the edge of his chair. "Why does Lily Archer's association with this Kendall fellow concern you so much? With all you've told us tonight, there's more that you aren't saying. Now would be the time to speak up."

Father was right. This would be the perfect time to speak up. But could he say aloud what he'd pondered in his heart since the day he returned to Anderson? Neal braced his elbows on the arm of his chair and made sure he had the full attention of both parents before continuing. "You're right, Dad. There is more...much more. I've never stopped loving Lily Archer, and before you succumb to shock over that statement, let me assure you that, yes, I did love Helen. I fully realize how contradictory that concept sounds, but it's also the truth."

"Oh, Neal. That's adultery. It says so clearly in Matthew." Mother rifled through the pages of her Bible. "Yes, right here...Matthew chapter five, verse twenty-eight, 'whosoever looketh on a woman to lust after her hath committed adultery with her already in his heart.'" She folded her hands atop the Bible on her lap, seemingly satisfied that she'd made her point and dared him to defy God's Word.

Neal bit his top lip and took a long breath. "Don't even go there, Mother. In the first place, I hadn't seen Lily for eight years so there was no *looketh* involved. Secondly, how many times have you reminded me that *God's Word is sharper than a two-edged sword*? Do you really want a sword fight? I can parry with the best. I won a first-place trophy for memorizing verses in Sunday School. Remember?" He turned to Father. "Hand me your rapier, if you will."

"My what?"

"Your Bible, Dad. Hand me your Bible."

Father reached across the space between the two chairs and handed Neal his Bible. "This is foolishness. Complete foolishness."

"Mother took the first jab. I'll take the second." He searched for the verse he wanted, then stood and assumed an *en garde* position, the Bible his sword. "James chapter four, verse seventeen. 'Therefore to him that knoweth to do good, and doeth it not, to him it is sin." He made a forward thrusting move. "Or how about James chapter two, verse twenty? 'But wilt thou know, O vain man, that faith without works is dead?' Your turn, Mother."

Tears rolled down Mother's face, but Neal ignored them. "For the record, I was never unfaithful to Helen. Never. Not until I drove into Anderson knowing this was now my home again, did I even admit to myself that I still loved Lily. Did I think about her over the years? Yes. But never with even the slightest idea or hope that the opportunity to see her, court her, perhaps renew a relationship with her would even exist. And she made it very clear tonight that she doesn't want me to ever return to the Archer farm."

"Oh, well, then." Mother smiled through her tears. "You know there are plenty of young ladies here in Anderson. Take Florence Bow—"

"No, Mother. I will *not* take Florence Bower." Neal's heartbeat pulsed in his ears and his legs tingled, a sensation he experienced every time he stood at the edge of a precipice with no safety rail. If he could, he'd desert his post at the bank, pack up Rosie, and go back to Kansas City. He'd used that cut-and-run tactic before, and yet here he stood, once again at the very edge of the cliff with only two alternatives—

jump or retreat. If he jumped, he'd undoubtedly end up a broken heap at the bottom of the hill he'd chosen for battle. But if he retreated…

With a vengeance, the words he'd so proudly spouted about winning a trophy for memorizing verses came back to haunt him. *Proverbs chapter twelve, verse fifteen…The way of a fool is right in his own eyes: but he that hearkeneth unto counsel is wise.*

Lily had made it quite plain tonight…he'd been a fool, was still a fool. Though it would mean retreating from the immediate battle in order to gain any semblance of wisdom, he had to take the first step toward counsel, which included swallowing a huge lump of pride.

He turned to Father. "After my long rant, I know I have no right to ask this of you. I have an appointment with Kendall in the morning and I have no idea how to handle it. We all know that Lily's name is not on the deed to her farm. I'd appreciate you sitting in on the conversation. I realize we can't save her property but there has to be something we can do to make the transition less painful for her and less confusing for Ruth. Wouldn't you agree?"

A slow smile lit Father's face. "I'll be there. What time?"

"No set time, but what little I know about Kendall, he'll be there first thing. Maybe you could come with me in the morning early enough to grab a cup of coffee and one of Milly's cinnamon rolls before we go to the bank."

Father's face softened. "I'd like that, son. I'll be ready."

LILY LOWERED HERSELF to the porch floor, hung her legs over the side, and hiked her nightgown above her knees in a desperate attempt to get some relief from the heat. She couldn't sleep. Not with the house like an oven, and Mama lying on her mattress with her eyes wide open, clutching the pink lace-edged handkerchief. When Neal and Rosie left, the light dimmed in Mama's eyes. If only she could explain to her that Neal's little girl was not Lily…that Lily had never left…that *she* was Lily, not *girl*.

After years of having no one who seemed to care, no one with whom to talk, no one to hold her, knuckle away her tears, or even try to kiss her, she'd managed, in the space of twelve short hours, to send away not one, but two such candidates. Maybe it was a good thing she couldn't sleep. Every time she shut her eyes, Joe Kendall's pain-etched face filled her vision. Oh, if only she could erase the memory of the way the corners of his eyes crinkled when he smiled, the gentle voice he used with Mama, his long strides and tanned, muscular arms, and…She pounded her fist on the porch. And the way he smelled, of all things. Wouldn't Daisy get a good laugh with that little bit of information?

She unbuttoned the top button of her gown and swiped the perspiration from her neck with the hem. Heat lightning flashed above the horizon in the east, far beyond any hope that rain would come her direction anytime tonight. What difference would it make if there was a downpour? It was too late to help the corn, the one crop that might have at least given her enough money to make some kind of good-faith effort to pay on the mortgage.

The mortgage. The bank. Neal. *Oh, Neal. If only you'd never walked away. If only you'd never returned.*

"Papa knows."

Lily's heart thumped at the sudden interruption of the quiet night and she scrambled to her feet as Mama pushed open the screen door and stepped onto the porch.

"Papa knows what, Mama?" This was the same statement she'd made when Neal showed up a couple of nights ago. Would she ever know what Mama meant?

Mama walked to the nearest porch post, wrapped her arms around it, the handkerchief still clutched tightly in one hand, and peered off into the distance.

"Mama? What does Papa know? Please. Can you tell me?" Lily

held her breath. Would Mama talk, or recede back into her own world?

"Mr. Fancy Britches." Mama moved away from the post and padded back to the kitchen door. "That girl made Bruce leave, too." She opened the door and slipped inside.

Lily's throat tightened. Papa had always called Neal *Mr. Fancy Britches*. How was it that Mama could remember so much, and yet so little? Lily leaned her head against the closed screen and fought the tears and words that threatened to choke her. For now, *that girl* was Mama's enemy, and Lily didn't much like her, either.

Fifteen

MILLY POURED COFFEE into the cups she set in front of Neal and his father. "Good to see you again, Ed. This young whippersnapper in trouble already?" She nudged Neal's shoulder with her hip. "You two look like you either had a sleepless night or were in a fight."

"Guess you could say both." Neal chuckled and handed the sugar to Father.

"Huh! I guarantee your day is about to get better." Milly pulled her order pad from the pocket of her apron. "What can I get you two gentlemen this morning? You want the works?"

Neal shook his head. "I think we'll be fine with a couple of cinnamon rolls, and cream if you have it. Is that okay with you, Dad?"

Father grinned up at Milly. "I thought your cinnamon rolls were the works."

"Only if you ask for extra frosting." She winked and stuffed her order pad back into her apron.

Neal laughed. "Then bring us both the works."

"Two cinnamon rolls with extra frosting coming right up." Milly set the coffeepot on the table between them. "I'm going to leave this for you. Believe me, you're gonna need extra—"

"Neal? Neal? Oh, my goodness. I'm so glad I found you." Florence Bower's high heels stuttered across the floor as she scurried to their booth. "Oh, and you, too, Mr. Murphy." She fluttered her hands. "Silly me, you're both Mr. Murphy, aren't you? Well, then, I'm not sure who, or is it to *whom*…oh, anyway, you need to come to the office right away. I tried to ring your house but Clarice, over at the phone office…you know Clarice Timmons, the girl who took my place when I got the job at the bank? You don't have to answer that. Everyone knows Clarice. Anyway, I gave her your number. I said, 'one-hundred please', in my most professional voice, and she said, 'I can ring it, Flo, but if you're looking for Neal I saw him and his father go in to Milly's Diner, and I thought to myself, '*my goodness, if both Mr. Murphys are together this early in the morning, then something very important must be going to happen*', but then I told myself, '*now Flo, dear, it's not all that unusual for a father and son to have coffee together*'." She took a deep breath and fanned her face with both hands. "Anyway, of course I hung up and I nearly ran, except I can't run in these shoes, all the way down the street, and here you are sure enough, drinking coffee, but you really need to—"

Neal grabbed Florence's fluttering hands. He was out of breath listening to her. "Now slow down. You found us. Why do we need us to come to the office right away?" He looked at his watch. "It's only eight-thirty. I didn't think you opened the doors until nine o'clock."

Red splotches appeared on Florence's neck. "Well, you needn't get snippy, Neal. I…I had some work I needed to finish and…well, since I was already there, I didn't see any…I guess, well, anyway, you have a client waiting and he's not one bit happy."

"Joe Kendall?" Neal frowned. It didn't sound like Kendall, but maybe the man got wind he wasn't the only visitor Lily had yesterday and wanted to make sure he was the first one seen this morning.

"No. No. Oh, goodness no. Mr. Kendall would never—"

Father tapped his spoon against the table. "Enough chatter, Florence. Who is waiting at the bank and why are you in such a panic?"

Florence straightened the jacket of her suit and jutted her chin. "Bruce Archer. That's who."

"Bruce Archer? Here in Anderson?" Neal and Father spoke in duet.

Florence slammed her hands on her hips. "That's what I'm trying to tell you."

"You want me to wrap those cinnamon rolls to go?" Milly nodded to Neal as she put her arm around Florence's shoulder. "You run back to the bank, Florence, honey, and tell Bruce that Mr. Murphy will be there shortly. Can you do that?"

Florence gave a toss of her head. "Of course I can. I *am* the bank secretary, after all. Oh, but which Mr. Murphy?"

Milly's eyes twinkled with mischief. "Which one did he ask for?"

"Just Mr. Murphy." Florence's hands fluttered again.

Milly rolled her eyes. "Then tell him that Mr. Murphy will be there soon."

Florence put one hand on her cheek. "Oh. Oh, yes. Of course. That will do. Mr. Murphy will be there soon."

Neal winked at Milly. "Wrap the cinnamon rolls, Milly. And Florence, when you get back to the office you might put on a pot of coffee."

Father nodded. "And make it strong, Florence."

Neal waited until Florence left before addressing Father. He'd observed a slump of his shoulders and heard the whoosh of air that escaped his lips when Bruce's name was mentioned. "Is there something I need to know, Dad? Does Bruce's return mean trouble?"

Father gave a wry smile. "You were so busy admiring Lily all those years, I doubt you remember much about her brother. In my past experience, anything to do with Bruce Archer usually contains a whole lot of trouble. I have a feeling he knows the Archer place is vital to the lake project and is here to demand his share of the profits."

"He can't do that, can he?"

"Right now, he has as much legal right as Lily." He scooted from the booth and pulled his wallet from the inside of his suit coat. "I'll get the bill this time. I have a feeling we'll be having coffee and cinnamon rolls many a day before this is settled."

Neal stood and patted Milly on the shoulder. "You left the pot of coffee because you knew Bruce was in town, didn't you?"

She poked at Neal's temple. "Oh, you catch on real fast. He was in earlier, wondering when *old man Murphy* would be at the bank."

"Old man?" Father huffed. "That boy has needed an old man in his life for a long, long time but Paul spoiled him. Now we'll more than likely have to deal with the rot."

Milly laughed and planted a kiss on Father's cheek. "Well, the joke is on him when the two of you walk in. I doubt he counted on Neal being with the *old man.*"

Neal shook his head. "And you got some kind of wicked satisfaction by not telling him I was back in town, didn't you?"

"Not near so much as I'm getting right now." She nodded toward the big window at the front of the diner. "While you two were discussing Bruce Archer, Joe Kendall walked past going in the direction of the bank. Were you expecting him this morning?"

Neal groaned. "We were, but not this early. What now, Dad? Do we face them both at the same time, or divide and conquer?"

In an unexpected move, Father slid back into the booth. "Neither. Let's finish our coffee. Milly, bring us those cinnamon rolls."

Neal seated himself across from his father. "Are you sure this is the best idea, Dad? I mean, once those two fellows figure out the identity of the other one, there could be a real dog fight."

"Nah." Father spooned sugar into his coffee. "More like two strays, circling, sniffing, and growling, but I doubt there'll be any bloodshed. Kendall's too much a gentleman, and unless Bruce has changed, he'll—" He licked his spoon and set it on the table, then yelled across the diner, "Milly, what is it you told my son he did after the Archer girl turned him down?"

Milly laughed. "You mean tucked tail?" she hollered back.

"Yes, that's it, thank you." He shook his finger at Neal. "Believe, me. Bruce Archer will tuck tail before he fights the likes of Joe Kendall." He took a sip of his coffee. "Enjoy your coffee, son. Trust me on this one." He winked. "Welcome home."

JOE HESITATED AS he stepped into the lobby of the bank, surprised the doors were unlocked so early and certainly not expecting to find a well-dressed, vaguely familiar, young gentleman already seated and a pencil being swallowed by Miss Bower's hungry sharpener. He nodded at the young man but was greeted with a huff and a scowl. There were some things even a good suit couldn't disguise, a nasty disposition being the most obvious.

Florence looked up from her task, a bounce accompanying each turn of the crank. "Uh...please have a seat, Mr. Kendall. Mr. Murphy will be right there. I mean...*here*. Mr. Murphy will be right here, but this...oh dear...well, I mean...this man is—"

Joe smiled at the flustered secretary. "It's all right, Florence. I'll wait my turn."

She pulled the stub of pencil from the throat of the sharpener. "You wouldn't have to wait if Mr. Murphy would let me keep an appointment book." She plucked a new pencil from the holder on her desk and inserted it into the jaws of her grinding machine. "This isn't Milly's Diner, you know, where people can walk in and expect first-come-first-serve." She grabbed the handle of the sharpening tool with her thumb and next two fingers. "I went to business school, you know." She gave a crank. "Two years at business school." *Crank.* "And I took first place in appointment-book-keeping." *Crank. Crank.* She was gaining speed. "Then I come back here, and Mr. Murphy sees no need." *Crank. Crank. Crank.* "'Keep the customers happy, Miss Bower', he says."

Joe put his hands over the sharpener. If he didn't stop the poor girl, she'd have every pencil within reach ground to a stub. "It's okay, Florence. Waiting will give me more time to plan my day."

The stranger stood and waved a newspaper in the air between them. "Plan your day, huh? And what poor farmer are you and this bank going to swindle today?"

Joe pulled himself to his full height, satisfied that he stood head and shoulders above the man…though man-child would be a better description. "Excuse me?"

The newcomer took a step toward him. "Oh, I know who you are." He slapped the front page of the newspaper with the back of his hand. "Mr. Big Shot Foreman, Joe Kendall. Your picture and everything. Bet you're surprise to know the Archers can read."

Ahh. No wonder the man looks so familiar. Lily took the same stance, waved a newspaper in the air, and spouted the same angry words at me three days ago. "And you are?"

"Huh! You don't know who I am? Well, for the record, I'm Bruce Archer, part owner of the land you're trying to sweet-talk my sister into selling to you."

Joe rolled his lips to still the retort that burned to be released. "I'm not sure who you've been talking to, Bruce, but they've given you some misleading information." He fought to keep his voice steady when what he wanted to do was knock the smart aleck on his rear for abandoning Lily and their mother. "Since we both have appointments with Mr. Murphy, I suggest we talk with him together. I've heard your accusations. I think it only fair you hear the truth."

He turned to Florence, who was studying the most recent pencil stub as if it had her fortune written on its remaining two inches.

"Perhaps when Mr. Murphy arrives, you can inform him that he has two clients who would like a joint meeting. Oh, and I hope I'm not overstepping any protocol, but a pot of coffee might be nice."

"Ooohhh!" Florence jumped from her chair. "I was supposed to…Mr. Murphy told me to…oohh…" She ran from the room crying.

"You have quite a way with women, Kendall." The arrogant young Archer sneered as he sat down and crossed his legs. "You wouldn't be so sure of yourself if Neal Murphy were still around." He puffed his chest. "They were sweethearts, you know, Lily and Neal. Neal's the banker's son. He's sure to come into a lot of money when old man Murphy kicks his silver bucket." He sniffed and brushed the sleeves of his jacket. "Yes, sir. Neal will be hanging around here for life and you'll be moving on."

For the first time since entering the bank, Joe wanted to laugh. Though he didn't find the reminder of Lily and Neal's past romance in the least funny, he couldn't wait to see Archer's face when he realized their joint appointment was not with the *old man.* "You're overlooking one important piece of information, Bruce. You see, it's not my job to have a way with women, nor does it include sweet-talking anyone out of anything. I'm sure after our visit with Mr. Murphy, you'll see things in a different light."

"Oh yeah?" Bruce doubled his fists and punched the air. "Well, I'm here to tell you, you try taking advantage of me or my family and I'll make sure all you see are stars."

Joe returned the threat with a smile as he sauntered to a chair across from Lily's brother. No need for the wise guy to know he still held the record for the fastest knockout round in the annals of his college boxing club. But oh, how he hoped there'd come a day.

Sixteen

NEAL WAITED FOR Father to unlock the back door of the bank that led directly into his office, bypassing the lobby. The sensation of power Neal had so readily claimed in the few days he'd occupied the tall-backed leather chair behind the massive walnut desk dulled upon entering the office of the bank president behind his father. Why did it take his father's presence to bring back the awe this room had imparted to him as a child?

For a moment, he was the little boy who lined his toy cars around the perimeter of the parquet floors or counted the squares in the tin ceiling. The floor-to-ceiling bookcases held more books than he'd wanted to count as a kid. The stacks of file cabinets, however, had been a source of childhood curiosity. Not until he'd attained the key to unlock the secrets did he understand why he'd so often witnessed Father withdraw a file, heave a long breath, and settle back at his desk with the countenance of a judge about to pronounce a life sentence knowing all too well that the accused was innocent.

Neal leaned one shoulder against the closed door and watched as Father swiped both hands across the top of the desk, as if shoving unnecessary papers from its premise. He straightened his tie and unbuttoned all but the middle button of his suit coat. Then he brushed one hand through his hair, sat, pulled the chair close to the desk, folded his hands on top, and bowed his head.

Father had a ritual that Neal had, with a great sense of irritation, likened to worship. Today, he involuntarily closed his eyes. It *was* worship, in a sense. How had he never equated his father's bowed head to prayer? Why had he not noticed that he talked to the Lord before he greeted clients? Maybe that's why his own few days here had been so chaotic. What did his father ask of the Heavenly Father? Wisdom? Strength to get through the day? A miracle, perhaps? Was he praying now for his son, the one who thought he could waltz back into Anderson and expect everyone to dance to his music?

Not until a rush of air hit his face did Neal open his eyes and raise his head. The final act of the ritual was to stand and pull the chain to start the ceiling fan above the desk.

Father nodded toward him as he sat back down, an unexpected mischievous twinkle in his eyes. "Open the door, son. Let's inform Florence that we're ready to receive our esteemed guests." He chuckled. "Pull one of the chairs here beside me so we can enjoy their entrance into our presence together. Kendall expects to meet with you, Bruce thinks he's facing me. Let's see what happens when they face the mighty Murphy Mob."

Neal laughed as he opened the door, then pulled a chair from the three that occupied the space in front of the desk and scooted it so he could sit beside Father. "Two of us hardly makes a mob, Dad."

"I know." He poked Neal with his elbow. "But I won't tell if you don't." He thumped his knuckles on the desk. "Florence? Are you out there?"

A very subdued Miss Bower appeared at the doorway. "I'm here and…and now Mr. Kendall is here, too, and he said I should say that you have two clients who want to see you at the same time. Well, I'm not supposed to say it at the same time, that would be silly, but they want to meet with you at the same time…together."

Neal smiled at her. "Then send them both in. Oh, and perhaps bring us that pot of coffee and cups to go around, please."

Florence clasped her hands in front of her. "And whom shall I say will see them?"

Neal folded his arms atop the desk and leaned forward. "I think 'Mr. Murphy will see you now' will be sufficient, Florence."

The secretary's face flushed. "I know, but…oh, you needn't be so snippy, Neal."

"I…I'm sorry. I…I—"

Thankfully, Father came to his rescue. "Send them in, Florence. I'm sure they are expecting to be seen by a Mr. Murphy. There's no need to elaborate."

"Yes, sir." Miss Bower flipped her hair over one shoulder and turned with a huff.

Neal raised both arms as if to surrender. "Was I snippy?"

Father's shoulders shook with laughter. "If you haven't learned by now that what a man says and what a woman hears is often two different statements, then I'd say you've just been schooled." He pulled a handkerchief from his inside jacket pocket and wiped his face.

Neal's shoulders drooped. To say he was a slow learner would be an understatement. Things might have been much different had he learned that lesson eight years ago.

"Well, this is a surprise. Good morning, gentlemen." Joe Kendall's entrance into the office brought Neal back to the task at hand.

Joe shook their hands. "Good to see you again, Ed." He turned to Neal and nodded. "You, too, Neal. It's good to see you both." He seated himself, leaned against the back of the chair, and stretched his long legs in front of him.

Neal rolled his lips. If Kendall was the least bit intimidated by the Murphy Mob, it would take someone with a keener eye than his to discern it. He wanted more than anything to dislike this guy, but he had to admire the confidence he exuded.

"I take it you've met Bruce Archer," Father addressed Kendall. "I thought he would come into this meeting with you."

Joe gave a wry smile. "Oh, yes. We've met. I think he's waiting to make an entr—"

"Mr. Bruce Archer to see you, sir." Florence stood at the doorway wringing her hands. "I'll…I'll be right back with the coffee."

Neal gave a quick perusal of the guy as he entered the room. Though he was much larger in stature than he remembered, he recognized the arrogant demeanor. If only he could discern the look on Kendall's face. He certainly didn't seem threatened by the man's appearance.

Bruce brushed past the secretary, took two steps into the room, then turned back and shook his finger at her before she could leave. "What is Neal doing here? I thought I told you I wanted an appointment with *old man* Murphy."

Father pounded his fist on the desk and stood. "If you ever refer to me as the *old man* again, I will personally haul your behind out of this bank. I did not tolerate that behavior from my son, and I certainly won't tolerate it from the likes of a smart-mouth kid like you. Is that understood?"

Bruce glowered, his face so red it was nearly purple, but he sidled to the chair next to Kendall and lowered himself into it.

"I did *not* give you permission to sit, young man." Father spit out the words through clenched teeth.

Neal rolled his lips. Oh, how he wished there was a newspaper handy. Father was so much more formidable with a rolled newspaper in his hand.

Bruce rose to his feet, his hands clenched at his sides.

Father sat down and folded his arms across his chest, eyes shooting a warning. "Now, then. Let's start this over again. If you think for one minute your rude entrance into this room made you appear important, I'm here to tell you that it did nothing but confirm to me that you are still the brash, cocky, rude, undisciplined, lazy, little boy who left town six years ago."

Bruce jutted his chin. "I'll have you—"

Father ran his fingers across his lips from corner to corner. "Zip it. You'll not utter another word in my presence until I give you permission. Is that understood?"

Archer's eyes darted between Neal and his father.

Neal shrugged. "I'm here to tell you, Bruce, you won't win this one. My father may appear old to you, but I guarantee he's an expert rear-end hauler." He planted the palms of his hands on the desk and leaned as close to Archer as he could get. "And I'll help."

"Now, then," Father continued. "I think that's settled. You may sit and state the reason you wanted an audience with me today."

Bruce lowered himself to the chair, but his face was still red, his eyes full of daggers, and his hands clenched.

Neal stole a quick glance at Kendall, who'd remained quiet and, by all indications, detached from the scene. Yet, behind the stoic façade there was an aura of dominance. He had no doubt that Joe Kendall could hold his own in any battle, including and especially one that involved Lily Archer. And that concerned him more than the reappearance of Bruce Archer.

JOE BRACED HIS elbows on the arms of the chair and tented his fingers, determined to remain as aloof as possible while the Archer boy stated his case. He'd sensed Neal's eyes on him throughout the parley between Bruce and Ed Murphy and had steeled himself to give no outward signs of the battle that was raging in his mind...and heart.

His mind, because until he heard Bruce's entire concern, he'd have no way to defend his stance. His heart, because anything that involved Lily, in any way, now involved him in ways he hadn't anticipated.

Bruce squared his shoulders. "As the man of the Archer family, I felt it only right to come back and defend our family farm against the likes of this…this," he pointed to Joe, "man whose sole objective in this project is to swindle farmers out of their land and put money in his own pocket. I know for a fact that Anderson can't build the lake without the water from Willow Creek and we Archers own that creek. It's gonna cost a pretty penny, Mr. Joe Kendall, great and mighty foreman, to get me to sign any papers over to you."

Joe bit his tongue. The longer he could stay out of this foray, the more ammunition he could stockpile.

Ed Murphy folded his hands atop his desk, a picture of authority that, by the look on Bruce's face, he hadn't expected. "First of all, Bruce, I believe that Mr. Kendall is a big enough man to defend his own actions against your accusations, so I will allow him time to do that when I finish this conversation with you."

Bruce sneered. "Yeah. Well, I've already told him what he can expect from me if he tries to swindle the Archers."

Ed raised his hand, palm out, a clear sign he wanted Archer to stop talking. Joe could hardly wait to hear what the man had to say next. "My second point is this, and listen closely, the owner of the Archer property, until such time as the mortgage is paid in full, is this bank."

"What do you mean, *the mortgage*?" Bruce scooted to the edge of his chair. "That farm has been in the Archer family for generations. Are you telling me it hasn't paid for itself over and over again?" He ran his hands over his face. "Pa should never have left Lily in charge. She's nothing but a girl. What did she know about running a farm?" He pointed to the elder Murphy. "What's your cut of the profit, old man?"

Joe watched in awe as Ed Murphy and his son rose from their chairs simultaneously and in slow motion. If he were called into court as a witness to this scene, he'd swear an oath that the men each grew six inches in the doing. Bruce must have sensed it also, as he wilted in direct proportion, a mere pebble about to be swallowed by a landslide.

"Leave this place. Now!" Ed Murphy's mouth barely moved but the muscle in his jaw rippled like a sheet in the wind.

Bruce paled. "You can't kick me out. This bank is a public establishment and I know my rights."

"You either get to your feet and walk out of this office on your own, or we will haul you to the sidewalk, which is another *public* entity and allow anyone passing by, or watching from their place of business, to witness this meeting. Your choice."

Bruce stood and buttoned his suit coat. "Oh, I'll leave. But you better believe I'll be back. I have connections, you know. I'll take you to court so fast this town will experience another dust storm." He straightened his tie, brushed a hand down each sleeve, then turned on his heel and sauntered out of the office as if his departure were chosen rather than ordered.

Joe took a deep breath and exhaled slowly. He'd grossly underestimated Bruce Archer. Where did that leave things?

Seventeen

WAS BRUCE ARCHER the threat he tried to portray? Did Lily know he was back in town? Was he capable of doing harm to his family…to anyone? Like water over a cliff, questions tumbled through Joe's mind in the awkward silence that followed Bruce's departure. He gave a sigh of relief when the rattle of cups on a tray and the aroma of freshly brewed coffee announced Florence's return.

"Thank you, Florence." Ed Murphy swept his hand across the desk. "Set it here." He indicated a space in front of him. "By the way, I asked Bruce to leave. Should he return, please have him wait in the lobby until I ask you to bring him in."

Her hands shook as she set the tray holding the coffeepot and cups atop the desk as instructed. "But…but how will you know he's here?" She glanced sideways at Neal.

"Florence." Ed rapped his knuckles on the desk. "I will know he's here because you will inform me of his presence. However, he is not to come into this office until I invite him to do so. Do you understand?"

Tears welled in her eyes. "Yes, sir, but you…ohh…" She glared at Neal, then scurried out of the office.

Neal turned to his father, his face a picture of little boy orneriness. "You were snippy." He grinned at Joe. "A long story for future discussion."

Joe leaned forward. "I knew there must be something behind that remark. Maybe we can grab lunch at Milly's sometime and you can regale me with Anderson trivia." He flicked an imaginary piece of lint from his pantleg. "Until then, do you think Bruce will follow through with his threat?"

Ed filled the cups with the hot liquid and scooted them to Neal and Joe. "Who knows what the dumb kid will do."

"What kind of connections do you suppose he has at his disposal?" Joe settled back into his chair and wrapped his hand around the cup of coffee.

Neal shook his head. "Probably the same guy on the street corner who sold him the suit."

"Neal." Ed frowned.

"Come on, Dad." Neal smirked. "Do you honestly think Bruce Archer paid for that suit with money he earned by putting in a full day's labor of any kind? By the way, you have no idea how badly I wished you had a newspaper in your hand when you were addressing him."

"What does a newspaper have to do with anything?" The elder Murphy rubbed his forehead. "Wait. I know, I know. I roll it when I'm angry, don't I?"

"Roll it and pin every word of your lecture into the air with a jab." Neal laughed and nodded to Joe. "Don't ask how I know that little piece of information."

Joe chuckled. "A wooden spoon placed squarely on the seat of my pants was the lecture I normally received." He took a sip of the coffee and tried hard not to grimace when he swallowed. He doubted Florence took first place in coffee-making at business school. "All kidding aside. Do you think Lily and her mother know that Bruce is back in town?"

Ed shrugged and looked at Neal. "You were there last night. Did Lily mention anything about his return?"

Joe clenched his teeth. So, his hunch was correct. Neal and his little girl were on their way to the Archer farm when he encountered them on the road last evening. Now that he knew it for fact, there was the familiar kick to the gut again.

"No. Nothing about Bruce." Neal tilted his head toward Joe. "She did inform me, however, of your kindness to her and especially Ruth."

Joe shrugged. "Mrs. Archer thinks *I'm* Bruce."

"Yes. She mentioned that also." One small wrinkled skated across Neal's forehead and disappeared into his hairline.

Joe detected no animosity from Neal, but something in that revelation certainly bothered him. "Did Lily also tell you that she doesn't trust me? She thinks everything I do for her is to somehow convince her to sell her land."

Ed Murphy's eyebrows arched. "You're saying that isn't the case?" He shot Joe a condescending smile.

Neal grabbed a clump of hair in both hands and groaned out a long breath. "Really, Dad? You want to go over this again?"

Joe steeled himself to remain calm. Neal's question of *again* signaled this was not the first time his attention to Lily's mother had been discussed. The last thing he wanted to do was stir the elder Murphy's ire, but he would defend himself against an unwarranted accusation. "I'm saying that I'd never use Ruth Archer's situation for my advantage." He hated using Aunt Hazel for an argument, and this was the second time in as many days. If he were to get these two to listen to him without their preconceived ideas of his intentions, however, then he figured his beloved relative would forgive him. He set his cup of coffee on the edge of the Murphy's desk, then raised his hands in surrender. "Look, I was raised by an aunt whose last years mirrored the behavior that Lily's mother exhibits. Never, ever, would I desecrate the memory of the woman I loved as my mother in such a deceitful manner." *Take a breath. Allow that bit of information to sink in before you charge ahead.*

Ed hung his head. "I'm sorry, Kendall. I…I didn't know. On the other hand, not knowing is no excuse for my sarcasm. As my son so creatively and angrily pointed out when this matter was discussed in our home last night, at least you're doing something. Will you forgive my suspicions?"

"Of course. Believe me, had I known how very personal this job would become, I'd have—"

"Tucked tail and ran?" Neal rubbed his hand over his chest as if in pain. "If by *personal* you mean Lily Archer, I've been there and done that and I'm here to tell you that tactic didn't work."

Joe wrapped his hands around the lukewarm cup of coffee. Neal's words carried an element of regret, while his eyes conveyed an unspoken challenge. Yes, Lily and her mother were becoming very personal, but this was neither the time nor the place to have that conversation. He stretched his legs in front of him, hoping the Murphys would understand that he had no intention of leaving until this job was completed. "Neal, after our meeting on the road last evening, I've given a lot of thought to the *anything* you promised to grant me."

Ed peered over the top of his glasses. "You two met last night?"

"It was a chance meeting, Dad." Neal gave a quick replay of the encounter.

"And I turned over the keys to the vault to you." Ed laughed and turned his attention to Joe. "So, what did my son promise you?"

"Well, I wrote down my thoughts so I wouldn't get sidetracked." Joe set his cup of coffee on the desk. With luck, he'd not have to drink any more of the bitter stuff. He fished a paper from his shirt pocket. "We are all aware that Lily's signature is not on the deed. Now, as I understand it, even though by law the city could obtain the land through eminent domain, since Ruth's is the only legal signature on the deed, all money would go to her."

Ed nodded. "Ordinarily that would be the case. However, with Ruth's condition—"

Joe moved to the edge of his seat. "Exactly my point, so hear me out."

Neal took a swig of coffee, grimaced, leaned back in his chair, and crossed his arms. "We're listening."

Joe smoothed the paper on the desk. "When I found that the only names on the deed were those of Paul and Ruth, I searched for a will."

"And?" Ed toyed with a pencil on his desk.

"If there is one, it's never been filed." Joe sat back in the chair. The more he'd searched for answers, the more confused he'd become. It was clear that the Murphys were no better informed.

Ed raised one shoulder. "It wouldn't have to be filed to be legal, Kendall. Paul and I were lifelong friends, but he distrusted any form of government, including the bank, and certainly not the courthouse. The Archer place has been passed down from father to son for generations. Not until after Paul died was there ever a mortgage on it, that I know. Paul was always in good health. I doubt he gave writing a will a second thought."

Joe swallowed. "You say he was always in good health. Yet it seems he died at a fairly young age. I know this is going to sound harsh, but if Archer died on his deathbed, did he not have enough warning ahead of time to make some kind of arrangements to assure his family would be cared for? How could a man leave his family in such limbo?"

Neal pushed his cup to one side, leaned forward, and braced his arms on the desk. "Death*bed* is a misnomer, Kendall. Paul Archer died lying in a dirt field. He was snakebit and didn't stand a chance."

Joe gasped. "But I understood Lily made a promise on—"

Ed wiggled the pencil between his thumb and forefinger. "She did make a promise, kneeling beside him in the dirt."

"How…did he not see…who…" The back of Joe's neck tingled with the thought of what Lily must have endured.

Neal licked his lips and blew out a long puff of air. "All questions only Lily can answer, and maybe one day she will."

Joe shook his head. "You mean you don't even know what happened for sure? I thought you were—"

"Sweethearts?" Neal lowered his eyes and made circles on the desktop with his finger. "We were. From the time we were six years old until the night she refused my proposal the summer after we graduated high school." He rubbed both hands across his face, as if he could somehow scrub away the memory. "That's the night I walked away. I have yet to know what really happened that tragic afternoon."

Joe involuntarily recoiled. Hearing of Neal and Lily's relationship straight from the man himself only exacerbated the gut punch.

Ed drummed the pencil on the desk. "Talking about it now won't get any of us any closer to the answer as to what took place. However, we do need to get on with this discussion concerning what to do now in the best interest of the Archers. Continue with your ideas, Kendall."

Joe perused his notes, not wanting to leave anything out of the possible solution. "I think we were discussing the fact that Mr. Archer left no will, at least not one we can find." His chest tightened. This wasn't the outcome he'd hoped to have from this conversation. "So, without a will, Lily would have no way to access any funds from the sale of the property. Am I correct?"

Neal tilted his head. "You must have stayed awake all night to come up with these assumptions, Kendall. Is he right, Dad?"

"He's correct." Ed nodded. "Unfortunately, unless we can find a loophole, Ruth is the sole recipient of any and all monies accrued from the sale of the property, minus what is owed, of course."

Joe ran his tongue over his teeth. Neal was right. He had stayed up all night praying and searching for a solution and could only hope he'd found it. "Could Lily be appointed executor of the estate on the basis of her mother's health problems?"

Neal gave his father a playful shove on the shoulder. "I'm glad I asked you to come in today, Dad. I don't have a clue how to answer."

Ed shrugged. "It's a legality I'm not qualified to answer. While it seems reasonable, you need to talk to an attorney."

Joe's heart sank. For reasons he couldn't explain, he felt uneasy about any delay in finding a solution for Lily. "Is there an estate attorney in Anderson? And could I perhaps get an appointment today?"

Ed balanced the pencil across the top of his coffee cup. "You've met him, Joe. At least, you've seen him."

"I have? Where? When?"

"The night of the townhall meeting when you were introduced as the foreman of the lake project." Ed rubbed his chin. "If I remember correctly, he came in late and sat at the back of the room. Big, tall fellow. Overalls. Had his dog with him."

"He's an attorney?" Joe chewed on the side of his lip. He recalled seeing the man Ed described, but a lawyer was the last title he would have given the man. And because his company had a legal team, he'd never had the occasion to personally meet him in a professional role.

A looking of amusement bounced between Ed and Neal. "Estate attorney. Probate attorney. City attorney. Property dispute attorney. Divorce attorney." Ed leaned back in his chair. "Need I continue? Anderson is a small town. We can't afford a separate barrister for every little legality that might arise. Amos Pettigrew is our man."

Joe folded the paper and put it in his pocket. "So, how do I go about seeing your man?" Why did he feel as though he was about to become a laughingstock?

Ed cocked one eyebrow as one side of his mouth twitched in an impish grin. "Oh, one never *sees* Amos Pettigrew. No, sir. One *experiences* Amos Pettigrew."

Joe bit his upper lip. It was obvious Ed was enjoying this dialogue and was in no hurry to direct him to Pettigrew's office. "Could you, perhaps, tell me where I might experience this man?"

Neal chuckled. "Does he still live where he always has, Dad?"

Ed nodded. "Same place. It would be best if you took him rather than me trying to give him directions."

"But what if Bruce returns?" Neal stood and fished keys from his pocket. "You going to be okay here by yourself?"

Ed laughed. "On your way out, ask Florence to bring me the newspaper from the lobby and I'll be fine. If nothing else, I'll turn the kid over my knee and give him the latest news through the seat of his highfalutin britches."

Joe reluctantly got to his feet. "Don't we need an appointment?"

Neal pointed to the clock on the wall. "It's after eight o'clock and before noon, so he'll be home. Trust me."

What choice did he have? He needed an audience with this so-called all-around lawyer, and it was obvious the only way he would achieve that task was to go with Neal.

They stopped in the lobby only long enough for Neal to relay his father's instructions to Florence before stepping out into the midmorning heat.

Neal turned to Joe and winked as they walked to the car. "Hot as Grandma's fryin' pan."

Joe laughed. "And we sure could use some rain."

Eighteen

THE MIDMORNING SUN seared through Lily's work-worn shirt as she chopped at the cockleburs along the corral fence. How did such ugly, good-for-nothing weeds flourish while the crops needed to sustain families shriveled and died, some before ever poking anything alive above the rock-hard soil?

A quick glance to make sure Mama hadn't wandered off added yet another question to Lily's repertoire of wonderings. Until Joe Kendall had made his unwelcome presence known, Mama hadn't communicated anything beyond her normal *goodnight, Bruce* routine for nearly three years. Now in the span of a week she'd visited with Joe and chattered away with Neal's little Rosie. And the real puzzle...here was Mama sitting on an overturned feed bucket, her legs stretched in front of her, stroking and murmuring sweet nothings to the mangy yellow barn cat that was lopped across her lap and purring like a well-oiled machine. Even the cat drew more intelligent conversation than Lily had managed to glean in the last three years. It would be funny...if only it wasn't the least bit laughable.

Lily leaned her hoe against a fencepost and kicked the chopped cockleburs aside as she scuffed to the barn. "Are you thirsty, Mama?" She retrieved the towel-wrapped thermos of coffee she'd placed in the shade of the barn's interior. The coffee was cold, leftover from an early breakfast, but both she and Mama liked cold coffee, though she preferred hers with ice. But that was a luxury she didn't have at her disposal of late. She poured the thermos cup about half full and handed it to Mama.

Mama stopped petting the cat and held the cup with both hands. She took a long sip that was followed by a hiccup. "Oops! Excuse me, please." She placed two fingers across her lips, giggled as she handed the cup to Lily, and then went back to methodically stroking the cat from its fuzzy head to the tip of its tail, lost again to Lily but crooning to the mouse-eater.

Little things. Little things like manners Mama remembered. So why didn't she recognize the girl sitting on her haunches in front of her, making sure her thirst was quenched? Lily poured herself a full cup of the cold brew and plopped to the straw-strewn floor beside Mama. Dog padded to her side from somewhere in the darkened interior and Lily patted his graying head. "At least you know who I am, huh?"

Why was she even bothering to chop weeds when the entire forty acres would most likely be in a watery grave before long? She set her cup in the dirt, drew her legs to her chest, and laid her forehead against her knees. She didn't dare shut her eyes. Eluded sleep of nighttime had a way of stalking her once the sun climbed above the horizon. But maybe, with Mama occupied with the cat, and Dog standing—or laying—his usual one-eyed guard, she could rest long enough to relieve her hard-floor-induced backache and heat-provoked headache. She'd ignore the constant, ever-growing weight of worry and hopelessness on her shoulders and the shards of a broken heart that reopened the old wound of regret with Neal Murphy's return and made a new incision every time she envisioned Joe Kendall's pain-filled face declaring he couldn't and wouldn't say goodbye to Mama. Why Mama? Why not her...Lily Archer...the girl?

The sound of a car roaring into the yard interrupted her ponderings and propelled Lily to her feet. Not wanting to alarm Mama, she paced unhurried steps until she cleared the barn, then dashed to retrieve the hoe she'd left leaning against a fencepost. The black late-model roadster parked by the gate was not one she recognized, and though the hoe would do little to protect her or her property against an aggressive salesman, it might at least deter him in a way that Dog, old and lazy animal that he was, would never do.

She stood with one hand gripping the handle of the hoe, the other one around the latch of the corral gate, while she waited for the driver to exit the vehicle. Or should she greet the newcomer before he had an opportunity to open his door? While the neighbors around were familiar with her mother's condition, she didn't like the idea of a stranger observing what might be interpreted as silly at the least, or insane at the most. Mama could do little to disavow either label.

Lily lifted the latch on the gate as the man emerged from his fancy car and pain shot through her chest. Though it had been six years, the tilt of the head and the cocky sway of his hips as he sauntered toward her were unmistakable earmarks of Bruce. Mama's long-lost son had returned. She fought to swallow the bile that threatened to choke her.

"There she is." Bruce swiped his hat from his head and gave an exaggerated bow. "The favored Archer child herself."

Lily bristled at his sarcasm-laced proclamation but held her tongue.

"I knew I'd find you in the barn. That's why I didn't go to the house first." He reached the gate and folded his arms across the top rail, a frown above the eyes that searched her from top to bottom. "My lands, but you look old and...and more like a man than a woman. You do know Neal Murphy is at the bank, don't you? Is Ma in the house?"

Lily stepped to one side and motioned toward the barn. "Mama is in the barn but—"

He didn't wait for her explanation but pushed the gate open and strode toward the open door. "Hey, Ma! Guess who's back?"

"Bruce, wait." Lily hurried to catch him before he burst into Mama's presence.

He turned, a scowl so deep his eyes looked all squinty. "Wait? Sure, you want me to wait. You afraid Mama's going to be happy to see me?" He loped the last few steps and slid to a stop in front of an overturned feed bucket. "I thought you said she was in here."

For a minute, Lily's heart was in her throat. What a time for Mama to decide to wander away. But when her eyes grew accustomed to the darkened interior again, she caught sight of Mama huddled against the wall, her arms wrapped around the cat's middle and her eyes wide with fright.

"She's here, Bruce." Lily approached Mama slowly, thankful that she didn't bolt. "Mama, Bruce is home. Would you like to see him?"

"What's wrong with her? Why…what have you…is she going to die?" Void of the haughtiness he'd earlier voiced, Bruce was once again the scared little boy Lily knew all too well.

"Come, Mama." Lily laid her hand gently on Mama's shoulder. "Let's go to the house so you can visit with Bruce."

Mama's eyes darted between the cat she cuddled close to her breast and Bruce, who stood with eyes nearly as wide with fear as hers.

Lily understood Mama's anxiety…it mirrored her own, only she had nothing to hold close for comfort. "You can bring the cat with you, Mama."

Mama clutched the cat closer but took a wide, tentative step away from Bruce to follow Lily.

Bruce stepped in front of Lily. "Pa would never allow a cat in the house and you know I'm allergic to the rat-traps."

Lily poked a finger against his chest to move him aside. "Follow us and keep your mouth shut, little brother." *Better yet, go away and leave us alone. You didn't want us six years ago. We don't need you now.* She had six years of pent-up arguments and could only hope he'd give her an opening to bless him with them.

Surprisingly, Bruce did as he was told. Though his faced screwed up as if he smelled something offensive when he entered the house, it gave Lily more satisfaction to note the dust and bits of straw clinging to his shiny patent leather shoes and his fancy wool pantlegs. Wool in Kansas in July? Well, she'd see how long his ego lasted in the oven-like temperatures of the living room.

Mama stepped around the mattress on the floor and made a beeline to her favorite chair while Bruce stood in the doorway, no doubt taking in the fact that except for the mattress and sleeping pad on the floor, nothing had changed in the years he'd been gone.

He pointed to the sleeping arrangements. "Why?"

Lily brushed past him and took a seat on the piano stool. "You don't remember how hot it gets upstairs in the summertime?"

He sneered. "You ever hear of fans?"

Lily stood, reached atop the piano, and retrieved a cardboard fan with a wooden handle. It was one she brought from the church after Papa's funeral, but she'd not divulge that information. It wasn't stealing, was it? It had the name of the funeral home on it, and goodness knows she'd paid them enough money to vindicate the taking of one paper fan.

He gave an irritated *harumph.* "You still don't have electricity?"

"This one runs without electricity." She waved it in front of his face.

"I don't suppose you have a telephone, either." He tiptoed around Mama's mattress and perched on the edge of the couch. "What's wrong with her? Have you taken her to a doctor? How long has she been this way? How will you get help if she needs it?"

There was that wrinkled nose again. Regardless of what else might be wrong with Mama, she was not repugnant.

"I have taken her to the doctor. He calls it hardening of the arteries but doesn't know what causes it. For your information, she started going downhill shortly after you left. For the last three years she's not communicated for any length of time about anything pertinent." She'd not mention Joe's apparent breakthrough with her.

"Take her to a different doctor, then." He sneezed and scooted against the back of the couch. A puff of dust exited the cushion when his back hit against it. He coughed and brushed at his sleeves. "Mama would never have let this house get so dirty." He pointed at the smudge-streaked window. "What do you do all day, anyway? And what do you think Papa would say if he could see how rundown this place has become?" He sneezed again. "Get that cat out of here before I throw it out." His reached inside his suit coat, whipped out a handkerchief, and dabbed at his eyes.

"The cat stays. Take note that Mama is hugging the cat. Not you." Lily bit the inside of her lower lip. The fact Mama didn't recognize Bruce gave her more gratification than she cared to admit. "Why did you come back, Bruce? Does it give you some kind of pleasure to belittle me? Could you please talk to Mama?"

Bruce splayed his hands. "Talk? You mean carry on a conversation?" He scoffed. "I thought you said she's not had anything sensible to say for the last three years."

Lily rolled her lips. Was he really that dense? "I didn't say talk *with* her. I asked you to talk *to* her. Bruce, after you left, she cried for days. Then suddenly the crying stopped and instead she started making excuses for you."

"Why did she feel the need to make excuses for me? I didn't do anything but leave this forsaken part of the country." He crossed his legs and wiggled his foot. In days past, it signaled agitation.

She wanted to slap the arrogance out of him but shook her finger instead. "Yes, you left, Bruce, and we had no idea where you were. People would ask, 'What do you hear from Bruce? Is he in school? Working? When do you expect him home?' And Mama would say, 'Oh, my boy Bruce is doing well. Busy, you know. He probably won't be able to get time off from his good job to come home very often.' They were lies, all of them, but she would check the mail every day for anything that would tell her the truth. Even now, she makes the trek to the mailbox every single day."

He sniffed and swiped the handkerchief under his nose. "I'm here now, for all the difference it makes. Ma hasn't even acknowledged me."

"What did you really expect?" She'd not give him the satisfaction of knowing that Mama didn't recognize her, either. Or that she called her *Bruce* every bedtime. "You came charging in here like you're the guest of honor at some grand reception, expecting this farm to be a showplace, the house company-ready, and Mama fawning at your feet. Well, guess what. I'll not kill the fatted calf for the prodigal son's return."

Bruce scooted to the edge of the couch and placed his hands on his knees. "Before you go riding off into the sunset on your high horse, I came back to save this place."

Lily clenched her teeth to keep a most inappropriate laugh from escaping. The nerve of this brash, cocky little brother thinking he was somehow the promised messiah of the Archer family farm. "Save it? Really? And how do you plan to go about achieving that goal? You do know our names are not on the deed?"

His mouth dropped open. "What? What do you mean our names aren't on the deed? Didn't Pa...why didn't—"

"Questions I've asked myself over and over. But questions don't change the fact. For reasons we may never know, Papa never put our names on the deed. Only Mama's. And Mama is the only one who can legally contest selling this place or the city taking possession through eminent domain. Believe me, I know. There is nothing to prove that you or I have any rights to this land, little brother." Though she hated acknowledging that her papa had been remiss in guaranteeing ownership, it gave her a satisfying amount of vindictive pleasure to see Bruce's panicky dismay.

He stood but quickly lowered himself back to the edge of the couch again. "There has to be something. A will, maybe? Surely there's a will."

Why hadn't she thought of a will? But she wasn't ready to voice that concern. "I would imagine the powers that be have exhausted all means to prove ownership, or lack thereof, of this farm. But even if there is a will we don't know about, this will be the third year I'm unable to pay the mortgage. I've only been allowed to keep the place thus far because Mr. Murphy has been gracious and lenient."

"Ha!" He pounded the cushion and was quickly enveloped in another puff of dust with an ensuing fit of coughing and sneezing. He stood and pointed his finger at Lily, his face red with anger and his nose even redder. "There's nothing gracious or lenient about either of the Murphys. I'm telling you what I told old man Murphy before I came out here. I know people. I have connections. You say there's nothing to prove that part of this property belongs to me, and I say there is. You wait and see."

The whites of his eyes shining through his red face gave him the appearance of some kind of demon…the devil, perhaps. As evil as her brother appeared, there some something even more sinister about his threat. Surely he wouldn't try something illegal. She took a long, deep breath, balled her fists at her sides, and willed herself to remain calm. "Don't think for even one minute you can get around the legalities that are already in place, Bruce. I don't know where you've been these last six years, but I do know where you'll end up if you try to defraud the government, even the governing body of little Anderson, Kansas."

Bruce sidestepped around Mama's mattress and grabbed the cat by the nape of the neck. "The governing body of piddling Anderson, Kansas, can go to thunder as far as I'm concerned." He stomped to the doorway between the kitchen and living room and turned back to face Lily, the cat clawing and hissing. "And that's exactly where this cat is going if it's still here when I get back…and I will come back." Three long strides got him to the screen door of the kitchen. He kicked it open it and gave the cat a toss.

Lily followed him to the door, then watched in both amusement and horror as the cat hit the porch and then turned, ears flat against its head, and with one leap latched all four feet, claws open, onto the right woolen pantleg of Bruce's fancy suit. Not until she felt an arm slip around her waist did she realize that Mama had joined her to witness the one-legged dance exhibition between cat and man.

At long last, the slam of a door and roar of an engine indicated that Bruce had somehow dislodged the cat. There was a scrunch of tires and a cloud of dust as the car turned around, then came to a screeching halt again by the gate.

Bruce rolled down his window and crossed his arms through the opening. "You know what, big sister? I have a sudden need to go back to the bank and have a talk with the Murphys." He tapped his finger against his chin. "Hmm. I wonder what the fine people of Anderson would think if they knew what really happened the day Papa died?" He shrugged and gave her a sinister grin.

Lily's heart raced and she fought to keep her legs from crumpling beneath her. How did he know that one question would throw her into an abyss of abject remorse eight years deep?

"Think about it, Lillian Ruth." Bruce then gunned the engine of his fancy vehicle, leaving behind a bigger cloud of guilt than dust.

Lily released a defeated sigh. Why, oh, why was she always left with no choice, or even a shred of pride? Bruce could do nothing to save the farm, but he could do more damage with his tongue than all of the earth moving machines Joe Kendall had at his disposal. She slipped her hand into Mama's and gave it a squeeze. "Come on, Mama. We're going to town."

Mama smiled up at her. "That naughty boy needs a spanking." She pulled her hand from Lily's and descended the porch steps to where the cat sat, preening itself as if it was personally responsible for chasing the *naughty boy* off the land.

"He needed a spanking a long time ago, Mama." Lily sat on the bottom step, rolled down the cuffs of her overalls, and brushed at the straw and dust that accumulated there from her burr chopping. It wouldn't be the first time she went to town clad in work clothes. There wasn't time to worry about appearances, but she'd have plenty of time to agonize over the consequences if Bruce wasn't stopped.

Nineteen

JOE WOULD HAVE bet his job that he'd traversed every road surrounding Anderson, but he hadn't counted the cow paths that he'd not included in his forays. A sideways glance at Neal when they turned off the gravel road onto nothing more than two ruts down a dirt path barely wide enough to accommodate a vehicle gave evidence that the younger Murphy was enjoying this trip far too much.

Joe grinned. "Are you sure this is the way, or are you waiting for me to ask?"

Neal laughed. "This is why it's hard to give someone directions, and this is only the beginning." They topped a rise in the road and Neal pointed to a huddle of rooftops that could be seen off to the right and down the hill. "That's Pettigrew's place, but we have a curve or two before we get there. Hang tight."

Hang tight was all Joe could do as they bounced and bumped over rocks and through dips. The first curve, as Neal called it, was more of a switchback and Joe lost all sense of direction. They rounded a much gentler curve and were stopped by a gate barely wide enough to allow anything bigger than a horse to pass. There was no fence attached to either side of the gate, although a fence would have made little difference. He doubted anyone would have ventured out of the ruts to climb over boulders the size of the car. A hand-lettered sign hung on the gate its letters faded but the message still readable: *Narrow is the way which leadeth unto life and few there be that find it.*

"How…what now?" Joe swallowed. This reminded him of his first snipe hunt, and he didn't like it any better now than he had all those years ago.

"We walk the rest of the way, that's what now." Neal opened his door and stepped out.

"You're teasing me, right?" Well, now he sounded like a girl on *her* first snipe hunt. At least it was daylight.

Neal poked his head into the car. "Not teasing. It's all a part of the Pettigrew experience. You coming?"

Joe opened his door and slid out, wishing he'd worn his work boots instead of the dress shoes he'd put on for his visit to the bank. *Vanity of vanities; all is vanity.* Joe chuckled to himself. Served him right.

Neal grunted as he pushed the gate through the dirt to make a space wide enough for them to sidestep through. "It's really not that far. Give or take a mile or so." He closed the gate again. "I'd warn you to be on the lookout for snakes, but I suppose you're all too aware of their presence since you've poked through the countryside surveying and whatever all it is you do."

"You certainly know how to put a man at ease." Joe eyed the dirt and rock-strewn path ahead of them. "Encountered mostly black snakes along the creek, but don't mind telling you I'm not real fond of anything that slithers."

"Most of the ones around here are harmless, but we do have rattlers—predominantly massasaugas. Not as big at the prairie or timber rattler, and midgets compared to a diamondback, but don't let their size fool you. They still carry a deadly punch if cornered."

"I carry a snakebite kit with me in my car."

Neal laughed. "Well, then. I'd say your car is safe enough." He stuck his hands in the pockets of his trousers. "Relax and enjoy the journey, Kendall. I guarantee this meeting with Amos Pettigrew will leave an impression you'll not likely forget."

After what seemed the longest *mile or so*, Joe caught his first glimpse of the Pettigrew homestead. Neal was right. He'd not likely forget this experience. What had looked like a grouping of buildings from the vantage point of the rise above them earlier, could now be best described as one building with four varying heights and rooflines. Though obviously connected, each piece of the muddle of different types of sidings and roofing materials sported its own door, small stoop, and nine-pane window. Each door wore a different colored screen door and on its crossbar one hand-painted letter, which when read from left to right spelled SLEW. And beside each stoop, which was nothing more than a large, flat rock, was a tiny garden of sorts.

Before Joe could ask even one of the myriads of questions that crowded his mind, Neal stepped to the yellow door with the painted W and knocked three loud raps, which were promptly met by the baying of some kind of hound. "That's Barnabas greeting us. He sounds mean, but he's really a big old softie."

"Barnabas?" Joe slipped behind Neal. He could only hope the screen door would hold should the animal decide to join them. "Why the W door?" Something had to make sense.

Neal shrugged. "No idea. Just thought we had to start somewhere."

"What?" Joe took another step back. "I thought you'd been here before."

Neal glanced over his shoulder, one finger over his lips. "Oh, I've been here, but never this close to the house." He rapped on the door again.

"Quiet, Barnabas." A deep voice stilled the barking and startled Joe. A tall man dressed in overalls and a white shirt with the sleeves rolled above his elbows loomed in the doorway. In one hand was a pair of binoculars. "Come in. Come in. I've witnessed your approach for quite some time, you understand, so your appearance is no surprise."

Deep blue eyes seem magnified through the Benjamin Franklin-like glasses perched on the end of the man's nose. The man's face was so broad, the earpieces didn't hook behind his ears but stretched around his cheeks. If the man smiled too broadly, they'd likely pop off of his face.

He nodded to Joe. "You're Kendall, and I know why you're here. Have a seat. No need to waste time."

Joe wanted to ask how Pettigrew could know the reason for his visit, but it was Anderson, after all, and nothing seemed to remain private business for long. He looked at his surroundings and clenched his teeth to hold back a gasp. Polished walnut floors held a gold-black-and-red woolen rug. Two leather chairs faced an ornate walnut desk, and floor-to-ceiling bookcases filled three walls of the room. Above the desk hung a large kerosene lamp with a red glass shade surrounded by spear-shaped glass prisms. A ratcheted mechanism above the ceiling canopy allowed the lamp to be raised and lowered.

"As soon as you get your fill of gawking, we can get down to business, young man." A smile that reached clear to the man's eyes and threatened the fall of his eyeglasses met Joe as he settled into his seat.

"Now, no doubt junior Murphy here failed to tell you that the gate you had to wiggle through was put there to keep young ruffians like himself from poking around where they had no business being in the first place." Pettigrew peered over the rim of his glasses and shook his finger at Neal. "By the way, you still haven't returned the gas can or the door of my necessary you and your cohorts *borrowed* from me the Halloween of '29."

"Seriously?" Neal's face was brick red.

"Serious as a heart attack." Amos winked at Joe, then leaned back in his chair and tented his fingers. "Now, as for all the doors. S is where I sleep. L is where I live and let—"

Neal puckered his forehead. "Let? Let what?"

"You're interrupting, but I *let* God. Now, where was I—"

Neal snorted. "But what do you let God do?"

Pettigrew shook his head and grinned. "Why, I let God do whatever He wants. You should try it some time." He cleared his throat. "May I continue?"

Neal shrugged. "Sorry. Go on."

The big man nodded. "Thank you. I shall."

He turned his attention back to Joe. "E is where I eat, and W is where I work. You'll notice I can't go from one place to another without going outside. That's because I carry nothing from room to room except me and Barnabas. If you know anything at all about the Bible, you know Barnabas was an encourager." He scratched the liver-and-tan bloodhound behind its long, velvety ears. "That's what this faithful friend does for me. He either encourages others to leave or supports their staying."

As if on cue, the big dog nuzzled close to Joe and laid his head, slobber and all, on his knee.

Amos laughed. "Now that Barnabas has decided you may stay, let's talk about the Archer dilemma. Which, by the way, is not nearly as worrisome as you think."

Now it was Joe's turned to wrinkle his forehead. "You do know that the only names on the deed are that of Mr. and Mrs. Archer?"

"I do indeed." Pettigrew's glasses slipped forward with the nod.

Joe frowned. "And you don't find that worrisome?"

Amos pushed his glasses up on his nose. "Ordinarily I would find it most worrisome, except there's the little matter of the will."

"The will?" Joe braced his arms on the edge of the desk. "I searched for a will at the courthouse and found nothing."

"That doesn't surprise me." The attorney took off his glasses and laid them on the desk. "I know for a fact Paul Archer wrote one because I helped him write it one day sitting on the banks of the Willow with him and Benton Finley. He signed it right then and there and Benton witnessed it."

A new surge of hope rushed across Joe's shoulders. "If you helped him write it, then you know what it says. And if he didn't file it, then it must still be somewhere in the house. Right?"

Amos hooked his glasses on the side of his cheeks and gave a crooked grin. "One would think that would be the most logical reasoning only if one didn't know Paul Archer. He was particularly upset with Bruce that day and wrote it from that position of frustration. It wouldn't surprise me at all if he tore it up and threw it away once he had more time to think rationally."

Hope slid from Joe like butter off a hot knife. "And there's no copy? Please tell me there's a copy."

A groan escaped Pettigrew's lips and rumbled through the small room as he pulled a folded piece of lined paper from the pocket of his overalls. "I always carry a blank sheet of paper with me. One never knows when one might need to record something noteworthy. Paul wrote it on the paper I had with me that day, but we didn't make a copy." He wiped his hand across his forehead. "I'm an attorney. I know the importance of keeping good records. I should have insisted we make a second copy, but Paul was still fairly young and healthy...just frustrated with his boy. I never dreamed he'd leave us so soon."

If the man didn't already look so distraught, Joe would have questioned his competency. But what good would that do now? There was one last question that perhaps could possibly give renewed confidence. "Do you remember what it said? A list of beneficiaries, perhaps?"

A slow grin nudged the glasses higher on Amos's cheeks. "I do. I do, in fact. But unless that will is found, it would be my word against any other person who might decide to contest its validity. Take Bruce Archer, for instance."

Neal leaned forward. "You know he's back in town?"

"Oh, I know. Met him on the other side of the gate when I came home from fishing yesterday. Let's say Barnabas here didn't encourage him to stay. In fact, he very loudly discouraged him from stepping out of his fancy car."

Joe laughed. "And how did he take that?"

Amos shrugged and pushed his glasses higher onto his nose. "Well, he has people, you know. Connections, he calls them. Threatened to dim my lights, you might say."

"You think his threats are only threats, then?" Joe settled back into his chair. "He voiced the same warning to me this morning and again to Neal and his father. He's cocky, that's for sure, but I'm not convinced he's harmless."

The big man leaned forward and his glasses slipped to the tip of his nose. "Bruce Archer is as dangerous as a rattler under a rock. Only thing is—those evil, slithery reptiles can't hurt anyone as long as they stay under the rock. It's when they get exposed that they can become deadly. Even then, you chop off their head and what's left only makes noise for a while." He pulled open a drawer and withdrew a harness of sorts that he slipped around the dog's middle, then walked to a coatrack close to the door, lifted a battered felt hat from a hook, and plopped it onto his head with an extra pat as if he were demanding it to stay put. "That Archer whippersnapper isn't smart enough to contest anything on his own, but it's hard telling who might have convinced him otherwise." He handed Joe the leather strap lead on the harness. "Hold on tight to that, Kendall. If Barnabas catches a whiff of anything that interests him, he'll take off and take you right along with him. I only pretend to be the master, you know. One never owns a bloodhound."

Joe grabbed the lead with both hands. He liked dogs, but this one was the size of a small pony. "We're leaving? We haven't—"

"We're leaving, and yes, I do realize you haven't gotten your answers." Amos opened the door and motioned for Joe and Neal to follow him. "We're going to go see Benton Finley. I could send the two of you, but he doesn't know you, Kendall, and if I remember correctly, Neal, your band of hoodlums took the Finleys' outhouse door that same Halloween."

Joe poked Neal in the ribs with his elbow. "You've left quite a legacy, my man. Neal the Ripper...of privy doors."

Neal shoved back at Joe. "I can't believe they remember after all these years."

Amos's shoulders shook with laughter. "You'd remember, too, if you were the one sitting inside when the door was ripped off. It's hot enough to fry water out here now, but that Halloween the wind was blowing hard from the north, it was spitting an early snow, and it was colder than an old maid's feet." He winked at Joe. "Don't ask me how I know about the cold feet. Remember, I'm a lawyer and I can give a real good argument."

Joe had little time to ponder Amos's old maid reference as the trio trudged back to Neal's car. Pettigrew had the stride of a racehorse and, between trying to keep up with him, avoiding every flat rock that could potentially harbor a snake beneath its surface, and being pulled every direction by Barnabas, he gasped for air as if he were drowning...which he could very well be if one could suffocate in one's own perspiration.

When they reached Neal's car, Amos pulled a watch on a gold chain from his overalls. "It'll be noon by the time we get to town. You boys hungry?"

Neal swiped his arm across his forehead. "A glass of water would be nice."

Joe nodded. He was starved but too out of breath to give an audible answer.

"Then we'll stop at Milly's for a bite before invading Gladys and Benton. Never polite to show up uninvited at mealtime." He opened the back door and Barnabas bounded onto the seat, pulling Joe halfway into the vehicle. "Hope you don't mind sitting with my dog, Kendall. My legs are too long to sit back there. Oh, and you better keep the window rolled up. I swan that dog can sniff a trail through steel, and he'll be out any hole he can find to follow it." He bent his large frame, wiggled his way into the car, laid his head against the back of the seat, and pulled his hat over his eyes.

At this point, Joe wouldn't have minded sitting with the old maid with cold feet. He scootched the rest of the way into the car beside the hound. Neal was right. Amos Pettigrew was an experience.

Twenty

WHAT WAS SHE thinking? Lily gripped the steering wheel as she sped toward town in an attempt to stop Bruce from...from what? From reciting his version of what happened the day Papa died? Or was it because he threatened to go to the Murphys with the telling? What difference would it make? She'd never lied about the events of that day, unless her refusal to divulge every detail would be considered a lie. Did her brother not realize that her very reluctance to give a play-by-play report was as much for him as it was for her? Would chasing Bruce into town be considered a confession of guilt?

Lily stopped at the corner before turning onto Main Street. From that vantage point she could see what cars were parked in front of businesses and her shoulders drooped with relief when Bruce's fancy roadster was nowhere to be seen. But why were there little clusters of people gathered here and there along the street? Oh, yes. She closed her eyes and gave a sigh of exasperation. Town was always crowded on Thursday. Shopping day for nearly everyone who still had money to spend. Most businesses, at least those still open, tried to entice sales as best they could. Then there was the open market for those few who had garden produce to sell, or enough extra flour for loaves of bread or pies. Even Milly had half-price specials on Thursday.

So now what? With no indication that Bruce was in town, plus the crowd of spectators should she choose to go through with her original plan, it wasn't like she could burst into the bank to defend herself if there was nothing to defend. But what if her sneaky brother had decided to park somewhere off the main street? What if he was already talking with Neal and his father? If that were the case, she doubted Florence Bower would grant her an audience with them at the same time. And if...if...

There were empty parking spaces in front of the bank. She'd take one and wait. If Bruce was in the facility, he'd have to come out at some point. How long would it take for him to spill what he was so sure was proof that she was responsible for their papa's death? And how much would the Murphys need to hear, or see, before she was condemned in their eyes, also?

She edged the car slowly onto Main Street and then into a parking spot in front of the bank, switched off the engine, and rolled her window down a crack. The last thing she needed was for the cat to escape. What a picture that would make, Mama chasing the cat and Lily chasing them both. *Why didn't you think this through, Lillian? You do realize you are sitting in a virtual oven, don't you?*

Lily laid her forehead against the steering wheel. She knew they couldn't stay long in a hot car in the middle of the day. She was also painfully aware that she'd rushed to town looking like a vagabond. So now, here they were. She in her baggy overalls, a shirt worn gauze-thin and boots that were wrapped in twine to hold the sole in place. And Mama...Mama clutching a mangy barn cat while dressed in a housedress that was missing a top button on the bodice and the hem coming unsewn on one side. Some days it was easier to give in to Mama's whims than try to reason with her.

Over the years, Lily had managed to swallow her pride too many times to count, or even care. But today was not going to be one of those days. She couldn't, no matter what Bruce did, take one more chance of making a spectacle of herself or Mama. She'd go home. Go home and chop cockleburs until sundown, if need be, and wait for her world, as she knew it, to tumble down around her. Bruce had warned he'd return. The bigger threat was—with whom?

She started the engine but had to wait for an approaching car before she could pull out of the parking spot. When the vehicle pulled into the spot beside her, Lily's stomach churned and her legs tingled so much she couldn't even press on the accelerator. There was no mistaking Neal's shiny red car, nor its front seat occupants. Amos Pettigrew, of all people. Was the lawyer one of Bruce's *connections*? He would know all the aspects of legality involved. But why was he with Neal?

Lily fought to keep down the bile that burned in her throat. Of course Neal was involved because he knew there was no way she could keep the farm. And Bruce himself said he'd been at the bank earlier today. They must have reached some kind of agreement. Why else would the banker and the attorney be together? It was more than mere coincidence.

She wanted to leave, but instinct reminded her that running often instituted a chase and there was no way she could outrun Neal's car. Besides, he knew where she lived. Her only reasonable option was to stay and deal with the consequences. She turned off the motor, folded her arms across her chest, and willed her body to stop quivering. She'd talk. She'd answer all questions. But they had to come to her. Her legs wouldn't hold her if she left the car.

LOOKING PAST AMOS Pettigrew's big frame, Neal recognized the driver of the vehicle parked next to him in front of the bank. Lily's profile was so ingrained in his mind that it wouldn't matter how she was dressed or where he saw her sitting, he'd know her. He also was quite astute in discerning her moods simply by her body language. The crossed arms, the tilt of the head, plus the averted eyes were sure signs of distress, or anger, or maybe…

No. Wait. He clenched his jaw. Those were Helen's signals, too, and Florence Bower's, and Milly's, and most every other woman he'd ever known.

But he also knew Lily well enough to be most certain that with the clusters of people gathered between the bank and Milly's Diner, she'd not exit her car even if they were on speaking terms. Even in high school, Lily hated crowds and insisted they not show any public display of affection while in the midst of them, though she'd laugh at his feeble attempts. He swiped his hands across his face. How long had it been since he'd heard her laugh, or seen her smile? *Oh, Lily, Lily. If only…*

Amos slid the hat off his face and sat up straight. "Are we going to eat or…whoa! I know it's Thursday, but why are people standing as if they're waiting for a parade? And why are we sitting here?" He grabbed the door handle. "I don't know what's happened, but a normal Thursday crowd doesn't line the street this close to noon. You coming, Neal?"

Neal nodded toward Lily's car. "Not sure what to do. This is awkward."

Amos peered through his window, then turned back to Neal. "Since when have you been hesitant to speak to Lily Archer?"

Neal gripped the steering wheel. "Since she told me she never wanted to see me again—not in those words, but the same effect."

Amos turned halfway in his seat. "What about you, Kendall? You care to join me?"

Joe grunted. "Can't go anywhere until you get this hound out of my way."

Not wanting to take the chance Joe could get out from under

Barnabas and reach Lily first, Neal opened the door. "I'll go see if anyone knows what's going on." He stepped onto the street, but before he could get to the bank, Florence came running and threw her arms around him. "Oh, Neal. I'm so glad you're here. It's Benton Finley."

Neal's arms involuntarily tightened around her to keep them both from falling. "Benton? What happened?"

"Well, Clarice over at the telephone office, you know Clarice? Of course, you do. Well, anyway—"

Neal pushed away from her arms and gripped her hands. "I just want to know what happened to Benton, Florence."

She pulled her hands from his and clutched the front of his shirt. "I'm telling you. Clarice rang the bank about an hour ago and said that poor Gladys found him in the chicken house after he didn't come in for his midmorning break."

Neal fought to take a deep breath. This was not the news he expected to hear at all. "So is Benton...did he—"

"Dead. Benton is dead," she squeaked.

Other than when Helen died, Neal had never been affected by death. The sudden lump in his throat, the visions of the last time he saw Benton Finley, the regret of not insisting they sit down that very day for the visit the older man wanted and needed, added to the weight of the reality of it all and he closed his eyes against the confusion it brought. He barely knew Benton Finley, at least not well enough to mourn his passing, so why the sudden feeling of loss? Was it because now they'd never know what might have happened to the will Paul Archer penned all those years ago? Or was it guilt for not taking the time to become better acquainted? Benton and Gladys had braved heat, wind, and cold to attend every high school event that he could remember. While he certainly wasn't the only participant in the various events, their support of kids they probably never knew personally had made an impression. And by the crowd gathered now, containing both young and old faces, others had been touched as well. Yet, he'd never acknowledged their presence, never even nodded their direction, and never once thought of thanking them.

The sound of a car starting broke through the cacophony of his own thoughts and the voices of the crowd as news of Benton's death traveled through the throng assembled along the sidewalk. He opened his eyes, only to watch Lily back her car from the parking spot and turn toward the road that would take her home.

Not until that very moment did it occur to him that Florence Bower was still enfolded in his arms and that they stood directly in front of the empty parking spot. With a groan, Neal moved Florence away from him. "I need to find my dad. He and Benton were good friends."

Florence gave him a sly smile, then turned toward the empty parking spot. "Oh. Did Lily leave? I just happened to be looking out of the window and saw her park here a while ago. I wanted to say hello but then I saw you drive up and knew you'd want the news." She flipped her hair over one shoulder and giggled. "But it's probably for the best. Her mother was holding a cat. Poor thing...Ruth Archer, I mean."

Anger shot heat through Neal's body. "Then you knew Lily was parked here when you came running into—"

Color drained from Florence's face. "Well, yes, but you see—"

"And how is it you just *happened* to be looking out the window? Do you not have enough work to keep you busy?" He knew that question was rude, but it wasn't nearly as rude as the rising anger.

Red splotches polka-dotted Florence's face and neck. "I...I...well, I wanted to make sure if Bruce Archer returned he wouldn't burst into your father's office unannounced."

Neal clenched his fists at his side. "And you spent all morning peering out the window for Bruce's return?"

Her hands shook. "No, not all morning. After Clarice called, I—"

"Where is my father now, Florence?"

She hung her head. "I'm not sure. He said something about going

175

out to the Finleys' to see if he could be of any help."

Neal pressed the heels of his hands against his forehead. If he hadn't been in such a hurry to make sure he got to Lily before Joe Kendall, he wouldn't be standing in front of an empty parking spot right now. Though Lily had made it quite plain that she wanted nothing more to do with him, he could hardly bear the thought of what she must think seeing Florence in his arms.

"Neal! Neal, I could sure use your help." Milly's arms pumped as she ran toward him. "Is it true? Is Benton Finley really gone?" She put her hands on her knees and bent over to catch her breath. "Goodness. I'm getting too old to run." She straightened and her pink cheeks puffed with each breath. "Phil Hargrove came tearing into the diner announcing to everyone that poor Benton was found dead. Do you know that for a fact?"

Neal nodded. "That's the information I have from Florence, and she heard it from Clarice."

Tears gathered in Milly's eyes. "I'll never understand how God decides when a man's time on this earth is done. This town could use Benton Finley for many years to come." She swiped at her face with her apron. "Poor, poor Gladys. Whatever will she do? Well, we aren't doing anyone any good standing out here on the street. Think you could help me serve these good people free coffee, or tea, or whatever else they might want?" She nodded toward the clusters of people gathering along the street. "Not a single one of them is going to go home until someone reports back from the Finley place, and it's too hot to stand out here all afternoon." She ducked and shaded her eyes to look into Neal's car. "Who is that sitting under Barnabas?" She stepped off the sidewalk and peered into the side window. "Good heavens, Joe." She knocked on the window. "Roll this thing down before you swelter in there."

"Can't get this hunk of dog meat to move his heavy behind," Joe yelled back at her.

"Oh, for—" She yanked open the door and grabbed the leather lead of Barnabas's harness. "Come on, big guy." She pulled the dog out of the car and wrapped her arms around his neck. "You're such a good boy, aren't you?" She wiggled her forehead against the dog's head. "Yes, you are. Yes, you are. Wait." She squinted up at Joe. "Where's Amos?"

Joe slid out of the car and brushed dog hair off his britches. "He said something about being a volunteer and that he was going to the firehouse to see if he was needed."

"Well, the ambulance went out a long time ago, but I suppose they would want someone at the station in case another alarm comes in. He'll figure out where everyone went. I've never known him to leave Barnabas alone for very long. In the meantime, you two come help me." She gave Barnabas another hug, then stood. "You come too, fella. I'm sure I have a bone you can chew on."

"Uh. Uh. What about me?" Florence wrung her hands. "I could make coffee or something."

Joe gave an emphatic shake of his head and Neal rolled his lips to keep from smiling, thankful that Kendall's wide eyes and mouthed *no, no, no* couldn't be seen by Florence.

Milly's eyes held the smile her lips didn't convey. "Oh, well, I…I could use your help keeping the cups washed or tables and counters cleaned."

Florence gave Neal a look that could shrivel rocks and turned up her nose. "Thank you, Milly. At least *someone* realizes I can do something besides…besides sit behind a desk with an empty appointment book."

Neal didn't need to look at Joe to know that the guy's mouth was stretched from ear to ear. "I'm going to lock the bank, then Joe and I will be there."

A slight frown wrinkled across Milly's forehead. "It takes two of you to lock the bank?" She waved her hand as if to dismiss the question. "Oh, never mind. But don't take forever." She motioned for Florence to follow her as she marched back toward the diner.

Florence gave Neal one last glare, then flounced after Milly.

"Were you snippy again, Neal, my boy?" Joe's breath was hot on Neal's neck.

"Shut up." Neal poked at Joe with his elbow. "Snippy doesn't begin to describe what I'm feeling right now. That little display of Florence's was contrived."

"You think?" Joe laughed as he moved to get in step beside Neal.

Neal swung around to face Joe. "Look, neither one of us are in real good standing with Lily. I know it and you know it. But if I stood a chance to have an audience with her ever again, Florence just made sure that would never happen."

Joe's eyebrows arched high on his forehead. "You had your arms around her, Murphy."

"Not for the reason you think. We would have both fallen to the ground if I hadn't caught her and braced myself."

"Another one of those 'I know it and you know it' statements, Neal. But looking at it through Lily's eyes, and my own vantage point, I might add, it looked pretty convincing. Lily is so fragile right now it won't take much to break her apart. That little scene likely produced a pretty good size crack. But now, I'd say we have a bigger problem than wondering if Lily will talk to either one of us again."

Neal opened the door of the bank and waited for Joe to step inside before following him. "I'm going to check Dad's office to make sure he's really gone. Why don't you see if you can find some paper and write a note letting people know we're closed for the day. I'll tape it to the door."

A quick search of the office confirmed that Father was gone and Neal hurried back to the lobby. Joe stood at Florence's desk, a folder in his hand, his lips clamped and his face contorted.

Neal stopped in his tracks. "What's the matter, man? You look like you could chew nails."

Joe held out the folder. "You need to see this."

Neal took it. "Where did you find this?"

Joe pointed to the desk. "In the top drawer when I was looking for clean paper."

On the outside of the folder, in the bottom right-hand corner, were small, penciled letters, *ba*. And inside was a sheet of paper that contained handwritten entries concerning numerous bank clients. Neal perused the entries.

Lily Archer—can't pay mortgage for third year, no money in account.

Benton Finley—owes $500 for money borrowed for seed. Asking for extension on loan money borrowed against property. Doesn't want Gladys to know. Might be good bargaining tool.

Milly at the diner—paid $200 toward loan but is late paying rest.

Mildred Murphy—has nearly $5,000 in personal account.

Neal Murphy—unable to find his information. Will keep looking.

There were others, all owing money and asking for extensions.

Neal clenched his teeth so hard pain shot through his jaw. "You found this in Florence's drawer?"

Joe nodded. "Right where you told me to look for the clean sheet of paper. What are you going to do about it? You do know what *ba* stands for, don't you?"

"Doesn't take a genius, does it? But then, Florence was never the sharpest pencil in the box." Neal shook his head and slapped the paper against his hand. "And yes, that remark was definitely intended." He handed the folder back to Joe. "Put this back in the drawer where you found it. Wait. Let's check the other drawers, too. See what else she's hidden away."

With both of them pulling open drawers, it didn't take long to find the folders of every person listed on the paper. Neal slammed the last folder on the stack. "I can't believe this. These files are supposed to be locked away in my father's office when he's not here. As far as I know, except for Dad, I'm the only other one who has the keys to the file cabinets. How did she get them?"

Joe scratched the back of his neck. "I don't know. Maybe he left in such a hurry to get to the Finleys' place that he forgot to lock it?"

"There's a sure way to find out." Neal ran back to the office and pulled on the top drawer of a file cabinet. Sure enough, it opened with ease. "Joe, come look at this."

"I'm right behind you. I take it this isn't something your father would normally do."

"Never. These files are sacred to my father. He'd never divulge the information contained in them unless given a court order."

"So, what do we do now?" Joe leaned against the file cabinet.

"We're going to put them in my desk under lock and key until I can talk to Pettigrew."

Joe poked his chin toward the sheet of paper still in Neal's hand. "You going to put that with them?"

"No, I'm keeping this." Neal folded the paper and put it in his pocket. "I can show this to Pettigrew easier than if I have a stack of folders under my arm. You know what really upsets me? She told me she just happened to see Lily drive up because she was watching to make sure Bruce didn't come charging into my dad's office before she could stop him."

Joe smirked. "You believe her?"

"Oh, I believe she was watching for Bruce's return but it wasn't so she could keep him from charging into my dad's office. I think she must be in cahoots with Archer somehow."

"But why?" Joe's forehead wrinkled.

Neal leaned one hip against the desk. "This is going to sound pretty proud on my part, but she's upset with me, for sure, and it's my fault. I made the mistake of asking her to work late when I first came to town. I honestly only wanted to get more acquainted with the files and see where I might make some positive changes."

Joe raised one eyebrow. "You didn't think she'd see that as an invitation?"

"I knew after the first couple of sessions that she read more into it than I intended and should have stopped it then, but, quite frankly, her obvious interest in me boosted my ego by several degrees. But then there was an incident involving Lily, and, well, I finally was man enough to let her know my real intentions."

Joe gave a wry smile. "I can imagine how that was received."

"Yeah. Well," Neal patted his pocket, "I think this is her rebuttal."

Joe closed the file drawer. "Do you think Bruce asked her for the information, or is she acting on her own?"

"I don't know. I hate like everything to think that my behavior caused her such angst that she'd implicate so many others in whatever scheme Bruce might have in mind."

"Are you going to show the list to your father?"

Neal closed his eyes and shook his head. "I should, but I don't want to say anything to him yet. Benton Finley was a good friend. Dad doesn't need anything more to deal with. However, I will turn this information over to Amos as soon as we can talk with him again. There's more at stake now than finding Paul Archer's will. I'm beginning to think Bruce's threats were real. If so, we've got a problem on our hands bigger than anything I ever encountered in Kansas City. We better get those files put in my desk and get out of here before Milly sends Florence to look for us. I sure do wish Amos were here."

Twenty-One

THIS WAS NOT Joe's first encounter with tragedy, but it was the first time he'd experienced such community. The crowd was subdued, with tears present on many faces, but there was an overall atmosphere of peace. Though his death had not been confirmed, whispered eulogies soon became voiced memories of a kind and gentle man as one after another shared the impact Benton Finley had made on their lives.

"He and Miss Benton were at my baseball game last week," one freckled-face youngster shyly reported.

"Loaned me money more than once," a man offered.

A young man with a little boy riding on his hip stepped from the crowd. "Paid my hospital bill after my tractor accident. Don't know how me and my missus woulda fed our young'uns if he hadn't helped. Wouldn't let me pay him back. Said I should pass it on to the next one who needed it."

Several nodded, evidently recipients of the same gracious generosity.

"I ain't never been a church-believin' man." A big, burly man with a scraggly beard slipped from his stool at the counter and tucked his hands under the bib of his raggedy overalls. "Ain't got nothin' against the church, just never saw me much evidence of Jesus bein' there 'til I met Benton Finley." A tear rolled down his farmer's-tanned face "But I reckon that good man comes about as close to bein' Jesus as anybody I ever come acquainted to."

"Never missed a Sunday."

"How will we know when church starts without Benton ringing the bell?"

"Saw him just yesterday. Guess one never knows when their time is up."

"Remember how he would shout out *number seventy-three* every time we had third Sunday singalongs?"

From the back someone started singing, "*When peace, like a river, attendeth my way,*" and slowly it spread until everyone in Milly's stood arm in arm as their voices swelled in harmony, "*It is well, it is well with my soul.*"

The crowd began to murmur and circle the intruder.

The burly man pulled his ham-sized hands from the bib of his overalls and stepped in front of Bruce.

Neal's shoulders tensed and he balled his fist.

"Steady, man. Don't do anything stupid. Let that guy take care of him," Joe whispered. "You'll have your turn, but let's wait and let this play out."

The big man punched one finger against Bruce's chest and forced him to take a step backwards. "Ya ain't only the not-honored guest, young buck, ya ain't neither a welcome guest 'less ya think ya can keep them lips from flappin' one more word what ain't respect for Benton Finley."

Bruce paled. "You…you can't tell me—"

"Reckon I just did." A slow smile stretched across the man's face as another push of his finger forced another step back. "But if ya wasn't listenin', I don't mind repeatin' it."

Bruce widened his stance and jutted his chin. "I got as much right to be here as you do. Besides that, I know people. I got connections. You won't be so big when—"

Joe rolled his lips. Archer didn't know when to back off. The atmosphere in the diner was so charged all it would take is one more spark of impudence from Bruce to set the onlookers into a fiery rage. Men from around the room began to shoulder past wives to draw closer to where Bruce and the big man stood nose to nose.

"Ya know what, little boy?" The burly man pulled himself to his full height and rolled his shoulders. "I done been this size long b'fore ya was borned and I ain't figgerin' on shrinkin' any time soon." He unbuttoned the cuffs of his sleeves and hitched them above his elbows. "Now, ya can either stay here and act like ya had some raisin' up, or you can skip on outta here and go find your so-called people. I reckon they's enough of us here to make some connections of our own." He nodded to the crowd. "That be what y'all is thinkin'?"

One tiny woman, someone Joe had never seen in town before now, stepped forward with a scowl so deep it drew her eyebrows together. Pearls adorned her black checkered dress. A red felt hat sat atop her snow-white hair and she carried a bright yellow handbag that was nearly big enough to hold her. "Bruce Paul Archer. "She reached into her purse and withdrew a wooden ruler. "Don't make me use this."

Bruce bent to the little lady's height. "Yeah? You and who—"

The circle tightened and Bruce paled. He did a slow turn, then elbowed his way through the crowd and reached for the door as Amos stepped in, blocking his exit.

Milly shoved her way through the onlookers to reach Pettigrew, and he put his arm around her shoulders.

Joe nudged Neal with an elbow. "Are those two a thing?"

Neal grinned. "For as long as I can remember."

"Huh." Joe gave a low chuckle. "*Love me, love my dog* makes a lot more sense now."

"Glad you're all here." Amos nodded to the crowd. "Neal, your father took Gladys to the hospital in Wichita. I've already contacted your mother."

"To the hospital?" Neal rubbed the back of his neck. "Did something happen to Gladys, too?"

Amos shook his head. "Oh, no, no. He took her so she could be with Benton."

An audible gasp went through the bystanders.

Amos looked around the room. "The last report from Ed was that Benton has a long road ahead of him, but with time, patience, and the good Lord willing, he'll recover."

As if on cue, all eyes turned to Florence, who stood with both hands on her cheeks, eyes wide. "How…how could…but Clarice said—"

"Clarice said what?" Amos peered down at Milly. "Did you think…is that why you're all so…Florence, exactly what did Clarice say?" His eyes narrowed. "That girl has got to stop divulging conversation she hears through the phone lines or we'll have to find someone else to man the switchboard. Did she tell you that Benton was dead?"

"Well, not exactly." Florence folded her arms across her waist. "She said…she said Franklin said when he found him, Benton couldn't talk or…or move and I supposed…I figured…he must be…ohhh!" She covered her face and stumbled blindly through the crowd right into Bruce Archer's embrace. Without a word, Bruce opened the door, gave one last smirk to the crowd, and led her from the diner.

Neal pushed past Joe, but Joe yanked his arm. "Don't."

"What do you mean, *don't?*" Neal turned on Joe, a vein on his forehead bulging. "You saw them."

"Shh. Keep your voice down." Joe pulled him away from Amos and the questioning crowd. "There's not another person in this place that would see that little scenario as anything but what it was. There's no sense getting them more riled by what we suspect."

Neal pulled the paper from his pocket and waved it in Joe's face. "I'm supposed to ignore this?"

"Not at all." Joe widened his stance and crossed his arms. "For now, let's do what Florence asked us to do. Even though we now have an idea what's happened with Benton, there are no signs the people in here are ready to disperse. There'll be time afterward to talk with Amos. By the arm he has hooked around Milly's shoulders, he's not going anywhere anytime soon. If we forge ahead without some kind of counsel, we could do more damage than good. Remember, *the way of a fool is right in his own eyes, but he that hearkeneth unto counsel is wise.*"

"So, you think quoting the Bible is counsel? Are you calling me a fool?" Neal shoved the paper back in his pocket.

"Not at all. Archer is the fool, but we are only a step away from him if we act before seeking counsel. And by counsel, I mean legal advice. What we found in that folder could very well be considered extortion, but until that is proven it is nothing more than notes on a piece of paper. We can't prove intent until something intentional is actually carried out." Joe clamped his hand onto Neal's shoulder. "Come on. Let's pour these good people a cup of coffee."

IT WAS WELL past Milly's normal closing time before the last citizen reluctantly closed the door behind them. Though she'd served more than coffee—on the house—someone had salvaged a jar, stuck it on the first table by the door, and labeled it for Gladys and Benton. One by one, as the crowd had dispersed, they dug into pockets or purses and stuffed dollars and coins into the jar. For some, Joe reckoned, that money represented bills that wouldn't get paid or food that would not grace their tables, and for all it was most likely a sacrificial gift of love.

Amos plopped onto a stool at the far end of the counter and pulled Milly onto his lap. "You, my lady, need to get off your feet." He winked across her shoulder at Joe and Neal. "You two are standing there with your mouths flapping like gills on a fish out of water. Let me tell you a secret." He folded his arms around Milly. "True love, like good wine, gets sweeter with age."

Milly laughed. "Look at you two—blushing like schoolboys." She slid off Pettigrew's lap, then turned and kissed him on the cheek. "I'm so hungry I could take that bone away from Barnabas and not even feel guilty about it. What say I fry us up some pancakes?"

"You stay put, Milly." Joe pulled the dish towel from Milly's shoulders. "Neal and I will whip up something. You…you two enjoy some time together."

"What do you mean, *Neal and I?*" Neal hissed as he followed Joe to the kitchen. "Have you forgotten we need to show Amos what you found in Florence's desk?"

They reached the kitchen and Joe leaned against the sink. "You saw what I saw." He raised one eyebrow. "You really think now is the time?"

Neal stuck his hands in the pockets of his britches. "No, I suppose not. But what if Bruce—"

"What if Bruce what? Listen," Joe moved closer to Neal, "I don't know who that boy is listing as *his people*. But I'm as certain as I can be that his so-called connection is none other than Florence Bower. When Florence realizes that the paper we found is missing from her folder she'll do one of two things—either panic or—"

"Or flutter her hands until she takes off." Neal shot a devilish grin toward Joe.

Joe laughed. Oh, how good it felt to laugh. "Now that, young Mr. Murphy, was snippy. Let's try to get through the rest of this day with no more drama. I'll flap the jacks, you scramble the eggs."

"Flap the jacks?" Neal shoved Joe to one side. "Better wash our hands first."

THE SETTING SUN cast a rosy glow up and down the street as Joe and Neal left the diner. "Kinda glad Milly offered to see Amos home." Neal pulled his car keys from his pocket. "Wasn't looking forward to that drive again…especially in the dark." He stepped off the sidewalk and unlocked his car door. "You need a ride to your boardinghouse?"

Joe rotated his neck and shoulders. "No, but thanks. The walk will give me time to unwind before stepping into a hot room."

"The walk to Pettigrew's didn't unwind you?" Neal opened the car door.

"If you remember right, I rode all the way back to town with a hundred-pound bloodhound on my lap." He stretched his arms above his head. "Do you think your father will get home tonight?"

Neal leaned against the open door. "I've been wondering that myself. If he does, it'll be late."

Joe stifled a yawn. "You won't bother him with—"

"No. Not tonight. While you were putting the last of the things away in the kitchen, however, I did mention to Amos that we needed to talk with him, and that it was rather urgent. He said he'd meet us at the bank in the morning, first thing."

"First thing, like usual-unlocked-doors-time first thing?" Joe checked his watch. "Pettigrew will not get a lot of sleep tonight if he's going to make it back in that early."

Neal rolled his eyes. "I don't think we have to worry about that. Milly doesn't have a car."

"What?" Joe's jaw dropped. "But she said she'd see him home."

Neal's face split with a grin. "She didn't say what home, though, did she?"

"You mean...?" Joe shut his eyes. "No. You know what? I don't even want to know."

Neal laughed. "If it's any consolation, Milly lives with her mother, Evangeline Wright, and her mama is the little lady who threatened to use the ruler on Bruce. It's none of our business in the first place, but that tiny wisp of a woman was my third-grade teacher. I can assure you she runs a tight ship...a very, very tight ship." He slid into the seat. "Hope you get some sleep. See you in the morning."

Joe waited until Neal drove away before he started his trek to the boardinghouse. The more he was around the guy, the better he liked him. If it weren't for Murphy's prior relationship with Lily, he'd not be the least threatened by him. And maybe it wasn't Neal himself who intimidated him. Maybe it was observing Lily's reaction, the pain he saw etched on her face, even through a car window, when Florence stood wrapped in Neal's arms earlier. Couldn't she see through Florence's deliberate attempt to engage Neal? He had to admit, however, that the scene appeared very convincing.

The events of the day rolled through his mind like water running downhill, and by the time he reached the boardinghouse, he'd made a decision—probably not a wise one, but a decision, nonetheless. He didn't stop to greet the other boarders sitting on the porch but went straight to his car. Some hills were worth dying on.

LILY SPREAD THE quilt under the willow tree, drew Mama down beside her, wrapped her arms around her bent knees, and watched the last rays of sunlight turn the waters of Willow Creek pink. Would she ever have a time in her life when her every move didn't include making sure Mama was okay? She longed for the days when this spot was hers alone, with no thought of anyone becoming too agitated to sit still. A place where she could cry, or laugh, or lay for hours looking at the sky, imagining faces in the clouds by day or counting stars by night.

She'd chopped cockleburs until her arms burned with fatigue, keeping one eye open for Mama and the cat. She'd scrubbed the kitchen floor on her hands and knees while Mama napped with the cat curled beside her. And even though Bruce had shown up this morning, Mama still made her afternoon trek to the mailbox, only today she carried the cat with her, and Lily had trudged after them both. All were daily activities that mortared together the bricks of fear, anger, and regret the day added to her already weighted shoulders…Bruce's threats…Neal's arms around Florence…while she still had food in the cupboard, there hovered the overwhelming knowledge that once it was gone there was no money for more…and she'd sent the one person who seemed to care the most away for good.

She pressed her forehead against her bent knees. She had no more tears. She'd spent that account dry on the way home from town. Witnessing Neal's arms around Florence was one thing. But observing Joe Kendall in the car next to hers with a smile clear across his face took away all hope of ever having anyone believe her over whatever Bruce might choose to divulge. Now all that was left was a pain so sharp and so deep it was as if a knife had been thrust into her chest.

Arms around Lily's shoulders startled her.

"Papa knows." Mama's soft declaration. One she'd voiced several times over the last few days. "Papa cares. Tell Papa." She patted Lily's back. "Papa fixes everything."

Lily gripped Mama's hand. "I know, Mama. I know."

Mama pulled her hand from Lily's. "Here." She plopped the cat onto Lily's lap. "Cat is soft. Cat sings." She scooted closer to Lily, took her hand, and together they stroked the cat's silky back. "This is Lily's Pond." Mama looked dreamily toward the water rippling by a rare soft breeze. "I like this place."

And while she knew it wouldn't last long, Lily savored what minutes she had to be the one comforted...by Mama.

Twenty-Two

NEAL WATCHED UNTIL Joe turned to the corner toward the boardinghouse, then backed out of his parking spot, drove around the block, and parked in the alley behind the bank. He needed time to ponder on the events of the day before heading home to what would be a sure lecture from his mother for being late, having to keep his supper warm, not spending enough time with Rosie.

Thankful for the darkness of the alley, he rolled down his window for much-needed air and slouched in the seat. His car being parked behind the bank wouldn't alarm anyone, but the fact that he hadn't gone into the office might make some wonder. Truth was—he could think better for himself if not sitting at Father's desk.

How could so much happen in one day? Bruce back in town, introducing Kendall and Pettigrew, Benton Finley in the hospital, and then there was the overall weight hanging above his head...standing in front of Lily's car with his arms wrapped around Florence Bower. Joe Kendall could attest to his innocence, but would he?

Neal linked his fingers together and braced his hands atop his head. His past history with Lily never included competitors—at least the years before he left Anderson. During high school it was a given that he and Lily were a couple and pity the poor guy who might try to muscle into that relationship. Then enter one Joe Kendall whose only reason for being in Anderson was to oversee the lake project, and in the doing secured a spot in Lily's life. There was no way Kendall had any prior knowledge of either Lily or Neal. Yet in the short time in this town, his charm, care, and compassion had melded into one word...action. And that one word had made more difference in the life of Lily Archer than the twelve years of his devotion.

If it were anyone else, he'd hate the guy. He did hate the thought of Joe winning Lily's affections, but try as he might, even after dissecting the guy from every direction, he couldn't deny the fact that they could very well be friends. Perhaps, the only real friend he could muster in Anderson.

Headlights from an oncoming car lit the alley and Neal scrunched as far as he could onto the seat. *Well, this certainly won't look suspicious, Murphy.* Neal clenched his jaw and prayed the car wouldn't stop. If so, could he feign sleep?

The crunch of tires against the sandy alleyway slowed to a crawl, hesitated, then sped away, leaving grit pinging against the side of his car and dust filtering through the open window. Neal jerked upright but only caught a glimpse of the backend of the vehicle as it sped around the corner.

He'd never been one to scare easily, so why was his heart pounding like a jackhammer? He wasn't doing anything illegal, nor could he prove the slowing down and subsequent speeding away of the vehicle was anything more than natural curiosity. He shivered and goosebumps prickled down his arms. One thing sure, he'd not sleep tonight unless he voiced his concerns to someone. With Amos busy with Milly, Kendall was his best option. He started the car and forced himself to exit the alley in a manner that wouldn't arouse suspicion. With luck, he'd catch Joe before he settled in for the evening.

Three cars were parked in front of the boardinghouse, but Neal didn't recognize any of them as belonging to Kendall. He parked beside one, stepped onto the street, then nodded to the three men sitting on the porch. "Evening, Ernie. I didn't know you lived here." Neal leaned against a porch post.

Ernie folded his hands across his chest and leaned back in his chair. "Don't."

Neal moved away from the post. "Uh, you don't live here, or I shouldn't lean against the post?"

The men laughed. "He don't live here but he pays Miz Lloyd to fix his meals. Lazy old grease monkey." One of the men punched Ernie in the shoulder. "What brings you here, young Murphy?"

Neal grinned at the speaker. "Good to see you, too, Levi. I'm looking for Joe Kendall."

Levi bent forward, placing his hands on his knees. "Say, you hear anything new 'bout Benton Finley?"

"Nothing but what Amos reported this afternoon." Neal could appreciate their concern but was in no mood to chat.

"Mighty nice of Milly to feed us all, weren't it?" Levi picked at a hole in the knee of his britches.

"It was, most certainly." Neal leaned back against the post. "Uh, about Kendall."

Ernie cocked his head. "What 'bout him? Seems like a nice enough fella. Real polite, that one. Does up the dishes every night for Miz Lloyd."

Levi looked sideways at Neal, a big grin across his scruffy face. "Sure can tell he's had some raisin'."

"Real good lookin', too. Hear tell he's been spendin' a lot of time out at the Archer farm." Ernie pulled a pocketknife from his pocket and cleaned his fingernails. "You lookin' for him or somethin'?"

Neal licked his lips. "Okay, you guys. I asked a simple question and you've beat around the bush long enough. I have some business to talk over with Joe, that's all. So, are you going to tell me where I can find him?"

Alice Lloyd opened the screen door and shook her finger at the men sitting there. "I just pulled a pie from the oven, but not a single one of you will get a piece of it unless you stop this nonsense." She winked up at Neal. "I should spank them all and send them to bed without supper. Joe isn't here but I did see him leave a few minutes ago. He didn't come to the house, so I don't know where he went or when he'll be back. And Ernie, you'll pay double for your supper tonight."

Ernie jumped to his feet. "Why? We was only havin' us a little fun. And I weren't the onliest one."

She snapped her dish towel at him. "It's only fun if it's fun for everyone, Ernie. Besides that, I know you well enough to know you were the ringleader." She held out her hand. "That'll be a dollar, and supper is on the table."

Ernie grumbled but pulled a dollar bill from the pocket of his greasy overalls and nodded to Neal as he followed the others into the house.

Neal pushed away from the post and gave what he hoped was a friendly smile to the boardinghouse proprietress. "Thank you, Miss Lloyd. I do think they were having fun."

She flipped the dish towel over her shoulder. "Fun at someone else's expense is never fun. It might be funny, but it's not fun. And my name is Alice. You know that."

Neal nodded. "I do know that but didn't want to be disrespectful since the others were calling you Miss Lloyd." He turned to leave, then swiveled back. "If you're still awake, and happen to see him when he returns, would you please tell him I was looking for him?"

"I will do that, yes." She opened the screen door. "And, oh, um, do you know if anyone has told Lily Archer about Benton? I think she'd want to know."

"I...I don't really know but, well, maybe I'll make sure she's informed."

Alice gave him a sly smile. "Yes. I think that might be a good idea. Now, I best get in there before those men decide to hunt for the pie."

"You hid it?" Neal laughed. "Serves them right."

She joined his laughter. "I did hide it…under the dishpan. They won't even touch that thing for fear I'd catch them and make them do dishes." She gave a flick of her hand. "I'll tell Joe you're looking for him."

Neal gave one last wave as he took the steps two at a time. So Joe left a few minutes ago, whatever *few* might mean. Was she suggesting that perhaps Joe was on his way to Lily's? Is that why she asked if Lily knew about Benton? She said Lily would want to know. Why?

CONFUSION HEAPED UPON guilt plus a healthy, or unhealthy, mix of jealousy fueled Neal's drive to the Archer farm. Was it just last night that'd he made this same trip? Only last night he was headed back to town after being thoroughly stripped of all pride. What would make this night any different? News of Benton Finley? And what if Bruce was there?

He slammed on the brakes and his car fishtailed to one side. A younger Neal Murphy would gun the engine again so he could throw debris and slide the other direction. Maybe the fact he was thankful he stopped before he hit the ditch meant he was growing up.

You want to grow up, do you? Then turn around. Go home. Take the lecture that is awaiting you. Love on Rosie. Listen to her prayers. Then do some praying of your own. Remember, fools rush in—

Fools rush in? There was that word again, only this time he couldn't accuse Kendall of calling him a fool, or bristle at God's word being quoted. He laid his forehead against the steering wheel. *Fools rush in.* He had no idea whether this was in the Bible or not. But what he did know was that when something popped into your mind more than once, it should not go unheeded. He turned the car around. He'd go home. He'd take the lecture, love on Rosie, and listen to her prayers. It had been a long, long time since he'd spent time in prayer on his own, but he'd try. He'd try.

JOE STOPPED AT the Archer mailbox and switched off the engine. Yesterday he'd promised Lily that if she'd allow him to buy her groceries for her that he'd leave and never bother her again. What made him think he could go back on the promise twenty-four hours later? Did his word mean nothing?

He stepped out of the car and leaned against the front fender. The moon crawled from beneath the purple quilt of dusk and a rare soft breeze rustled the dry grasses along the lane. It was as if Kansas were apologizing for the chaos of the day, and Joe wrapped his arms around his chest as if he could somehow capture the peace it offered.

Not normally given to impromptu decisions, being here was not one of his better ideas. While his intentions were good, he had to admit they were not entirely without ulterior motive. It was not his place to explain the real nature of Florence and Neal's little exhibition. When Neal rushed to get out of the car ahead of him so he could be the first to greet Lily, he'd felt the all-too-familiar kick in the gut. Then when he witnessed Florence's rather pitiful but convincing performance to persuade any onlooker that Neal Murphy was her man, the kicked gut changed to a belly laugh…until he saw the effect it had on Lily. Did he really think that by defending Neal's actions it would somehow cause Lily to look on his reaction with more favor?

He paced between the mailbox and his car. Reluctant to retreat yet knowing to stay could well do more harm than good, he finally shuffled back to his car, turned it around, and headed to town.

197

Before he got to the end of the second mile, two red pinpoints of light made him aware there was a car ahead of him and he dimmed his headlights. The road was rocky and narrow, and he was in no hurry to get back to the boardinghouse and field the questions of Ernie and his cohorts, so he'd keep a distance behind the other driver. He rolled his window down, braced his elbow through the opening, let up on the accelerator, and willed his shoulders to relax.

When they got to the edge of town and passed under the first streetlight, Joe recognized the car he'd been following was that of Neal Murphy's, and when Neal turned down the street to his house, Joe followed. Had they both had the same idea, and both chickened out? Instead of the kick in the gut that thought would normally have brought, there was a more urgent need to talk to the guy and he pulled into the drive behind him.

They exited their cars at the same time. Neal shook Joe's hand. "Did you talk to Lily?"

Joe huffed out a breath. "Was going to, then realized it wasn't one of my finer decisions. Were you headed that direction yourself?"

Neal stuck his hands in the pockets of his britches. "I went to the boardinghouse looking for you. It's kind of a long story, but when I realized I was being followed, I hoped it was you."

"You went looking for me?" Joe crossed his arms and leaned against the trunk of Neal's car. "Why? Look, man, I wasn't trying to cause trouble between you and—"

Neal raised his hand like a stop sign. "No, no, that isn't why I was looking for you." He hitched one foot onto the back bumper. "Listen to this and tell me what you think."

Joe listened to Neal's alley escapade and his scalp prickled. "You didn't see the car?"

Neal shook his head. "Only a glimpse. It looked dark, but then it was dark in the alley and natural light that time of evening is so, well, so unnatural."

"What does your gut tell you?"

Neal rubbed his hand across his forehead. "My gut says—"

The porchlight flipped on and Mrs. Murphy stepped onto the porch. "Neal? Is that you?"

Neal moved his foot from the bumper. "It's me, Mother. I'll be in for supper in a minute."

"Oh, well, Florence Bower stopped by earlier, looking for you. Said she left her purse in the bank and wanted you to come let her in. She said to tell you she'd be waiting in the alley."

Neal stepped closer to Joe, his eyes wide. "She has a key," he hissed. "What do you think she really wants?"

Joe shrugged. "I don't know, but you're not going down there alone." He stepped to the porch. "I'll take him to the bank, Mrs. Murphy."

"Oh, well, I suppose that's all right." She wound her hands in her apron. "Goodness, I do wish Edward were here, but I know the Finleys needs him, too. Don't be too long, Neal. I've already kept your supper warm beyond repair."

"Don't worry about me, Mother." Neal smiled. "You know Florence. Once you get her to talking it's hard to get away."

They waited until she went back into the house, then Neal crossed his arms atop Joe's car. "What are you thinking?"

Joe motioned for Neal to get in. "First of all, we're not going to the bank. And secondly, I'm thinking it's time we pay a visit to your third-grade teacher."

MILLY'S MOTHER PULLED the ruler out of the yellow purse hanging on the back of her chair and slapped it against the dining room table. "Amos Pettigrew, you sit down. This table isn't Jericho, and you marching around it isn't going to bring anything tumbling down except you and maybe me. I'm dizzy watching you."

Joe watched in awe as Amos stopped in his tracks and slid onto the nearest chair, looking the world like a schoolboy instead of an overall-clad attorney.

"Sorry, ma'am. I think better on my feet."

"Mother." Milly stood and moved behind the older lady. "I think maybe we should leave these gentlemen alone to discuss whatever they need to discuss."

"Nonsense." Mrs. Wright jutted her chin. "They came in here bringing trouble with them and I aim to sit right here until they take it right back out with them."

Milly patted her mother's shoulders. "But it's none of our business."

The older woman shoved at Milly's hands. "Maybe not. But I can tell you right now, I don't have any idea what's on that sheet of paper that seems welded to Amos's hands, but I can sure as fire is hot tell you who wrote it. Florence Bower. That girl thinks you have to put curlicues on everything. I guess she thinks it makes her look fancy or something. Looks silly to me. Don't know how she ever got through business school."

"There's more than just the paper, Amos." Joe kicked Neal's shin under the table.

"More in the folder or more information of a different sort?" Amos peered at Joe over the top of his glasses.

Joe held up two fingers. "Both."

"Well, then." Amos reared back in his chair. "Let's hear it."

Neal folded his hands atop the table. "It's probably nothing but Joe feels you should know." He retold the incident in the alley.

Amos leaned forward, a frown creasing his brow. "But you didn't see the car?"

Neal shook his head. "No. I—"

"He's not telling you everything." Joe scooted to the edge of his chair. "Tell them what your mother said, Neal. You know, about

Florence calling and wanting you to meet her in the alley and let her in the bank so she could get her purse. And make sure he knows she already had a key." He nudged Neal's shoulder. "Tell him."

"*Humph.*" Mrs. Wright looked down her nose at Joe. "You did the telling, young man. We don't need to hear it twice."

Amos's glasses pushed up on his face when he laughed. "No, I don't need to hear it twice." He pushed his glasses back down on his cheeks and wiped his eyes. "I say we let her wait there tonight and we keep our appointment to meet in the morning like we planned. A simmering stew brings forth more flavor than a hasty meal every time."

Joe rankled. "What does cooking have to do with this?"

Amos leaned back in his chair. "You know how you take a good beef roast, add some potatoes and carrots and an onion, maybe some cabbage or corn or whatever? You hurry that along and all you have is a pot of half-cooked meat and vegetables. But you cook it real slow-like and all those things meld together into something downright mouth-watering. Right now, all we have are bits of pieces of things that look suspicious but no real proof. But if we're patient and wait long enough, we'll have us a real nice pot of evidence."

Joe braced his elbows on the table. "But how long will it take? My superiors are already grumbling because we don't have all the necessary land purchased. It leaves a bad taste in my mouth knowing I'm going to have to make some very hard decisions."

Amos shrugged. "I can't tell you how long. But don't do anything yet. I'll be your defense if you need it. It sure would help if we could find that will Paul made." He scooted his chair closer to Milly and lobbed his arm around her shoulders. "Benton sure picked a bad time to go down."

Mrs. Wright's ruler hit the table. "Shame on you, Amos Pettigrew. It isn't like the poor man planned it."

Amos gave a curt nod. "That's true. He didn't plan it but he is the only one who might know what became of Paul Archer's will."

"Oh, bunny feathers." She tilted her head and sent a devilish grin around the table. "Gladys Finley knows as much, or more, about Benton's business than he does."

"I don't think so, Mother. I've heard him—"

"And you believe everything you hear?" She tweaked Milly's nose. "Your father, Mr. Wright—God rest his soul—thought I didn't know what was going on either, but he was wrong." She put her hand in front of her mouth and giggled. "Get it? Mr. Wright was wrong." She reached down the front of her dress, pulled out a handkerchief, gave her pearls a pat, and fanned her face. "Oh. My. Sometimes I surprise even myself."

Joe's chin wasn't the only one hanging loose as he looked around the table. Then, as if finally given permission, laughter filled the room. And in the laughter, he experienced renewed hope.

Twenty-Three

EARLY-MORNING LIGHT filtered through the open kitchen door, and Lily had yet to sleep though she was so very, very tired. Mama had been up and down all night, mumbling to the cat, pumping water but putting no glass to catch it, repeating '*Papa knows*' over and over. She'd finally shuffled back to her favorite chair and settled down.

As loud as her body groaned for rest, it would be full daylight soon. Lily rolled to her side and pushed herself to a sitting position. Mama was still in her chair, Papa's Bible clutched against her breast with one hand, the other hand methodically stroking the cat, though seemingly sound asleep…at last.

Lily tiptoed around the mattress and gently pulled the Bible from Mama's grip. If it fell on the cat, who knew what bedlam might occur? As she pulled it away, the envelope fell out and what looked to be a blank sheet of paper slid from the envelope. On closer inspection, she could make out writing, but the dim light in the living room prevented her from deciphering the inscription.

She hurried as quietly as she could to the porch where the light was better, lowered herself to the top step, and unfolded the creased paper atop her lap. There was a short, penciled message, nearly faded, but by squinting, she could read it.

Should anyone find this after I am dead, show it to Benton Finley. He'll know what to do.

What mystery did this message hold? Why Benton Finley? The Finleys were good neighbors and friends with Mama and Papa. Then Papa died and…

Her head pounded and her chest was so tight it hurt to take a breath. Did she dare show the paper to Benton? She'd kept her promise to Papa, but would Benton keep his promise to her? There was only one way to find out and that was to follow Papa's directions. If only she didn't have to worry about Mama and the cat, and both of them in Gladys Finley's fine home.

By eight o'clock, Lily had dressed herself, fed and dressed Mama, fed the cat, and had everyone in the car headed to the Finleys' place. It was early, perhaps too early, but if she had to wait any longer she'd lose her nerve. Besides, she knew from past experience that Benton was up and around long before daylight…a habit that used to vex poor Gladys, at least to hear Mama tell it.

The Finley farm was less than three miles from Lily's home, but it lay well above the ground needed for the lake. Even though the grass was brown and the trees were already shedding dry leaves, the farm had a *Green Gables* air about it. After reading the story of Anne and her adventures, Lily had often wondered what it would be like to live in such a grand house or to have a close friend like Diana. And she'd lain awake at night imagining Neal to be Gilbert Blythe and giggling over the idea of Gladys Benton and Ed Murphy being attracted to one another in their younger years.

Lily hesitated before switching off the engine. Though the Finley vehicle was in the garage, there was not the usual activity. In years past, Gladys would be at the gate greeting anyone who drove in, and this early in the morning Benton would be coming from the barn. Did she dare leave Mama in the car long enough to go knock on the door? And if Mama followed her, and there was no one home, would Mama get back into the car without a fuss? For that matter, if Gladys was home, how would Mama *or* the cat behave in a new environment?

With questions that outweighed the option to stay, Lily slowly backed away from the gate. Whatever it was that Benton Finley was supposed to know or do would have to wait.

Before she reached the end of the drive, another car drove in. Lily's shoulders tensed. She hadn't done anything wrong, so why did she feel guilty to be found leaving the Finleys'? She pulled to the side as far as the narrow driveway allowed and waited to let the other vehicle pass, but when it got even with her it stopped. Recognizing the driver didn't do anything to lessen the apprehension but there was no pretending she didn't see him. Ed Murphy was not a person one ignored.

He rolled down his window and motioned for her to do the same. Lily did so. This was worse than sitting in his office.

"You're out bright and early, Lily." His voice was friendly and held no question.

She swallowed. "I…I know. I—"

His eyes narrowed below puckered brows. "You probably haven't heard about Benton."

"Something happened to Benton?" One more twist of the rope around her chest and she wouldn't be able to breathe.

Mr. Murphy's sad eyes met hers. "Oh, my dear. Yes. He had a stroke and is in the hospital in Wichita. I was with Gladys and was stopping by to check on things. We left in such a hurry yesterday and…Lily? Lily, are you all right?" He jumped from his vehicle and was beside Lily before she could answer. "Lily, why are you here so early? It must be important. Is there anything I can do?"

Was there? Could she trust him? "Bruce is back."

He rolled his lips and nodded. "I know. He was in my office yesterday, but he was arrogant and rude, and I sent him away."

The rope around her chest loosened a notch. "Then you didn't...you haven't—"

"Lily." He tilted his head toward her. "Haven't I always been fair and honest with you?"

His gaze was so kind and his voice so gentle she felt another knot slip. "Yes, Mr. Murphy. But I can't—"

"I'm your banker, Lily, and I was your father's banker before you. I know there's no money for the mortgage again this year. But I'm also a friend, or at least I want to be. Your papa and I were high school buddies. I know he'd want me to do everything I can to help you, but you have to trust me."

She reached for her purse and pulled out the envelope that held the note and handed it to him. "I found this just this morning. I don't know what it means. That's why I'm here."

Mr. Murphy opened the envelope and withdrew the sheet of paper. His forehead wrinkled as he read it, glanced up at her, and then appeared to read it again. "You've never seen this before today?"

She swallowed. Maybe if she'd read the Bible like Papa would have wanted, she'd have found it earlier. "Not the note. The envelope was in Papa's Bible for as long as I can remember. I thought it was a bookmark."

"Knowing your papa, I would have thought the same thing." He gave her a wistful smile. "He'd find a use for a horse feather...if horses had feathers."

She returned his smile. "*Why buy new when what you have will do* was his constant reminder. Well, I've not bought new, but have very little left that will do." She hung her head "I've tried so hard—"

He opened the door and sank to his haunches. "Lily, look at me." He clasped her hands. "The lack of money to pay the mortgage doesn't have anything to do with how hard you've worked. Don't you see? The farmers around you who have so readily agreed to accept the purchase price for their land did so because they could no longer pay their mortgages, either. It wasn't because they, or you, didn't try. Dust storms and drought have taken away the hopes and dreams of so many. It's those same catastrophes that have forced the city to purchase your lands for the much-needed water supply. Wells are dry. Businesses are closed. People all over the country are hurting."

She fought, in vain, to hold her tears. "But I have nowhere to go. The farm, the house, it's all…and there's Mama and people don't—"

Tears filled his eyes, too. "Will you give me a chance to do better? Please? There's a reason Paul left this note and we need to find that reason as soon as possible, especially with Bruce back in the picture."

She swiped at her cheeks with the back of her hand. "But how? With Benton so ill, he can't tell us anything."

He nodded. "Joe Kendall was in my office when Bruce was there yesterday and raised some good questions that I couldn't answer. I sent him and Neal out to Amos Pettigrew's place. I'm assuming they met with him. If not, he's definitely the one to help us now. Will you come back to town with me?"

The rope tightened again. She glanced at Mama sitting next to her, so far content with the cat in her lap, but she couldn't guarantee how she'd react to being in a bank office. "I…isn't there some other way we could talk with him? Mama doesn't…Mama sometimes—"

He squeezed her hands. "I'm sorry. I wasn't thinking. I tell you what. I'm going to go in and use the telephone to call Neal. You go on back to your place and I'll be there was soon as I know anything."

Fear threatened to choke her. "What if Bruce comes again? He said he would be back."

He rose from his haunches and smiled down at her. "Then we'll deal with Bruce together. You go home and try not to worry. I'll be there shortly." He put the note back into the envelope. "If you don't mind, I'm going to keep this. I think it might be safer with me."

The trip back home didn't seem so long this time, nor was her chest so tight. She didn't look forward to seeing Neal Murphy or Joe Kendall again, but if it meant the help she so sorely needed then so be it.

NEAL UNLOCKED THE back door of the bank and stepped to one side to let Amos Pettigrew and his hound enter before him. "You're sure this is the right way to handle this?" He followed the attorney in and locked the door behind him.

Amos lowered himself to one of the leather chairs beside the desk. "Trust me, Neal."

Barnabas sat dutifully beside his master, his big head nuzzled against Pettigrew's leg.

"Oh, I trust you." Neal chuckled. "It's Florence Bower and Bruce Archer I no longer trust."

"Shh." Amos put one finger of his lips. "Let her know you're here and wait for Joe to make his entrance. Leave the rest up to me." He scratched behind the dog's ears.

Neal raised his hands in surrender. "Whatever you say. I'm more than a little nervous. I just hope it doesn't backfire." He straightened his tie and stepped into the lobby.

"Oh! Florence!" He put his hand over his heart in feigned surprise. "Goodness. I didn't expect to see you here this early."

She plucked a pencil from the holder and proceeded to rat-a-tat-tat it against the top of her desk. "I work here, Neal."

He leaned one hip against her desk. "Oh, I'm quite aware of that, but you see, I didn't get the message that you needed your purse until late last night. You know a gentleman doesn't call after nine o'clock, and I didn't get home until after eleven, so I opted to get here early to let you in." He shook his head. "How is it you beat me here?" It wasn't a total lie but was still close enough to earn his mother's wrath.

The familiar red splotches popped onto her face and neck. "I…well, silly me, I remembered I had a key at home." *Thrum, thrum, brrrrrr, thrum.*

Neal tilted his head and smiled at her. "I see. Perhaps next time, that is, if it ever happens again, you might let my mother know your problem was resolved. Poor dear stayed up until I got home." *Neal Murphy, you're going to have a sore on your tongue so big you won't be able to shut your mouth.*

Florence's lips trembled. "I never…I mean, I didn't want her to—"

"No harm done. She said she knew how important a purse was to a girl. Seems like you ladies must carry everything but the kitchen sink in those handbags." He chuckled, and it sounded false even to his ears. Pettigrew better know what he was doing. "Now that I know you're here, I'm expecting Joe Kendall this morning." He checked his watch. According to the plan, Kendall should be stepping into the bank right about—

The door opened and a smiling Joe Kendall entered. "Well, it's a sign of a friendly town when the banker himself greets me." Joe pulled the door shut behind him. "You know, someone needs to tell that sun it doesn't need to start burning until at least noon. *Whew,* it's hot out there."

Neal gripped Joe's hand. "Good to see you again, Kendall. You're right on time." He swiveled toward Florence. "Perhaps you could fix a pitcher of iced tea since Mr. Kendall here is already complaining of the heat."

The telephone ringing stopped Pettigrew's plan but seemed to increase the incessant pencil drumming. When it rang the second time, Neal cocked his head. "Are you going to answer that, Florence?"

"Oh. Oh. Well, I thought since you…oh, you needn't be so snippy." She cleared her throat and picked up the phone. "Anderson City Bank, Florence speaking. Oh, it's you, Mr. Murphy." She covered the speaker. "It's your father."

Yes, he'd surmised that since she addressed the caller as Mr. Murphy, but this wasn't the time to add one more *snippy* remark to his growing list of insults. "I'll take it in my office. Do you mind, Joe?"

Joe sent him a knowing smile. "Not at all. I'm not going anywhere."

Neal suppressed a smile in return. "Thank you, I'll only be a minute. This is probably an update on Benton."

JOE SAT IN the chair closest to Florence's desk. Pettigrew's timing had been good—it was the phone call that might cause a problem. At least the pencil drumming had stopped. In fact—

He stood and sauntered to Florence's desk. "I think you forgot to hang up the receiver, Miss Bower." He reached across her arms and hung it up for her, then stepped back to his chair and picked up a magazine from the table beside it. He could at least pretend to look at it while waiting for Neal to return. He had no idea what the two Murphys were talking about, but he was quite sure Florence intended to listen in on the conversation. He made a mental note to alert Neal.

Before he finished looking at the pictures, Neal was back in the lobby. "You can come in now, Joe. Sorry about the interruption."

Though the words were innocent enough, Neal's countenance revealed much more, and Joe didn't hesitate to follow him back into the office.

Neal turned to Joe as soon as they got into the office. "That call from Dad—"

"Wait, Neal." Joe walked to the door that led to the lobby and closed it, making sure it clicked shut loud enough to be heard.

Neal raised one hand and a frown slid across his forehead. "What?"

Joe stepped away from the door and moved closer to the other two men. "Let's keep our voices down. I think Florence intended to listen to that call. She left the receiver off the hook, but I caught it and hung

210

it back where it belonged. It wouldn't surprise me if she has her ear pasted against the door now."

"There's one way to find out, you know." Pettigrew stood and walked to the back door. "She doesn't know I'm here. What say I walk in the front door and announce I'm waiting for Joe Kendall?"

Joe rolled his lips. "Isn't that sneaky?"

Amos let out a low huff. "Having files in desk drawers that just happen to contain the information recorded on a separate piece of paper is sneaky, Joe."

Neal's eyes widened. "Wait. That will work. That phone call wasn't an update on Benton. Dad seemed in a hurry and I'm not sure I understood all he was saying. One thing was clear, though. If I saw the two of you, I was to send you to Lily's as soon as possible."

Joe's stomach quivered. Not the usual gut punch he received whenever Neal and Lily were mentioned in the same breath, but more of a flutter of anticipation. "Me and Pettigrew? What about you?" He couldn't imagine how he'd feel if he were the one left behind. Especially going to Lily's, where they'd both been banned.

"I asked the same thing and he told me not to argue. Said he wanted you, Joe, because Ruth seems calm around you, and Pettigrew because well—" He motioned for them to form a huddle. "He said something about a note that Lily found stuck in an envelope in Paul Archer's Bible."

"The will? Glory be!" Amos clamped his hands over his mouth. "Sorry, but I couldn't help myself. Don't tell me it's been there all along."

Neal shrugged. "He said he didn't have time to explain but wanted you out there as soon as possible."

Amos rubbed his chin. "This will work to our favor, Neal. I'll still go out the back and come in the front and say I'm looking for Kendall. There'd be no reason for Florence to suspect anything." He glanced toward the door. "And the rest of the plan you can carry out yourself, except you won't have witnesses." He rubbed his chin. "You do have the list you made from the original one Kendall found, don't you?"

Neal nodded. "I do. Do you have the other one?"

Amos reached inside the bib of his overalls and patted his shirt. "Right here in my pocket. Now remember to play the missing files as a mystery. Don't let her know you suspect a thing. Do you think you can do that?"

Neal gave a sinister grin. "Trust me." He flicked his hands toward Amos. "Go. Get out of here. My father doesn't like to be kept waiting."

As soon as Amos left, Neal turned to Joe. "Look, Kendall. I'm going to address what we know is the truth regarding Lily Archer. I've loved that girl since I was six years old. I was dumb and all kinds of stupid to walk away from her like I did. But I'm here now and even though she has pretty much told me she doesn't ever want to see me again, I'm not going to give up so easily this time." His eyes narrowed. "Just so you know."

Joe leaned against the desk and crossed his arms. "It's been a long, long time since I've had even the slightest hope of finding the right girl, getting married, and settling down to raise a family. I understand all too well where you're coming from, and I respect that. But since getting acquainted with Lily and her mother, and with this town of Anderson, hope has been restored."

Neal frowned. "Then am I right in assuming that you're saying you don't give up easily, either?"

Joe met Neal's creased brow with a smile. "What I'm saying, my friend, is may the best man win."

Twenty-Four

*M*AY THE BEST *man win.* After Joe and Amos left, Neal pondered those words over and over again. In past years, he wouldn't have had a doubt about the outcome of that contest. Neither would he have questioned Lily's affections. Those were good years— years when there was no uncertainty as to whom the best man in Anderson was. He braced his elbows on the desk and rested his head in his hands.

Those were indeed sweet years, Murphy, but you were not yet a man. A real man doesn't run at the first sign of rejection. If he truly believes in something, he fights for it.

He fights for it. Neal let out a big puff of air. He'd never had to fight for anything. Academics, athletics, and looks were all wrapped up in one big package.

And that package was a gift, Neal. A gift given to you by the Lord, and not anything you earned or even deserved.

He jerked upright and looked around the office, quite certain his mother was somewhere in a corner. How many times had she preached that same message? Why was he only now understanding it? She was right. He'd never even had to look for a job. Helen was the banker's daughter. Naturally, her daddy had a job for him. After all, she was his baby girl. But when Helen and her parents were all killed coming home after a relative's funeral…

You turned tail and ran.

He pushed away from the desk and paced around the perimeter of the room. He'd hadn't really turned tail, had he? He had reasons to come back home. Helen had never been to Anderson. There was nothing here that would remind him of her. Could anyone understand the pain of going home to a cold, dark, empty house? He had a daughter to raise. A little girl who seemed to understand the concept that her mama was in Heaven with Jesus much better than he. He'd questioned God. Oh, not about Helen being in Heaven. But why, why, why would a loving God take one so young, so full of life, so much to live for, when there were people like Ruth Archer who…

He groaned and sank to the floor with his back against a wall. So, Ruth Archer was going to determine the best man? If he were put on a witness stand, having taken the oath to tell the truth, the whole truth, and nothing but the truth, he'd have to admit that her condition frightened him. And the thought of raising Rosie with someone with Ruth's condition frightened him even more.

"Neal?"

Florence's voice and knock on the door jolted him back to the present. The last thing he needed was for her to walk in and find him on the floor wallowing in self-pity. "I'm fine, Florence." He hoisted himself to his feet, wiped his face with his hands, and hurried to unlock the files. "Come in."

Florence stepped into the office and sauntered to his side. "I'm sorry I didn't get the tea fixed that you requested."

"That's quite all right. As it happened, Kendall had business elsewhere and wouldn't have been here to enjoy it."

She rung her hands. "Would…I could still do it for you, you know."

"No, no." He pretended to look through the folders. "These files are alphabetical, aren't they?"

"Yes. Alphabetical. Why? Is there a problem?"

A slow flush crept up her face, but Neal ignored it. He needed to stay calm and collected if Pettigrew's plan was going to work. "No, no." He shot her a quick smile. "That phone call from my father wasn't an update on Benton Finley after all. He asked me to pull some files for him and I can't seem to find them. But you know me, Florence. I'm great with numbers but never did well in things that required me to put the ABCs in order. I must be overlooking them."

"Here." She gave him a bump with her hip. "Let me help."

"Oh, would you? That would be great." He stepped back to his desk. "I hate to admit to Dad that I can't find my way through the files."

Florence stood with one hand on her hip, her lips in a pout. "You do know I can't read your mind. Do you remember the folders you were to pull for him?"

Neal slapped his hand against his forehead. "Now why didn't I think of that? I don't remember all of them, but I did scribble the names as fast as he gave them. I hope I didn't miss anyone, or I'll be in trouble." He handed her the list he'd recopied.

Florence retrieved the paper and color drained from her face as her eyes scanned the list. Neal sat at his desk. This would be the time she'd either be forced to confess she'd removed the folders or feign innocence. He'd give her all the time she needed to decide.

Sooner than he expected, Florence looked up from the paper, her chin thrust forward. "I think your father forgot he had me pull these same files for him yesterday."

"Oh?" Neal cocked his head. "So why aren't they on his desk?"

"I…he left in such a hurry to go be with Gladys Finley that I put them in my desk for safekeeping."

Neal wiped his hand across his forehead. "What a relief, Florence. I was ready to think I failed file-fetching altogether. Now that we have that mystery solved, you can bring them here and put them on the desk. He said they were important. He'll be in later today, but I don't think we should mention his apparent lack of memory."

A tinge of color returned to her cheeks. "No, we shouldn't mention it." She gave a nervous giggle. "Wouldn't want him to think he's getting old or anything like that. It will be our little secret."

"No, Florence. No secrets. I've found that things kept hidden are often revealed in the harshest of light. Now, let's go get those files." He stood and stepped around her, then bowed and gave an exaggerated swoop of his arm toward the open door. "After you, m'lady."

Florence strode ahead of him with such a confident air that he felt sorry for her. Was she so certain that her ruse would never be discovered that she'd not checked to make sure the files were still where she put them? He had to admit, she'd come up with a reason they were in her desk in the first place without much hesitation. It would be interesting to hear her explanation of why they weren't there now.

Florence sat at her desk, flipped her hair over one shoulder, and pulled the first drawer open. What confidence she's displayed earlier wilted as she frantically shuffled through the contents of drawer after drawer.

Neal leaned across the desk. "Is there a problem, Flo?"

"I...I don't understand. They were right here."

"Maybe check the middle one, Florence."

Red splotches crawled from her neck to her hairline. "There isn't...no room for..."

"Check it anyway, Florence. The first thing Dad will ask is if we've looked everywhere."

Her hands shook as she opened the drawer that revealed the file Joe had discovered.

Neal held out his hand. "Hand it to me, Flo."

Panic filled eyes met his as she gave him the folder. "You found it, didn't you?"

Neal didn't answer. They weren't done yet.

Her eyes were wide with fright. "Aren't you going to say anything?"

Neal opened the file, withdrew a clean sheet of paper, and handed her a pen. "Write it all down, Florence. Everything. I don't know if Bruce Archer asked for the information, threatened you, or if you decided on your own to do everything in your power to hurt these people. Don't leave anything out."

Tears ran freely down her face and she made no attempt to wipe them away. "Does your father know?"

"He will. Kendall and Amos Pettigrew are on their way to meet him as we speak. Oh, and in case you are wondering, Amos has possession of the original list, and your handwriting has been verified by a very reliable source."

She fluttered her hands. "I…I can—"

"No, Florence, you can't. I don't know what you were going to say but if you thought you could explain your way out of this, you can't. Now write." He sat on the chair beside her desk and crossed his arms. "We have all day."

JOE CLENCHED HIS jaw. It was one thing to have Pettigrew's big hound sitting between them. It was quite another to have the mutt licking his face like he was a piece of meat. Besides that, he couldn't even give the mongrel a dirty look because he couldn't tell if the dog's eyes were open or shut. Droopy was a given. Bloodshot and droopy like he'd been on a real doggie bender, and his breath gave credence to that observation.

Amos leaned around his dog's big body. "You seem to know your way out here." He grinned. "Business, I suppose."

Joe chuckled. "Yep, business. But none of yours."

"Naw. I don't suppose it is." Amos put his arm around the dog's neck. "How do you think Neal's getting along? I'm wondering if we should have left him there alone, but it's too late now."

Joe glanced sideways. "He'll be okay if he doesn't forget the plan. I'm more worried about what will happen when we get to Lily's. What if Bruce shows up?"

"One look at Barnabas and he'll settle down." Amos nuzzled the dog's head. "Bruce is afraid of this big hunk of dog meat. Could be because he got a chunk taken out of his behind once."

"Barnabas bit him?" Joe raised his eyebrows. "I'm surprised Archer didn't turn you into the sheriff for having a dangerous animal on the premises. Of course, that was probably before he knew people or had connections."

Amos laughed. "You got that right. No, he wouldn't turn me in because the key word is *premises*, and he was on mine."

Joe sobered. "Speaking of premises, the last time I was on Lily's I promised her I'd go away and leave her alone. I wonder if she knows Ed Murphy asked us to meet him here?"

"You needn't worry. Ed, Paul Archer, and I go back a long, long ways. I don't think she'll cross Ed's judgement in this matter. Let me do the talking and you keep an eye on Ruth. Oh my, it would break Paul's heart if he could see his wife. She was a fine and beautiful lady in her day. More than one young buck was hoping to catch her eye, but she chose Paul."

"Do I hear regret in your voice?" Joe glanced toward Amos but all he could see was Barnabas.

"No, not at all. Milly was, is, and always has been the one for me."

"Then why aren't you married?"

Amos wiggled his eyebrows. "Who's to say we aren't?"

Joe cocked his head. "Business, I suppose?"

Amos cackled and reached across his dog to punch Joe in the shoulder. "Yep, business. But none of yours."

Joe staid his laughter as they stopped in front of the Archer's gate.

His pulse thumped at the prospect of seeing Lily again, but would she tolerate his presence? Would she understand he was there because the elder Murphy deemed it necessary?

Amos opened his door but stopped before he exited. "In case you don't already know, Dog won't be a problem." He winked at Joe as he climbed out of the car and pulled Barnabas out after him."

Joe grinned at him. "Oh, I already know that. I'm more concerned about what Barnabas will do with Dog."

"This isn't the first time the two have met." Amos patted his dog on the head. "Besides, Barnabas is trained to tolerate other dogs when I have him on a leash."

Joe exited the car, walked to Dog, then bent down and put his arms around the animal's neck. "Good dog, Dog." He patted the animal's head.

Amos winked at him. "Business, huh?"

Ed met them at the bottom of the porch steps. "I was wondering if you were going to sit out here all day." He shook their hands. "Thank you for coming. Lily is too fragile right now for me to insist she go into town."

Joe nodded. "Lily is tough as nails, but she's also been as fragile as fine crystal since the day I met her. Does she know you asked me to come?"

"She knows." Ed grabbed the pipe handrail and took a step up to the porch.

Joe joined him on the step. "Then she's okay with me being here?"

Ed shrugged. "She knows I asked you to come. Whether or not she's okay with it is something for the two of you to discuss later. We have more important business right now." He motioned for Joe to go ahead of him.

As they stepped into the kitchen, Lily looked up from her seat around the table. Dark circles under her eyes told of more than a lack of sleep but her gaze met his and signaled a welcome her lips didn't form. Instinct warned him to proceed with caution. "Where's your mama, Lily?"

Her eyes didn't move from his. "On her mattress. Sleeping. She was awake most of the night."

Joe gave a slow shake of his head. "And if she doesn't sleep, you don't sleep. Right?"

A half-smile answered his question.

"Lily, you have to get help. You can't—"

Ed cleared his throat. "I hate to barge into this conversation, but we need to get on to the reason I called you both out here."

Joe scowled at Ed, but he pulled a chair from the table and sat beside Lily. He'd know soon enough if she wanted him to move.

Ed handed Amos a piece of paper. "This slipped from an envelope in Paul's Bible. Read it and tell me what you think."

Amos gave a quick scan of the paper, then scooted it back to Ed. "I can tell you what I think. I think that Benton Finley knows where we can find Paul Archer's will."

"His will?" Ed's eyebrows hit his hairline. "Where? And why Benton?"

Amos recounted the day Paul wrote the legal missive.

"There's a will? Papa had a will?" Lily grabbed Joe's hand and squeezed so hard it hurt, but he welcomed the pain. "Does this mean—"

Ed shook his head. "We don't know what it means until we see the actual document, Lily. And unfortunately, Benton can't tell us anything. At least not yet, and maybe never."

"Never?" She looked around the table, landing her focus on Joe. "Please, please, tell me I won't lose this farm."

Joe's heart plummeted into the depths of unanswered questions. "I can't tell you that, Lily." He turned to Amos. "What *does* this mean? Can you give her some kind of...of hope?"

Amos rested his forearms on the table and folded his hands. "I can only tell you this for absolute certain, Lily. Nothing that will contains can save this—"

"No!" She clung to Joe's sleeve. "Why? Why is finding it so important then?" Tears filled her eyes.

"Lily, dear." Amos waited until she raised her eyes to him before continuing. "Hear me out. Please. The will won't save your farm, but it can tell us how and by whom it is to be divided and distributed. If I remember correctly, and I seldom forget something this important, your papa named you as executor of his estate. Unfortunately, until we find the actual document, we can't forge ahead on my memory alone."

"Executor? What does that even mean?" She wiped her hands down her face. "If I can't save this place, what *can* I do as executor that will result in anything good?"

Joe took a chance and slipped his arm around her shoulders. "Let's listen to him, Lily. Then you can ask questions." She slumped against him and he drew her closer. Was she so exhausted she didn't care, or was she allowing him into her life? "Go ahead, Amos. We're listening."

Amos turned to Lily. "An executor has many duties, but for now I think we need to concentrate on the two that concern you the most, those being managing the deceased property and distributing the assets to the beneficiaries named. Hiring an attorney is also vital but I'll take a giant leap here and assume you will allow me to fulfill that obligation."

Panic filled Lily's eyes. "Hire you? With what? You tell him, Mr. Murphy. Tell him how much money I *don't* have in my account and see if he still thinks I can hire him, or anyone, for that matter."

"No one is asking you to pay for anything, Lily." The muscle in Ed's cheek twitched.

"Then it's charity?" She straightened and Joe cupped his hand around her shoulder to keep her from bolting. He knew all too well her aversion to anything that smacked of a handout.

"Not at all." Amos peered at her over the top of his glasses. "When this is all said and done, I'll send you my bill and we'll worry about payment then. Agreed?"

Lily folded her arms across her middle. "And if there's nothing left?"

Amos gave an impatient huff. "Like I said, Lily. We'll worry about payment then. In the meantime, Ed, there's something you need to see." Amos reached into his pocket and produced the paper Joe found in Florence's desk and handed it to Ed. "You read this and tell me what you think."

In the stillness that followed, Joe's mind wandered in every direction…Lily allowing his arm around her…the conversation with Neal before leaving his office…the pressure from his superiors to get on with the lake project…Bruce Archer's threats…Amos and Milly's marriage, or not…Milly's feisty little mother.

"Wait! Wait!" Joe pulled his arm from Lily's shoulders and jumped to his feet.

Ed shot daggers Joe's direction. "Wait on what? I'm not through reading."

"Then you keep reading while I talk to Pettigrew." He nodded to Amos. "Remember last night at Milly's?

Amos shrugged. "Sure. I remember. What about it?"

"Do you remember Mrs. Wright stating that Gladys Benton knows as much about Benton's business as Benton himself?"

Amos's eyebrows arched and the glasses slipped upward with the big man's grin. "Kendall, if you weren't so ugly, I'd hug you right now. Her actual words were 'Gladys Finley knows as much *or more*'. I can't believe I didn't think of that.'"

Lily tugged on Joe's arm. "What does this mean?"

Amos pulled Joe back down onto his chair. "It means, Lily, my dear, that Ed and I are going to Wichita to visit with Gladys, but Kendall and Barnabas will stay here with you. We don't want you alone should Bruce decide to cause trouble."

Joe swiveled on his chair. Amos hadn't given her a choice, but he would. "It's up to you, Lily, whether I stay or not. I know I promised—"

A slight flush pinked her cheeks and her eyes met his. "Don't go."

His heart tripped and he bit the insides of his cheeks to keep from grinning like a schoolboy. "I'm staying, Ed." He couldn't tear his gaze from hers.

"Yeah, we heard." Ed chuckled. "We'll get back as soon as we can."

Joe merely nodded, reluctant to take his eyes from Lily. Now, if only he could discern whether she asked him to stay because she was frightened, or out of a real desire for his presence. If he were a betting man, he'd lay his money on the fear card. But for now, he'd take every minute with her as a gift.

Twenty-Five

*D*ON'T GO. LILY took a long, deep breath and released it slowly. Had she just uttered the very words she regretted not saying yesterday? She couldn't have voiced a simple *stay* or given a nod? Should she try to explain she was too tired to argue? She could, of course, but it wouldn't be the truth. The truth was...she didn't want him to leave. She hadn't wanted him to leave last night but she was too proud and stubborn to release him from the promise he'd made.

"Lily." Joe gripped her hands. "I know this is awkward but hear me out. I don't know how long Murphy and Pettigrew will be gone, but I do know it will be long enough for you to get some sleep. So, here's what we're going to do. You are going to go in on your pallet and sleep while Barnabas and I hold down the fort here in the kitchen."

If only his eyes weren't so blue and his voice soft as melted butter. "Mama won't sleep much longer. I can't—"

He rubbed his thumbs over her knuckles. "You can and you will. Your mama will be fine with me and," he smiled at her, "I know what groceries you have in your cupboard so if it gets late, I'll be the chef tonight." He stood and pulled her out of her chair. "And I also know how to milk the cow. Remember?"

"Are you ordering me?" She hadn't had anyone to care enough to give her orders for ever so long, at least not anyone whose eyes seemed to search her very soul.

He ran his fingers along her forehead and tucked her hair behind her ears. "I'm ordering you." He gripped her shoulders and turned her toward the living room, but not before she saw a desire in his eyes that could well be a reflection from hers. She walked to her pallet on tired, wooden legs while her heart raced and her head seemed to float. Was she that exhausted, or could it be that Joe Kendall awakened the woman inside…not the girl of eight years ago but a woman waiting to be birthed?

JOE BALLED HIS fists at his side and his shoulders shuddered with a deep draught of air. Only a power greater than his had kept him from pulling Lily to him. Even now, his arms tingled, aching to hold her close enough to feel her heart pulse against his. Had he only imagined that she'd not have objected, or was his own desire so strong it reflected in her gaze? He rubbed both hands down his face. *Fragile as fine crystal.* Isn't that how he'd described her less than an hour ago? Fine china could shatter and, while his arms ached to hold her and his heart thumped with the possibility, he had yet to prove if he was the better man.

He leaned down and patted Barnabas's bony head. "Come on, fella. Let's you and me get some fresh air."

THE SCRATCHING OF Florence's pen across the paper and the ever-present hum of the ceiling fans were all that broke the silence following Neal's edict for the tearful secretary to write her confession. The only problem now was that they still had the bigger part of the day to get through before he could lock the doors. Though the plan had worked, he was the only witness, and unless Florence's missive contained the whole truth, it would be her word against his in any court. The fact he'd lied in order to force her to reveal the evidence did nothing to alleviate his guilt for being so deceptive.

After what seemed an eternity, Florence scooted the paper to him.

He scanned the two-paged missive. "Is this everything, Florence?"

She nodded.

Remembering Amos's analogy between a hasty meal and gathering a big pot of evidence, Neal folded the paper and stuck it in the empty folder Florence had produced earlier.

"Aren't you going to read it?" Florence's voice shook.

He rested his forearms on the desk. "What did he promise you, Florence?"

She folded her arms across her chest and made circles on her elbows with her fingers.

"You might as well tell me." He pointed to the folder. "We'll find it out anyway."

One shoulder twitched into a shrug. "He promised me a way out of this sorry town. He said he knew people. He had connections. He told me…he told me things no man has ever told me."

"Oh, Florence." While the familiar red splotches seemed to grow, there was no life in her eyes. No sparkle. Not even tears. "What you heard as a promise, Bruce used as a threat to Dad, Kendall, and me in the office. Did it ever occur to you that *you* might be the connection? He used you, Florence. I do hope you have that recorded."

The telephone ringing stilled her answer. "I'll answer it." He lifted the phone and perched on the side of the desk. "Anderson City Bank. This is—"

"I know who it is, but why are you answering the phone?"

"Amos? Where are you? Hold on." Neal covered the mouthpiece. "Florence, if you don't mind." He flicked his hand toward the nearest bank of chairs and waited until she seated herself into one of them. "Okay, Amos. Go ahead."

"Don't be alarmed when the sheriff shows up. I've called him and he knows the details. It's a long story, but Ed and I are leaving the hospital as soon as I finish this call, and we have Bruce Archer in tow."

"What? He was at the hospital?"

"Yep. No more questions. Just do what I say. Oh, and Clarice, I know you are listening to this conversation. I have someone relieving you of your duties shortly and I expect you to be in the bank lobby when I return. Give her five minutes, Neal. If she's not darkened your door by then, go after her. Then lock your doors for business after she arrives. No use getting the whole town alarmed if a client should walk in with the sheriff standing guard."

Neal put the receiver back on its hook, set the telephone on Florence's desk, and checked his watch. Five minutes, Amos instructed. Clarice. What had the scoundrel promised her? Florence and Clarice were roommates, so it made sense that they'd be in on this together, but did the cad woo them separately? If so, he knew more than one man who'd pay good money to learn that stunt. Of course, it could mean sudden death if one was stupid enough to try.

At four-and-a-half minutes, Clarice stepped into the lobby. She took one look at Florence and all color drained from her face. Neal acknowledged her presence with a nod and she quickly averted her eyes and took a chair to the far side of Florence.

When the *William Tell Overture* popped into Neal's head, though not at all humorous, he rolled his lips to quell a smile as he locked the door.

SOMETHING WET SLIDING across her cheek woke Lily and she shot upright only to come nose to nose with Barnabas. Joe Kendall knelt beside her, grinning behind the big dog's floppy ears.

"I thought that might get your attention." Joe chuckled.

Lily wiped her hand across her cheek. "You couldn't call my name or shake my shoulders?"

Joe screwed his mouth to one side and his eye slid into a wink. "Yeah, I tried that, but it didn't work." He twirled a feather between his thumb and forefinger. "I even pulled this from your pillow and got a slap on my hand for the effort."

"I'm sorry." *Drat those teasing blue eyes.* "I didn't mean—"

In an instant the mischief she'd detected in his gaze was replaced with something much more compassionate, and soft, and—

"Lily, there's no need to apologize. I was the one who made you lie down in the first place, knowing full well how badly you needed the rest." He wrinkled his nose. "And if it weren't for Ed and Amos sitting in your kitchen, I'd let you sleep until morning if you could."

Her heart thumped. "They're back already?"

He tapped his finger against his watch. "It's later than you think, but yes, they are back."

She grabbed his wrist and checked the watch. "Six o'clock? The chores? Mama?" Why did it take this long for her to think of Mama? When had she ever awakened without Mama crowding her mind? For that matter, when had she ever fallen asleep without worrying about where Mama would be by morning?

"Shh, shh, shh." Joe put his finger against her lips. "Did you forget that I told you I'd take care of the chores *and* your mama? I even made sandwiches. Are you hungry?"

"Sandwiches?" *Is there anything this man can't do?* "With what, pray tell?"

He shook his head, mischief once again filling his eyes. "Nope. A gourmet chef never reveals his recipes. However, I think even you,

Miss Lily Archer, will be impressed by my creation." He stood and reached for her hands. "Here. Grab hold and I'll help you off the floor."

Painfully aware that her dress had climbed above her knees and wouldn't allow for her usual mode of rising rump-first, she had little choice but to *grab hold* as he requested. He lifted her with ease but didn't release her hands. "Get your sea legs before you try walking, Lily. I think I pulled you up too fast. You're pale."

How could she be pale when at the touch of his hands every beat of her heart sent a rush of heat through her body? She smiled at him but couldn't look into his eyes. "I'm fine. I think I just slept too hard." She tried to pull her hands from his, but he only released one.

He put his finger under her chin and forced her to look at him. "Like it or not, Lily, I'm going to hold onto you until you're at the table."

Stepping into the kitchen did nothing to stop her thumping heart. Had Joe conveniently forgotten to mention that Neal was also present? Not only was he present, but his eyes, after searching her face, now seemed locked on her hand entwined with Joe's. And Joe's tightened grip signaled that he wasn't the least intimidated.

Ed Murphy stood and pulled a chair from the table. "Lily. I'm glad you had a chance to rest. Take a seat, if Kendall will let go of you long enough for you to sit."

Joe's warm hand on her back nudged her to the chair and he took the seat between her and Mama…Mama with no cat in her arms and her head down. Barnabas edged close to Lily and laid his head on her lap.

Lily ran her hand along the dog's velvety ear and his tail thumped against the floor. "How did you get the cat away from Mama?" Lily whispered to Joe.

He leaned closer to her ear. "I wasn't sure how Barnabas would react to a cat, so I took a chance and slipped it from her arms while she was still sleeping. She hasn't seemed to miss it."

Lily continued to stroke Barnabas. "She probably doesn't even remember she had it in the first place. But if she does, she'll hunt frantically for it."

Joe slipped his arm around the back of her chair. "I told you I'd take care of her so don't worry. If she misses the cat I know where to find it. You concentrate on what news these men brought."

Amos leaned back in his chair and folded his arms across his chest. "Okay, now that you've joined us, Lily, and if we aren't interrupting your conversation with Kendall, let's catch you up on what has happened."

"I was asking about Mama." Lily clasped her hands in her lap. Why did she feel the need to defend talking to Joe? "Did you talk with Gladys? Did she know why—"

Amos shot her a friendly smile. "I'm going to tell you everything we know, but you need to let me talk. And Kendall, perhaps you could refrain from engaging her in conversation until we're through." He winked at Joe.

Lily nodded. "I'm sorry." Not wanting to risk Neal's frown of disapproval, she focused on the attorney.

Amos flicked his wrist at Neal. "You go first, then maybe we can fit all we know together."

"Sure." Neal folded his hands on the table. His eyes met hers but the questions she'd detected in them earlier were no longer there. Even as he explained all that happened, starting with Florence's hanging on him like grapes on a vine, to Amos and Ed's return from Wichita with Bruce, she only detected concern.

"Now, Amos. It's up to you to fill in the rest," Neal finished. "Lily, I'm so sorry that…that things are so complicated. Please know we are all doing what we can to get to the bottom of this situation."

Amos cleared his throat. "Okay, thank you, Neal." He swiveled on his chair and faced Lily. "When we got to the hospital and inquired as to how we would find Benton's room, we were told we'd have to wait because his son was in with him at the time."

"His son?" Lily gasped. "But he doesn't have a son."

"Exactly." Amos nodded in agreement. "When we showed them proof that identified us as Benton's attorney and banker and reiterated, in no uncertain terms, that Benton Finley had no son, they immediately called for security and asked us to follow them to Benton's room."

"Bruce." Lily searched the faces of the men seated around her. "It was Bruce, wasn't it?"

"Bruce?" Mama looked up, her eyes wide, and tugged on Joe's sleeve. "There you are. Where have you been?" She looked around the table as if she were only now noticing the others. "Oh." She giggled. "I didn't know you brought your friends."

Joe turned on his chair and put his arm around Mama's shoulders. "They're your friends, too, Mama."

"Oh." She tilted her head and her brow puckered. "Do I know them?"

Lily rolled her lips and bit down hard. How would Joe handle this? And what were the other men thinking?

"Yes, you know them. This is Amos Pettigrew and Ed Murphy and Neal Murphy." He pointed to each one.

Amos smiled. "It's good to see you, Ruth."

"Ruth." Ed's voice was husky. "You…you look good."

Mama blushed and looked up at Joe. "Do I look good, Bruce?" One hand went to her cheek.

He leaned his forehead against hers. "You look good, Mama."

Neal gave a curt nod. "Ruth. Always good to see you." He glanced at Joe and Mama, his lips drawn tight.

Lily held her breath. What would she do if Mama called Neal *Mr. Fancy Britches*? The thought brought an inappropriate smile to her lips and she covered her mouth in a feigned yawn.

Mama squinted her eyes at Neal. "Girl. Papa knows."

"What's your papa supposed to know, Lily? That I'm back in town?

Doesn't she remember he's dead?" Neal's face was red and drawn.

Lily shrugged. "I don't know if she remembers Papa is gone, Neal. She says that over and over again, but I don't know what she means, and she doesn't seem able to tell me."

"Paul never liked me." The corners of Neal's mouth turned down into a pout.

Ed shook his head. "Neal, this is not the time nor the place."

Amos cleared his throat. "As an attorney, Neal, let me remind you that unless you can prove Paul told you that he didn't like you, you're putting your own perception into a dead man's mouth. That's unfair to Lily and Ruth and would never hold up in court. Now can we get back to the reason we're all here?"

"Go right ahead." Neal slumped back against his chair and swept his arms wide.

Amos turned to Lily. "To answer your question, yes, it was your brother."

Lily's heart pounded. "But how did he know to go to Gladys?"

"He somehow charmed Clarice into thinking that listening in on any conversation between the Murphys and the other people of this town was doing a great service. He promised her, as he did Florence, a life of every small-town girl's dreams."

What hope Lily had on finding what the note revealed plummeted to the pit of her stomach. "Then you didn't talk to Gladys?"

"No, but we will." Amos pushed his glasses higher on his face. "Gladys is under a tremendous amount of pressure right now and the little scene involving Bruce didn't help. But Lily, this is far from over. With Bruce out of the picture, at least for now, we have more time on our side. We will eventually be able to sit down with the dear lady. Trust us."

"Bruce is out of the picture?" Lily's stomach roiled. "How? Is he in jail?"

Amos nodded. "He is in jail. Seems your brother is in big

trouble—car theft, breaking and entering, supplying liquor to underage kids. You name it and Bruce has tried to get away with it. There are warrants for his arrest from several surrounding counties. It will be up to the courts as to who gets him first."

"He confessed?" Lily couldn't remember her brother ever acknowledging any wrongdoing.

Amos sighed. "Not at first. Once Clarice realized that he'd used the same line on both her and Florence, she babbled away."

"But he said he came back to save the farm." Lily clutched at her stomach to keep it from erupting. "How could he do so much in so little time?"

"His coming back was only the tail end of his plot, Lily. According to both Florence and Clarice, he had them employed, so to speak, from the minute the news of a city lake being built was ever released. He's had plenty of time to come up with a plan, but when Florence told him that she thought you and Kendall here were becoming sweet on one another, well—"

Barnabas yelped as Lily's chair crashed to the floor when she stood. She clamped her hand over her mouth and stumbled out of the kitchen. She was going to be sick and the very last thing she needed now was to upchuck with an audience.

Footsteps behind her only added to her angst. She hit the bottom step but before she could go any further, all-too-familiar strong arms encircled her waist and steadied her as she retched with dry heaves. How much humiliation could she stand? Her brother a common criminal, revealed to the three most influential men in Anderson. And to top it all off, a proclamation that she and Joe were becoming sweet on one another.

Her legs felt like jelly and her stomach hurt but all she could do now was to turn and face the inevitable. She swiveled and met Neal's unsmiling face. "Kendall couldn't get away from your mother fast enough. Are you disappointed?"

She glared at him. "Really, Neal?" She turned on her heel and walked to the steps.

"Wait!" Neal caught up with her and grabbed her arm. "I'm sorry. That was rude."

She bit her lower lip and met his sad gaze with a slow shake of her head. "My papa is dead. My mother is no longer capable of making decisions or communicating in any intelligent fashion. I'm about to lose everything my parents and I worked so hard for. I just found out my brother is a…is some sort of crook who might very well end up in prison. And I'm penniless. Yet you have the nerve, based, I suppose, on silly Florence Bower's proclamation that Joe Kendall and I have some sort or romance, to ask me if I'm disappointed that it wasn't he who watched me humiliate myself once again? Yes, Neal. That *was* rude."

She took the steps as fast as her shaking legs would allow. *If only it had been Joe.*

Twenty-Six

HEAT STILL RADIATED from the lengthening shadows of evening, yet Neal wrapped his arms around his chest to fight the chill that engulfed him. Lily had gone back into the house without so much as a glance, her back ramrod straight and her shoulders thrown back in a clear signal that defied any further dialogue. How many times would he need to be reminded that words once spoken could never be taken back? He could apologize, even attempt to rationalize, but the truth remained, he'd made a jealous deposit into her memory bank that could now be withdrawn and spent at his expense. And to top it all off, he still needed to go back into the house and face the consequences.

Amos looked up as Neal stepped into the kitchen. "Good of you to join us again, Neal. We've made some decisions while you were gone. You want to hear them?" He waved his hand as if shooing a fly. "Never mind. I'm going to tell you anyway. You and your dad will go back into town for the night. You will open the bank as usual in the morning, *with* Florence. At this point, we don't need to draw unnecessary attention to all that has happened."

"Wait, wait, wait." Neal pulled a chair from the table and plopped into it. "What do you mean *with Florence*? You really expect me to carry on as if nothing happened? That's crazy. How can she be trusted?"

Amos pulled his glasses from his face and rubbed his eyes. "We have the confession she wrote. Plus, the sheriff made it very plain that should she try to leave Anderson, or pull any other stunt to help Bruce, he had an empty jail cell with her name on it. What she did was wrong, but I doubt she had any idea of the consequences."

Neal splayed his hands. "What about Clarice? Are you going to leave her at the switchboard?"

Amos shook his head. "No, her actions are more far-reaching. She listened in on private conversations and passed what information she gleaned on to someone whose intentions were to reap monetary gain. That's much more serious. Florence hadn't yet passed on her list."

Neal braced his forearms on the table. "I understand that Florence and Clarice were the connections that Bruce bragged about, but he also boasted that he *knew people*. Were any of those revealed?"

Amos shook his head. "Nope. Big talk from a little boy." He hooked his glasses on the sides of his face and folded his arms atop the table. "Now, if you don't have any further questions, Neal, I'd like to continue."

"Continue? There's more?"

Amos nodded. "There's more, but they need Lily's approval."

Lily tilted her head. "I have a choice?"

"You always have choice, Lily." Amos sighed. "We can't save your farm, but we will fight for your best interest as sure as dawn follows the dark of night. Listen to our plan. If you don't like it you have every right to come up with a something more to your liking. I'm only asking you to trust us."

Her gaze rested on each one seated around the room, landing on Joe. "I trust you."

Neal's throat tightened. Did she mean she trusted them as a whole or was her message directed to Joe alone?

Amos drummed his fingers on the table. "Ed will go back to Wichita in the morning to check on Benton and talk with Gladys again. Hopefully she'll be in a better state of mind and can give us some answers. In the meantime, Joe and I will stay here with Lily and her mother."

"Why?" Neal brushed his hand through his hair. "With Bruce in jail, why does it take two to guard this place?" Although, the idea of Joe spending the night at Lily's was acceptable only because Amos would also be present.

Father cleared his throat. "Think about it, Neal. Propriety dictates that Lily not be alone with a single man for the night. Caution dictates that we provide as much security as we can until we know exactly the full ramifications of both Bruce's actions and whatever the note on the napkin reveals. Ultimately, Lily's decision precludes any reservations you might have." His gaze challenged Neal to disagree.

His head knew the truth of his father's statement, but his heart warred against it. He was okay with Joe's challenge. There was still time to prove who was the better man. And he also knew full well that should any crisis occur, Joe could and would care for Ruth in a manner that went far beyond anything he could or was willing to do. But seeing the man's arm around Lily's shoulders, and her lack of visible discomfort with the arrangement, only added to his angst. Whatever happened to *there's always a choice*?

JOE STUDIED NEAL'S face during Amos's instructions and understood the anguish it displayed. He'd feel the same if he were the one being sent away from Lily. He'd challenged Neal, but he didn't want to win by default, nor did he think one night playing guard with Amos would determine the best man.

Ed stood and motioned for Neal to join him. "I wish there were some way to get Lily and her mother to a more secure setting, Amos. I don't like the idea of you having no way to get help."

Amos pushed from the table and slapped the elder Murphy on the shoulder. "I've lived nearly fifty years with no telephone. Barnabas can sniff out an intruder long before my eyes or ears can detect anything amiss. We'll be fine. Check in again before you go to Wichita tomorrow. Oh, and tell Milly where I am and that she's not to worry."

"You want me to tell a woman not to worry?" Laugh lines crinkled the corners of Ed's eyes. "I'll do my best. Come on, Neal, your mother is the next one I need to convince."

"I'll follow you out." Amos motioned for them to go ahead of him. "I need fresh air." He glanced over his shoulder and winked at Joe.

Amos's wink sent a silent message that shouted to Joe. Pettigrew didn't need fresh air near as badly as he understood Joe's need—awkward as it might be—to have some time alone with Lily. He gave her shoulder a gentle squeeze, then withdrew his arm. "You need to eat something." He stood and retrieved a plate of sandwiches from the icebox.

She waved the plate away. "I'm not really hungry."

"What? You don't want to try my culinary masterpiece?" He set the plate in front of her, then knelt beside her chair. "Look, Lily. I can't even imagine how hard this day has been for you, so I won't say all the usual *I know how you feel* platitudes. But you have to eat, and I'm going to make sure you do even if it means sitting here beside here until you at least take a nibble of one of these sandwiches."

Lily rested her elbows on the table and massaged her forehead with her fingers. "Has Mama eaten?"

He rose to his feet and rubbed his hand across her shoulders. "She has, and quite heartily, I might add." He bent down to her ear. "She thinks Bruce is a better cook than *that girl*."

Sad eyes met his. "In all honesty, Bruce *is* a better cook. He'd beg

238

to stay in the house with Mama and they'd come up with all kinds of new dishes."

Joe's heart wrenched. She looked so weary. "And that made you the one who had to work alongside your papa."

Lily ran her fingers around the edge of the plate. "Papa never *made* me work with him. I…I preferred being outdoors."

"Is that why you promised him you'd never leave this place?"

A small wrinkle took residence between her eyes. "I never thought about it like that. I promised because it made sense. I was the oldest. Bruce was still in school. Mama couldn't do it alone."

A new revelation wriggled across his mind. "But think about it, Lily. Maybe the reason your mama calls *you* Bruce, at least until I came along, was because your brother was the one who spent the most time with her here in this house. Could it be that she has more memories of him?"

Doubt etched her forehead. "But he's been gone for six years, Joe. He left before Mama's mind got so confused."

He settled onto the chair next to her and reached for her hands. "Have you ever thought about how God so intricately formed each one of us…so alike and yet so very, very individual? I'm not sure mere man will ever truly understand how our minds work. How will they ever determine why some experiences are forgotten nearly as fast as they happen, yet the smallest details from years ago remain etched in our memories forever? Only God could create something so infinitely complex."

Lily pulled her hands from his and stood. "I don't think about God much at all these days."

She turned to walk away, but he caught her arm before she could leave. Pain, anger, and confusion were all written across her countenance. He longed to take her in his arms but couldn't risk being locked out of her life again. This was not the time for words, but it was all he had. *Lord, please let her hear my heart.* He rose to his feet, placed his hands on her shoulders and forced her to turn to him. "Look at me, Lily. This time I can truly say I know how you feel. I was angry, too, after Aunt Hazel died. In retrospect, I was angry from the moment I realized she was never going to be well again. We both prayed for healing. Then later I begged Him to heal her, and it was as if the heavens were made of brass and my words became meaningless noise. I felt betrayed. She'd always been my rock and then she was tumbling downhill. It felt like she was taking me with her in one giant landside and no matter how hard I dug in my heels, I couldn't stop it. How could a loving God deprive me of both my mama and the woman who became my mother? Didn't He realize how badly I needed them?"

Lily lowered her eyes. "God doesn't answer my prayers, either. I stopped trying a long time ago."

"He answers, Lily. Not always the way we want or on our timetable, but He does answer." There was so much more he longed to say, so many verses he could quote to prove that God did indeed answer prayers. But he knew from experience that he had to allow her this time to be angry, to question, even to deny God's constant presence. For now, Lily didn't need a preacher, but she did need a faithful friend…one who would pray for her and whose actions spoke louder than words. God had used the arms of others around him, the tears shed with him, and the little acts of unconditional love for him that allowed him to see, when sight was so obscured by pain and anger, that God was good even when nothing around him felt good. Time proved that God loved Joe Kendall even more than all the love his mother or Aunt Hazel could render combined.

Her eyes filled with tears and she swayed toward him. "I'm so alone and so afraid."

Desire overcame any reticence he might have felt a few minutes earlier. He pulled her to him and pressed her head against his chest as she cried long, heart-wrenching sobs.

"You're not alone, Lily. I'm here and I'll always be here. You can

ask me, order me, or beg me to leave but I'm not going anywhere."
He cupped her face in his hands and looked deep into the brown
velvet eyes that haunted him from the first time he met her gaze. "Do
you hear me, Lily? You are not alone."

Even as her tears subsided, he didn't release her from his arms.
Neither did she attempt to move out of his embrace. Joe was afraid to
breathe. It would take only one false move, one wrong word, or even
one deep breath for the fine china pressed against him to shatter into
more broken pieces that he could ever put together again. He wanted
more than anything to feel her lips against his but chose instead to kiss
the top of her head as their bodies swayed to the rhythm of an unheard
melody. They weren't dancing. He didn't even know how to dance.
This was rather a communion of spirits. But he didn't dare allow
himself to think beyond this moment. Not until he was proven to be the
better man.

Twenty-Seven

JOE CUPPED BOTH hands into the bucket of cold water and splashed as much as they'd hold onto his face and neck. After three days of heat and no running water or hot bath, it wouldn't take a bloodhound to find him. He ran his wet hands through his hair in an attempt to not look so much like a wild man. While sleeping in the barn gave him and Amos the best advantage point to intercept anyone coming onto the property, plus the most privacy for Lily and her mother, it did nothing for maintaining any modicum of respectable appearance. He made a mental note to ask Ed Murphy to deliver clean clothes and a razor the next time he stopped by to give his morning report on Benton.

So far, Murphy's daily trek to Wichita had yielded nothing from Gladys. Not because she had no knowledge of what the note meant, but rather because Ed hesitated to ask. Benton was slowly recovering. He was alert, knew who they were, and in his usual good spirits. But his speech was still very garbled and his right side slow to respond. Gladys was weary and despondent but refused to leave Benton's side.

Barnabas let out a mournful yowl, his usual morning greeting to

Ed, and Joe hurried to the barn door to greet Murphy, but this morning it was a different vehicle that stopped at the gate. A sense of foreboding slid across Joe's shoulders as Earl Trinidad, his boss, stepped from the car.

"I'm out here, Earl."

Earl swiveled toward the barn. "Ed Murphy told me I would find you here, but he didn't mention you were living in the barn." He took a couple of steps, then stopped when Barnabas and Dog appeared. "Is it safe to come any further?"

"It's safe, Earl. Step around them. The small one is too lazy to move and Barnabas here won't do much but slobber all over you unless Amos gives him the word." Joe met the man with an outstretched hand. "Had your morning coffee?"

"I have, but could use another." He gripped Joe's hand. "You have somewhere we can talk in private?"

Joe laughed. "You mean more private than a barn?"

"Guess that was a silly question." Earl gave a sheepish grin. "Is Pettigrew still here?"

"I'm here." Amos strode in, fastening the buckles on the straps of his overalls. "Fancy man staying in a hotel won't understand morning ablutions out here in the sticks." He grinned and shook Earl's hand. "Good to see you again, Trinidad. We'd invite you into the house but—"

Earl waved his hand. "I know and I understand. Milly at the diner filled me in on the situation." He nodded to Amos and withdrew a paper from his pocket. "She also sent you a kiss." He unfolded the note that revealed a lipstick imprint of her lips and handed it to him. "I'm here to tell you, though, you're on your own returning the favor." His eyes twinkled with his laugh.

Amos blushed. "You needn't worry. I don't kiss by proxy. Has Joe offered you a cup of coffee? I'll fetch it, but want to make sure Lily's mother is dressed before I go barging in."

Joe stuck one hand in the pocket of his pants. "I offered, and we'd both like a cup if you don't mind."

Amos scoffed. "Since when have you gotten manners enough to ask if I minded?" He winked at Earl. "You take yours regular or loaded?"

Earl grinned. "I usually like a couple scoops of sugar, but I'm thinking this visit calls for something less doctored. That being said, I'll take mine straight."

Joe's shoulders tightened. Earl Trinidad never visited a jobsite unless there was trouble. His visit now wasn't entirely unexpected. He hoped the guy would let him explain before firing him.

Two overturned buckets were not the ideal boardroom, but for now they would do. Joe took a deep breath. The only way he'd know if he were going to sink or swim was to dive in. "I know why you're here, Earl. But—"

"No, I don't think you do, Joe." Earl's lips formed a friendly smile. "I got a call from the powers that be yesterday."

"Who's more powerful than you?"

"The call was from Howard Niles, but he spoke for the Anderson city council. Seems they are out of money, or at least don't think they have enough to finish the lake project. It took more money than they projected to buy up the necessary properties, and I understand there's still one in limbo. Unless we can come up with some kind of solution, this job is done."

Joe's bucket went sailing across the straw-strewn floor as he jumped to his feet. "What? They can't go back on a contract, can they? And what do we do with the properties that we've purchased? Where does that leave the workers we've hired? The city still needs water, doesn't it?" He paced. "Isn't there something they can do, like raise taxes or float a new bond? I can't believe they started this project without thinking through all the scenarios."

"Exactly the same questions I put forth. Sure, they could raise taxes, but who could pay them? The town has lost so many businesses, and those that are left are barely keeping their heads above water. And a bond would need to pass a vote. You can expect people to sacrifice only so much. I was in on their planning meetings, Joe, and I didn't see the problems." He scrubbed his hands across his face. "I had doubts going into this undertaking, but in the end I felt the need outweighed the risks. I should've known better. Truth is, if our company is going to stay viable, we need this project."

"I knew you doubted the farmers would sell without court hearings, but I didn't know you doubted the finished lake."

Earl stood and joined Joe's pacing. "You're right. I guess I didn't think it would be a complete failure."

"I take it Mr. Niles didn't have any quick fix to offer?"

Earl shook his head. "None. We talked at length and he finally agreed to give us another three weeks. But Joe, it will take a miracle to save this project."

Joe leaned his shoulder against the wall. "These are such good people. What do I tell them? Except for Lily Archer, no one fought the idea. They've already lost so much, Earl. We can't ask them to return the money. The only reason they sold is because they had no real choice."

"Believe me, Joe. I fully understand what you're saying. But that doesn't leave us with solutions, or money to continue."

"You say we have three weeks?"

"Three weeks. That's the agreement."

"You believe in prayer, Earl?"

"I do."

Joe grinned. "Then we pray. Where two or three are gathered, you know."

"A prayer meeting here in the barn?" Amos set a tray that held two cups of coffee on one of the overturned buckets. "Not a bad idea, seeing as how I made the coffee."

Earl chuckled. "I should have brought some from Milly's. But I'm afraid it's more urgent than coffee. We've been given three weeks to come up with a solution to save the lake project." He explained the situation to Amos.

"Three weeks?" Amos gave a low whistle. "Then I reckon we best get started." With a groan, he slipped to his knees.

Earl removed his hat, glanced at Joe and they both joined Amos.

Amos cleared his throat. "Here we are, Father. You made this whole world and everything in it in six days. Now, I don't know if those days were the same hours as our days, and I'm not going to argue with Your word. But we got us a problem and we have three weeks to solve it and those weeks are made up of twenty-four-hour days. I know, and You know, that the three of us kneeling here in this dirt don't have enough smarts to come up with a solution. But solving problems is what You do, God, so I'm asking, in the name of Your only Son, Jesus Christ, my Lord and Savior, to give us the wisdom of Solomon and the faith of the saints of old as we take one day at a time believing that You will answer according to Your perfect plan. Amen."

The other men echoed the Amen, then each grabbed an arm and tugged Amos to his feet.

"Now, we forge ahead and pray without ceasing." Amos brushed the straw from his knees, then motioned to the cups of coffee. "That's cold by now."

Earl slicked back his hair and lifted one of the cups from the tray. "I don't mind cold coffee." He took a sip, his eyebrows arching with surprise. "Not bad, Pettigrew. Not bad at all." He turned to Joe. "Now, there's one other little thing we need to discuss. Ed filled me in on what has happened here, but if we're going to forge ahead until we can't go any further, then we have to have access to this property, Joe. I'm aware that there is a possible conflict of interest, so if you're uncomfortable with pursuing the purchase of the Archer farm, I can handle it myself or appoint one of the other men to seal the deal."

Joe's shoulders slumped. "I never meant for—"

Earl clamped his hand on Joe's shoulder. "Look, man. I understand. I realize what I said came across harsh, and I'm sorry. From what I understand from Ed Murphy, Miss Archer will lose this farm whether she sells it or not. I also know you're waiting for an important piece of information that will sort out who can agree to the sale without having the property claimed through eminent domain. I tell you what. Since we are already dealing with one three-week deadline, how about I make this one congruent?"

Three weeks to convince Lily to sell. Three weeks to convince her that there was no ulterior motive to his promise to never leave. Joe rolled his lips and shrugged. "Not a lot of choice, is there?" Hadn't Lily voiced that same sentiment so many times?

"You married, Trinidad?" Amos interrupted the conversation.

Earl frowned. "Yes, as a matter of fact, I am."

Amos tapped his finger on his chin. "How long?"

"Uh, two years this coming January."

Amos put his hands behind his back and strode back and forth. "Two years. Hmm. You have kids?"

"Not yet." Earl scowled. "Where's this going, Pettigrew?"

"Does she have a job?"

"Not outside the home."

Amos stopped pacing and folded his arms across his chest. "And where's home?"

"Kansas City."

"You own your home?"

Earl scratched his head. "I guess we own it. It's the home she grew up in. Her parents gifted it to us when they moved to a smaller one."

Joe felt like he was watching a ping-pong match. He had no idea where Amos was going with his questioning, but he was in full courtroom mode and he wasn't about to interrupt the proceedings.

"Kansas City. Hmm." Amos held up one finger. "No job. Two, no kids. Three, own your own home. Four, you're newlyweds." He waved the four upright fingers in Earl's face. "Why doesn't she travel with you?"

Earl shrugged. "Her family and friends are in the city. The big city is all she's ever known. I can't ask her to give that up to travel to every little town across the country, living out of suitcases in cheap hotels or boardinghouses."

Amos teetered to his tiptoes. "Am I correct in assuming that you love her?"

"What?" Earl's eyebrows joined the wrinkle of his forehead. "Of course I love her. I love her with all my heart. What–"

Amos stopped Earl with a raised hand. "And because you love her, you can't bring yourself to ask her to leave her friends, family, and the only home she's ever known to be with you. But you miss her."

Earl's eyes misted. "I miss her terribly."

"And I'm sure she misses you." Amos gave a sly smile. "I tell you what. How about you give me three weeks to convince her that her life would be better and she'd make you happier if she'd agree to sell the house, leave all that's familiar behind, and travel with you. After all, there's no reason for her to stay home alone while you go gallivanting all over the country."

A gleam settled in Earl's eyes. "I object to this questioning, you old court hound. I should know better than to fall prey to your tricks."

Amos jabbed his finger in the air. "Objection overruled. And it wasn't a trick, Earl. I wanted you to see what Kendall is up against. Plus, unless your wife's mother is ill, you still have no idea what it's like. I've lived in Anderson all my life. I know these people. I've known Lily Archer since she was a gleam in her papa's eyes. Every farmer around here who gave up their land without a fight had someone who'd stood beside them year after year while they toiled through both victory and loss. They made hard decisions together. Not so with Lily. She knows she's going to lose this place. But what you might not understand is that in losing the farm, she loses her identity, who she is not only in the eyes of the community, but who she is in her own eyes. And in her own eyes, she sees herself only as a failure."

Earl raised his eyes to Joe. "You love this Lily Archer?"

Joe smiled. "Am I under oath?"

"No. Just curious."

Joe took a deep breath. Answering his boss's question meant voicing aloud what he'd not spoken of to anyone else. "I'm no expert on love, Earl, but I know I would like to spend the rest of my life convincing this woman she's no failure."

"And is the feeling mutual?"

Joe made circles in the dirt with the toe of his boot. "I don't know."

"I see." Earl's low laugh rumbled in the barn. "Afraid to ask, are you?"

Joe shook his head. "Don't know how to ask. Up until a few days ago, she read any interest on my part as a way to get her to sell. Until this whole mess with her brother and whether or not her father left a will is settled, I don't think she'll trust my affections."

"Or maybe she doesn't trust her feelings toward you."

Joe arched his eyebrows and shrugged. "Now who's the court hound? Yeah, there could be that, too."

"What say we forget about the deadline concerning the sale of this place?" Earl gripped Joe's shoulder. "I'm well aware that one can't legislate love. So, my good man, pursue your sweet gal at your own pace and God will do the rest. Oh, and we'll keep praying, of course." He shook hands with Amos. "Good to see you, Amos. Thanks for the insight. I'll check back with you in a couple of days. Don't want to pressure you, but I think you know how important it is that we come up with some brilliant ideas…soon."

Amos followed Earl out of the barn, but Joe stayed behind and slumped onto one of the overturned buckets. *Pursue at your own pace.* How did one do that? He'd done nothing but pace himself from the first time he'd set eyes on Lily Archer. If he went any slower, he'd be going backwards. Bruce was right. Once the lake project was done, one way or another, he'd be moving on and Neal Murphy would stay. Neal had the means to provide a home and stability for years to come, while all he had was this job, guaranteed only for the next three weeks, and nothing else in sight. What was he thinking when he challenged the younger Murphy with *may the best man win?* But would Lily be happy living in town, being hostess to the various functions that went along with being a banker's wife? He could see her being a mother to little Rosie, but what about her mama? What would become of Ruth in a different environment? Would she be accepted? If only there was a way—

Like water hitting a hot skillet, ideas sizzled through Joe's mind. His heart pulsed in his ears and his leg tingled as he pushed himself to his feet. The familiar edge-of-a-precipice sensation. But this time, considering the alternatives before him, he'd take a chance and jump.

Bring it on, Neal Murphy. I might not win, but I'll give you one good fight!

Twenty-Eight

NEAL STEPPED INTO Milly's Diner and plopped onto a stool at the far end of the counter. Milly was the only one he knew to whom he could voice his current concerns. He could guarantee he wouldn't like the advice she'd feel obligated to bestow, but his need to vent outweighed her unsolicited opinion. Though, if he were honest, he couldn't say any light she managed to shine on his problems could be labeled unsolicited.

Milly sashayed from the kitchen and set a pan of cinnamon rolls on the counter beside the coffee maker. "You're up bright and early, Neal."

"But not your first customer, I see," he pointed to the pan of rolls, "unless you're the one who stole the corner goodie."

She chuckled. "A great cook always makes sure her food is good before she serves it to anyone else. But this time, it wasn't me. The big boss of the lake project beat me to it."

"Joe Kendall is in town?" Oh, if only it were true.

She took the coffeepot from the warmer. "Not Joe the foreman, but Earl something or other, the even bigger boss. You ready for the works and a cup of coffee, or are you waiting for your dad to join you?" She set a cup on the counter in front of him and filled it with the steaming brew, then handed him a napkin.

"No cinnamon roll. Coffee is enough." He folded the napkin in half, then in half again before unfolding it and repeating the exercise.

She reached across the counter to feel his forehead "No cinnamon roll? And playing with the napkin. You sick?"

He tried to smile, but his lips quivered. "Yeah. I'm sick, but not doctor sick. Does that make sense?"

Milly set the pot of coffee back on the warmer, leaned on the counter behind her and crossed her arms. "Wanna talk about it, or would you rather sulk?"

"Will you keep it between the two of us?"

She glared at him. "Neal Murphy, when was the last time you heard anything from me that even came close to gossip, or chin wagging, as Ernie so eloquently calls it?"

"I'm sorry. After Florence's betrayal, I don't know who to trust."

"Well, you can trust me. Besides, I'll bet this diner that your problems all lie about six miles out of town, say the Archer farm, for example."

He rolled his eyes. Milly was no pushover. "What makes you think that?"

She laughed and shook her head. "Because when I said it wasn't Kendall back in town you looked like you'd been kicked in the gut."

"You won't lose your diner with that bet, Milly." He took a deep breath. "For the past three days I've been stuck at the bank, playing babysitter to Florence and pretending that everything is okay, while Joe Kendall spends his days and nights at Lily's."

Milly frowned. "He's not there alone, Neal. Amos is there with him. What are you implying?"

"I'm not *implying* anything. Kendall and I had a, well, we had a discussion pertaining to our feelings for Lily, and his challenge to me was *may the best man win.*"

She tilted her head. "And the unconquerable Neal Murphy is afraid he might lose. Is that your problem?"

Neal puffed out a long breath. "I love her, Milly."

Milly's countenance softened. "Oh, Neal. Not for one minute do I doubt that you loved her but I'm not at all sure that what you are feeling now is the same kind of love."

He already didn't like the way this conversation was going. "I loved her? Past tense? What do you mean, the *same kind* of love?"

She pointed at him. "You do know you're asking my opinion, don't you?"

He nodded.

"Okay, then. Here goes." She moved forward and leaned her elbows on the counter in front of him. "Yes, I meant loved in the past tense, and I think what you *think* is love now is really only memories of the past. The years when you were both young and carefree. You know, the years before real life took over. Sometimes it's easier to live in the past than to face the task of daily living or even think about the future. And believe me, Neal. Real honest-to-goodness life is daily. Very daily."

"She was my first love, Milly." That sounded whiney even to his ears.

"I know, dear boy. But she wasn't your last. You were gone for eight years and have only been back for what? A month? And look what all has happened in those thirty days. Relationships, even ones from the past, can't be maintained with memories alone."

Neal bristled. "And who are you to talk? What about you and Amos Pettigrew? Doesn't it concern you that he is out there with Ruth Archer? Who knows what could happen, and she certainly couldn't tell anyone."

Milly shot upright, her eyes snapping, and Neal ducked his head. "You've have crossed the line with that very unkind, thoughtless, and completely foolish remark." She didn't raise her voice, but the heat of her words singed his ears. "Do you see what is happening here?"

"Happening?" He wiped is hand down his face. "What do you mean, happening?"

"We started this conversation with you bemoaning the fact that you're stuck in town while Joe is at Lily's, and now you have made a very ugly implication that Amos would somehow take advantage of Ruth's condition. I'm angry, Neal. But I'm not nearly as angry as you."

He slapped the counter. "You're right. I am angry. Angry that I have to stay at the bank pretending nothing is wrong while Joe—"

"No, Neal." Milly reached across the counter and grabbed his hands. "That's not why you're angry. Deep down, probably deeper than you've ever allowed yourself to go, you're angry at God, but you're too well taught to shake your fist at Him. You'd much rather make sordid insinuations and wallow in self-pity."

Her words stung like the slap across his face she should have delivered seconds ago. He yanked his hands from hers. "Helen's death has nothing to do with this." A cacophony of sirens, hospital pages, hushed voices, and a little girl crying for her mommy engulfed him in the aftermath of his outburst.

Milly gripped his chin. "Look at me when I'm talking to you. I never mentioned Helen's name."

He closed his eyes. "Then why—"

"Helen's death has *everything* to do with your behavior. You're mourning, Neal. All the anger you feel is a natural part of grief. Until you allow yourself to grieve you can never truly love again."

He pushed her hands away and braced his elbows on the counter. "How long? How long does grief last?"

Her face softened. "If I could answer that question, I'd market it and retire. Grief is very, very personal. I can no more tell you how long it lasts than I can hold a sunbeam in my hand."

He ran his hands through his hair. "I thought coming back here would help because there's nothing here to remind me of her." He turned on his stool. "You know, that day I drove back into town after…after…when it was only me and Rosie, the first person I thought of was Lily."

Milly folded her hands on the counter beside him. "But who is the last person you think of at night?"

Neal swallowed. If he confessed that he still slept with Helen's pillow…that he still reached for her every time he turned over…that he still had her picture by his bedside and that he told her goodnight, every night, would that negate his love for Lily? He ran his tongue over his lips. His arms ached with the memory of holding Helen the night before she left with her parents for the funeral. The next morning, they'd prayed for traveling mercy and then he'd kissed her and stood in the driveway urging Rosie to *wave goodbye to Mommy, sweetie.* And as they drove away, she'd kissed her fingertips and wiggled then toward the two.

He raised his eyes and Milly's questioning gaze only raised more questions of his own. More questions and a pain that took his breath away as he tried to remember. Had he returned her parting sign of love? Had he told her he loved her…not to worry about Rosie while she was gone…that he'd be waiting for her? For that matter, when *was* the last time he told Helen he loved her? Not the mechanical statement that accompanied the quick peck on the cheek as he left for work, or even the murmured one after their lovemaking. But the one where he held her, looked at her, and told her all the ways he loved her, all the whys, and all the forevers. The words emptied his heart only to fill it again because there too many ways and whys and forevers to count or run dry.

Milly stood. "Your silence answers the question, Neal."

He ran his fingers around the rim of his still full cup of coffee. "It's not silence, Milly. Believe me. It's the farthest thing from silence."

Further conversation was stilled when Neal's dad hipped onto the stool next to him.

Milly turned to get the coffeepot off the warmer. "You want a cinnamon roll with your coffee, Ed?" She set a napkin and a cup of coffee in front of him.

He checked his watch. "I think I have time. Thank you, Milly."

As soon as Milly went to the kitchen, Neal leaned closer to Father. "I thought you already left for Wichita." Neal handed him the sugar. "Your car was gone when I left home."

"That's because I didn't come home last night." He swirled his spoon around in his coffee. "I was able to convince Gladys she needed to get away from the hospital and get a good night's rest and your mother, mind you, informed me that I was to stay at the Finleys' place and make sure the dear lady slept."

Neal laughed. "You mean my mother, Mildred Murphy, actually instructed her husband to spend the night with another woman?"

"Hush." He wiped a smile off his face. "No need for anyone else to know that little bit of information."

Neal leaned across the table. "Then you were able to ask Gladys about Paul's message?"

"We talked about a lot of things, some of which might interest you."

Neal cocked one eyebrow. "Oh? So, what is it you think might interest me?"

Ed swiveled on his stool to face Neal. "First of all, Gladys does know about Paul's will, but that's a conversation for Lily and Amos. But she also mentioned that she and Benton talked—"

"Whoa! You mean Benton is talking now?"

"No, talked is probably not the word I should have chosen, although someday you'll understand. Gladys did the talking while Benton either nodded or shook his head." He grinned. "It works, Neal. Believe me. It works."

Neal laughed. "Are you speaking from experience, Dad?"

A smirk crossed Father's face. "Years and years' worth, my boy. But that's beside the point."

Milly returned with Ed's cinnamon roll. "How was Benton yesterday?" She set the coffeepot on the counter.

"Better each day, Milly. If he continues to improve, the doctors are saying they might release him in a couple of weeks."

"Release him? Will Gladys be able to care for him? What about the farm? I know Frank Scott farms the land but there is so much more...the upkeep of the buildings...the animals...the orchard. Gladys can't possibly care for all that by herself."

Ed nodded. "That's a conversation I had with Gladys and was about to impart to Neal. Since you already know the ins and outs of this situation you might as well know what we talked about yesterday."

Milly pointed to the clock. "Make it quick, Ed. The regulars will be coming in before long."

"Well, I've already mentioned that Gladys and Benton had a long talk, and then the three of us had an even longer discussion. The end result is that Benton and Gladys have decided it's time for them to leave their farm."

"What?" Neal and Milly exclaimed in duet.

"I know. I know. Can you imagine how difficult a decision it's been? They plan to keep the farmland and hope it will continue to generate sufficient income. However, they want to sell the house and outbuildings plus a couple of acres and hopefully make enough from that sale to purchase the small home here in Anderson they've had their eyes on for quite some time. Well, after more conversation that included a long look at their finances, we were able to—"

The voices of Milly and Neal's father drifted into the background as Neal's mind whirled. If this news had come a day earlier, he'd have taken it as a sign that perhaps he could be the best man after all. It would be a great place to raise Rosie, and he knew for a fact that Lily had always loved the Finley farm. She had called it her *Lily of Green Gables some-day home.* He could sell his house in Kansas City and there was still some insurance money. Between what he knew and what he could pay, it shouldn't be difficult to purchase the property. That would give him an advantage toward being the best man, wouldn't it?

But the news didn't come yesterday. He wanted to put his hands over his ears to shut out the din of memories and questions screaming through his mind. How could he make a decision that included Lily with Helen still sharing his bed? Helen wouldn't have wanted to live in the country. Too many bugs. Too many wild creatures. Too many dangers for Rosie. No, she would much prefer the city and all its amenities. Not Anderson. Not this town where everyone knew everyone and their business. Not this place that held memories too precious to release yet impossible to hold. Isn't that how Lily described the what-ifs he'd presented to her? Like a breath of air puffed into your hands that disappeared the minute fingers unfolded.

A tap on his shoulder, accompanied by Milly's frown, brought him back to the present.

Father smiled, his eyes wide with excitement, and his hands shook as he gripped Neal's arm. "So, what do you say to that, Neal?

"Say to what?" If the man had a newspaper in his hand he'd have listened better, but as it were—

Milly thumped Neal on the head with her order pad. "Your father asked you a question, Neal. Were you listening at all?"

Neal shook his head. He'd been so lost in the what-ifs that he had to confess he'd paid no attention to the now. "I'm sorry, Dad. I guess I didn't hear the question."

Father grinned. "I wasn't punching the air with a newspaper, was I? Well, the question came after a lengthy revelation. After my discussion with the Finleys, your mother and I had a long talk by phone yesterday. Now that you and Rosie are back in Anderson, and you're busy at the bank, we decided that the Finley place would made a grand retirement home and we're gifting your childhood home to you and Rosie. Gladys, Benton, and I all agreed on a purchase price, and as soon as we're able to get all the papers in order and signed we'll start the process of moving." He slapped Neal on the shoulder. "The question was, what do you say to that?" He gave an extra squeeze to Neal's arms, then stood. "Never mind, son. I know this is a lot of information to throw at you this early in the morning. Look, Gladys is going to stay at her place for the day so I'm not going to Wichita. However, I've not seen your mother since yesterday morning so I'm going to go home, give her a kiss, and take a nice hot shower. Why don't you hang a sign on the door of the bank and meet me out at Lily's, say around ten o'clock. Will that work for you?"

Neal scrunched his forehead. "Hang a sign? And say what?"

"Oh, I don't know. Maybe something like *closed.* That should cover it." Father chuckled and pointed to his cup. "You pay for mine today. I got yours yesterday."

His mind boggled beyond rational thought, Neal watched his father leave, his shoulders erect and steps sure and lively. A sight he'd not witnessed since his return to Anderson. "I guess I need pay for our coffee and go hang a sign, Milly." He stood, pulled his wallet from his inside coat pocket, and retrieved a dollar. He gave it a toss to the counter and in the process sent his cup sailing, coffee sloshing, until it finally careened off the edge, hit the floor, and shattered into pieces.

"I'm so sorry, Milly." He pointed to the shards of pottery on the floor. "It's pretty pathetic when seeing that broken cup is like looking in a mirror, isn't it? I'll clean it up."

Milly stepped in front of him. "No, you go on to the bank. But first remember this—sometimes, Neal, sometimes we have to be broken before we can be made whole again."

"All the king's horses and all the king's men, Milly. You know the rest."

"That's Mother Goose, Neal. This is real life. God can do what all the king's horses and king's men can't do if you let Him."

'L is where I live and let—'

259

'Let? Let what?'

'I let God.'

'But what do you let God do?'

'Why, I let God do whatever He wants. You should try it some time.'

Neal rubbed his hand across his eyes. Amos had smiled when he imparted the same insight when questioned about his L door. It wasn't a smile of amusement. Rather, it was one a father might give a child when passing on a nugget of wisdom. It was an outward expression of certainty because the theory had been tried and tested and found to be true.

Now if only someone could teach him how.

Twenty-Nine

ERE? LILY'S HEART thumped against her chest. "You mean Papa's will has been in this house all these years?"

Ed Murphy nodded. "He said he gave the wills and his letter to your mama about a month after your papa's funeral. She said she would put it in a box in the attic where Paul kept other important papers. He assumed that you knew, thus he'd not asked any questions."

Lily's legs tingled. "Wills? There's more than one? What important papers? What box? Mama never said anything."

"Could it be your grandmother's treasure chest, Lily? You know, the one you called her ugly box?"

Neal's question held a familiarity that made her uncomfortable, especially with Joe sitting next to her. "I don't know. I haven't seen that box since she died. I don't know what Papa did with it."

"Do you know how to get into the attic, Lily?" Joe's warm breath on her neck sent a shiver across her shoulders. Did anyone notice?

Neal leaned across the table. "Remember that little door in your parents' bedroom, and how we liked to sneak into the attic and pretend—"

Ed held up his hand to still Neal. "This isn't about what you remember, Neal. You can reminisce later. Right now, we need to see if Paul's will is indeed in that box." He motioned to Joe. "Why don't you go with her? There's no need for all of us to be in the attic."

Neal's chair squawked across the floor as he stood. "But why Kendall? I know where to look and could be up and back before he could—"

Ed pulled Neal back down onto the chair. "Because Ruth needs to go with her, Neal, and right now I think Joe is the better person to accompany them."

"Is that okay with you, Lily?" Joe squeezed her shoulder.

She nodded. "We'll need a flashlight but I don't…mine doesn't have batteries."

Joe stood. "I have one in the car. Wait here and—"

Amos jumped to his feet. "I'll get it for you, Joe."

Once upstairs, Mama went straight to the bedroom she'd shared with Papa for so many years, as if she knew the nature of the mission.

There was a dresser in front of the door to the attic, but Joe moved it without any problem. "Here." He handed Lily the flashlight. "Let me know when you find it." He stood back as she turned the latch and ducked her head as she stepped through the opening.

On the first pass of the light, Lily spotted the box. It *was* Grandma Archer's pine treasure chest. Propped on the wall behind it was the oblong picture of Jesus kneeling in a garden. Memories threatened to choke her. For as long as she could remember, the picture had hung above the piano in her grandma's house, the box occupying the space beneath it atop the crocheted topper with the pointy edges. As a young girl, she was sure the picture's gilded frame must be pure gold.

She knelt beside the box and ran her fingers around the edges. The top was dusty and scratched, and one corner looked as if something had chewed on it. She'd asked her grandmother one time why she set such an ugly box under the picture of Jesus.

'Well, my child,' her grandmother's smile had beamed through the wrinkles of her pink cheeks, *'it's a reminder that God doesn't look on the outside of a person but looks on the heart. The treasure is what's in the box, not the trappings on the outside. Remember that, Lily Ruth. I've always been plain as a stick, but your granddaddy, God rest his soul, looked beyond my shortcomings in the beauty department. He said true love looks past the outer appearance but savors what's down deep inside a person.'* She'd rubbed her nose against Lily's. *'Outside beauty fades, my girl, and no amount of powder or lip rouge can cover an ugly heart.'* Then she'd cupped her hands around Lily's ear. *'Besides that,'* she whispered, *'your granddaddy heard Clara Sue Dillon say a naughty word. He knew he could never take her home to meet his mama after that, but he paraded me like I was the grand prize of the county fair.'*

Lily smiled, remembering the twinkle in her grandmother's eyes and the gnarled fingers that covered her mouth after a giggle escaped the confines of her lips when she added, *'And that's the only time I was ever glad to know someone used naughty words.'*

"Lily? Are you okay? Have you found the box?"

The concern in Joe's voice brought her out of her reverie. "I'm fine, and yes, I found it." She stood and cradled the box against her chest.

Mama met her and reached for the box as soon as Lily stepped from the attic.

"Mama Archer's treasure chest," Mama crooned as she clutched the box. "Papa knows." She titled her head and smiled at Lily. "See, Papa knows."

Joe's questioning eyes met Lily's.

Lily shrugged. "She's said that over and over these last weeks, but I have no idea what she means."

Joe pointed to the box. "Is this your grandmother's treasure chest?"

Lily smiled up at him. "It is."

"So, what else might we find when the box is opened? Are there other important papers that would prompt your mama's memory? Anything that might make sense out of *Papa knows*?"

Lily crossed her arms atop the dresser. "I…I have no idea. I never even knew what was inside the box while Grandma was still alive. My parents would have scolded me for asking, although I did ask why she kept an ugly box under the picture of Jesus."

"And what did she say? Anything that would give a clue?"

"I don't think so." She relayed the memory of their conversation. "I think it was like she said, a reminder."

"You do know that it's possible to have both, don't you, Lily?" Blue eyes locked onto hers and she was powerless to look away.

"Both what?" She couldn't get her voice above a whisper.

He trailed one finger down her arm before grasping her hands in his. "It's possible to be beautiful on the outside as well as the inside. I know because I'm looking at someone who possesses those very qualities."

Oh, if only she could believe those words. But Joe Kendall didn't know her. Not really. He couldn't see the anger and fear she harbored, and she could only hope he couldn't see the longing and desire he elicited. "You have no idea how my heart looks, Joe Kendall. If God truly looks on the inside, then what He finds looking at me is far from anything beautiful." She pulled her hands from his. "We better go down before someone comes looking for us. We've found the box. Now we need to discover the contents." She moved from the dresser and willed her legs to hold her. "Let's take Grandma's treasure chest downstairs, Mama." She reached for the box, but Mama turned away.

"Wait." Joe hurried to Mama's side and crooked his arm through hers. "You can carry the box, Mama, but let me help you down the stairs so you don't fall."

Mama handed him the chest. "You carry it, Bruce." She patted his arm. "You're such a good boy."

Lily clenched her jaw as she followed Mama down the steps. If God looked on her heart right now, He'd surely see a whole lot of regret. But could He also see the tears she prayed Joe wouldn't observe? She swiped at her cheeks. She didn't want Neal to see them, either, but for entirely different reasons. If Neal saw her tears, he'd most likely assume it was Joe's fault and would certainly have something to say.

If Joe saw them, he'd pull her close and murmur over and over again that he was sorry and he didn't mean for his words to make her uncomfortable, and he'd remind her that he wasn't going anywhere.

She also knew that once in his arms, she'd not want to go anywhere, either.

NEAL GLARED AND Amos winked at him as Joe set the box in front of Pettigrew. "Lily says this is her grandmother's treasure chest." He seated himself between Lily and her mother and took a deep suck of air. "Let's pray we find the necessary papers inside."

Amos folded his arms atop the table and dipped his head toward Lily. "I think it only right that I ask both you and your mother for permission to open this box. I know Ruth might not understand, but I think we need to give her the respect she deserves."

"Thank you. Papa would want that." Lily turned to her mother and took her hands. "Mama, may we open Grandmother Archer's treasure box?"

She smiled at Lily. "Papa knows, girl."

Lily lifted her eyes to Amos. "I think that is as much of a yes as you will get."

"Okay, then." Amos's chest heaved with a deep breath as he opened the box, then his cheeks puffed with a long exhalation as he withdrew the sealed envelope lying on top. "This is much thicker than what I expected, but we won't know until we open the envelope." He slid his fingers under the flap.

Joe sensed Lily's body tense and he put his arm around her shoulders. He'd ignore the glare still burning across the table from Neal, but knew it would need to be addressed at some time. The guy wouldn't go down without a fight.

Amos grinned as the first thing he pulled from the envelope was a sheet of lined paper. "This is the paper I'm looking for." He carefully unfolded it and his eyes scanned the contents. "You ready to hear this, Lily?"

She nodded and Joe closed his free hand around hers. She returned his grip with a strength he wouldn't have imagined could come from such a tiny hand.

"To whom it may concern." Amos raised his eyes. "I guess that would be us." He looked back at the paper. "This is to make sure that in case something should happen to me, I leave the Archer farm and all my earthly goods to Ruth Marlene Archer, my wife. Our daughter, Lillian Ruth Archer, has a good head on her shoulders and has worked alongside me so I want her to be the executor of my estate."

Amos brushed his hand across the paper. "It's signed Paul Wilbur Archer, March 11, 1929. And it's witnessed by Benton Finley."

"Is that all?" Lily's voice cracked. "What…what about—"

"Wait, Lily." Amos waved the envelope in the air. "There's more." He pulled out another sheet of paper, his eyes scanning the page. "Ahh, yes. There is indeed more." His glasses slid up on his cheeks when he smiled. "Listen to this. June 12, 1930. This is an addendum to what I wrote on March 11, 1929. Since that time, my son, Bruce Paul Archer, has made some very poor decisions that have caused his mother and I much grief, plus money to pay damages and bail him out of jail. Should Bruce not finish school, or should he decide to leave either before or after my death, then he forfeits all privileges and monies. Should Lillian marry and choose to leave the farm, then Ruth shall be the sole executor." Amos grinned. "This one is also signed Paul Wilbur Archer and witnessed by Benton Finley. It's the proof we need, Lily, to allow you to make any and all legal decisions. However, there's one more note." He slipped another missive from the envelope. "Since it was in with the other papers, it must be important." He opened the folded paper, then looked at Lily, his lips a taut line across his face.

"What is it, Amos?" Ed scooted next to the attorney. "You seem—"

"This one is dated Tuesday, July 12, 1931."

Lily gasped. "That's the day Papa died. How could he have written anything and gotten it to Benton? I was with him the entire day fixing fences that had blown down in the last dust storm. We were out from early morning until…until—"

Amos laid the paper on the table. "Your papa didn't write this one, Lily. This one is signed only by Benton Finley."

LILY SWOONED AGAINST Joe. Why would Benton write something the day Papa died, before Bruce played his hand?

Joe shook his head. "This is too much for her, Amos."

Amos refolded the missive. "Only Lily can determine if it's too much, Joe." He handed the paper to Lily.

Neal snorted. "This doesn't make any sense. If you have everything you need, then what is one more piece of paper going to prove?"

Lily's hands shook as she opened the note. What if it proved her guilty? She quickly scanned the contents, then handed the paper back to Amos. "Please read it for me, Mr. Pettigrew."

Amos tilted his head. "Are you sure, Lily? I'll do it, but only if you are absolutely sure this is what you want."

Though her insides quivered with the realization that what she'd kept hidden for so many years would now be brought to light, it had to be done. She couldn't continue to live with Bruce's threats hanging over her head. She met Amos's kind gaze. "I'm sure."

Amos squared his shoulders. "Okay, then." He hooked the earpieces of his glasses over his ears and braced his elbows on the table. "July 21, 1931. My good friend, Paul Archer, went home to the Lord today. I'm so sad I can hardly pen this document, but I was there, you see, so I feel it imperative to record, to the very best of my knowledge, what happened. I was helping Paul fix fence today. Lily and Bruce were also helping. I worked ahead of the three of them, clearing tumbleweeds from the fence line. Around the middle of the afternoon, I heard Bruce and Paul arguing. It wasn't unusual. Bruce has a hot head and has made it quite clear that he wants nothing to do with the any part of dirt farming. But this was more than a normal fight. Bruce threw his tools onto the wagon behind the tractor and took off, tractor, wagon, drinking water, everything, leaving Paul and Lily with nothing but the wire stretcher, a hammer, and a bucket of staples."

Neal scooted his chair from the table and crossed his legs. "Please tell me what fixing fence has to do with anything important we've thus far discovered?"

Amos looked up from the letter. "You don't have to stay in here, Neal, but if you do I expect you to keep your mouth shut. Is that clear?"

Neal smirked. "Yes, Counselor."

"Good, then I'll continue." Amos adjusted his glasses. "It wasn't long after that I heard Lily screaming. I ran what seemed like miles but was only about a hundred yards. Paul had reached down into a posthole to clear it of debris before setting a new post and pulled out a big rattler, its fangs still sunk deep into his wrist. I still had a pitchfork in my hands and was able to kill the snake. I took off my shirt for a tourniquet, but we had nothing sharp enough to make a cut through the bite, and no water. We couldn't even move him to a shady spot because there was none.

"Paul lived long enough to ask Lily to promise to keep the farm, to make sure Bruce finished high school, and to always care for Ruth. The Archers have no phone, and my farm is a good five miles away from where we were and my tractor at least a half mile. We had no way to get help sooner. I should've raced to my tractor and gone for help after Paul was gone, but Lily was so distraught, and it was getting dark. Gladys got concerned when I didn't show up at chore time and called neighbors and the sheriff. Frank Scott found us first.

"Bruce never came back. I don't know where he is, but Lily made me promise never to tell anyone about the fight. She's afraid Bruce will up and leave if the story gets out about what happened. Ruth is beside herself with grief. I don't know how Lily will manage, but she didn't want anyone to stay the night with her.

"Paul never trusted any kind of government so he asked me to keep his will, both of them. Me and Amos Pettigrew were with him the day he wrote the first one. He said he'd put a note in his Bible where to find it if anything ever happened to him, but I'm not to worry if no one asks because Lily has a good head and she'll know what to do.

"Paul Archer was a good man. A close friend. I miss him already." Amos folded the paper and took off his glasses. "Signed, Benton Finley."

Tears poured down Lily's face and she made no attempt to stop them. Benton's story was finished, but hers wasn't.

Ruth Archer stood and reached across the table to gather all the papers Amos had just read. She folded them, stuffed them back in the envelope, put them back in the box, then scooted the box in front of Lily. "See. Papa knows." She sat down again and smiled. "Papa knows."

Thirty

S O THAT'S IT?" Neal jumped from his chair and paced. "Benton Finley knew all this time there was a will and never mentioned it? You know what this means, Lily? You could have married me after all. Your papa's will specifically said *should Lillian marry and choose to leave the farm, then Ruth shall be the sole executor.*"

"Stop it, Neal." Father pounded his fist against the table. "You can't blame Benton. He gave the papers to Ruth. He had no way of knowing that she put them away without telling Lily. This all is a very unfortunate set of circumstances, but it's not for you to place blame. So, stop...just stop." Father placed his hands over his ears and braced his elbows on the table.

"No, Dad. I won't stop." Neal marched to Lily's side. "Don't you see, Lily? If Benton would have told you about the will to begin with, you wouldn't be stuck here now. With what? No farm. No money. Your mother calls you *girl*, and you have a brother who ran out on you and has—"

Joe's chair crashed against the floor as he stood and slammed his fist against Neal's chin. "One more word, Murphy. Please, say one

270

more word so we can end this right now."

Neal staggered backwards and rubbed his chin. It hurt like blazes, but he wasn't about to let this outsider win. No, sir. Joe Kendall was not the better man. "I have a whole lot more words, Kendall, and you're going to listen to every one of them and so is Lily."

Joe doubled his fists. "Then you're going to be talking out of the side of your head because I'm about to bust that smirk right off your face."

"You and who else, Kendall? Big man, aren't you?" Neal fisted his hand and brushed his nose with his thumb. "Come on. Let's see—"

Barnabas growled and strained against his leash. Amos scooted his chair from the table and gave the leash another wrap around his hand. "If either one of you takes so much as a deep breath, I'll unleash this hound. You have two choices. Sit your behinds back onto your chairs and keep your mouth shut or take this fight outside and duke it out like little boys on the playground. Is that understood?"

Joe sank to his chair, but Neal took a step toward Amos. "You loose that hound and I'll have you in court by the end of the day, Pettigrew. This isn't your fight. All I want are answers." He tossed his head toward Lily. "Why didn't you tell me what happened that day, Lily? All anybody knew was that your papa died from a snake bite. There was no shame in that. But neither you nor Benton Finley ever said anything about Bruce running off. Why was it such a big secret?"

"I thought I told you I didn't want to hear another word out of you, Murphy." Amos's growl was as menacing as his hound's. "You don't have to say anything, Lily. What happened is in the past. We've found the will and now we can proceed from here. It's up to you."

LILY REACHED FOR Joe's hand. She'd no doubt have to answer to Neal later, but if she were ever to get from under the cloud of fear that had held her prisoner for eight years, now was the time and she needed something to keep her from running. "I do need to explain what happened…not to curb your curiosity, Neal, but for me. Nothing you hear today will save this farm. I can only hope it will save me from one more day of dread. The letter said Bruce never returned, but he did. I don't know where he went when he first left, and I didn't know then that he'd returned, but he actually came back two different times. I will never know how he was able to hide from us, but he found a way. The first time he came back, he saw Benton kneeling beside Papa with his shirt off. He thought it was funny, I guess, and figured if he could record it he could somehow use it against me. The second time he returned, he later confessed, he brought his camera."

"His camera?" Neal huffed. "What was he doing with a camera?"

Lily sent him a scathing glare. "His birthday is in June. He'd begged Mama and Papa for a Brownie camera and they got it for him."

She took another deep breath and released it slowly. Every face around her held wrinkled brows, and she knew they were waiting for the rest of the story. She squeezed Joe's hand, hoping he understood the worst was yet to come. He needed to keep her from bolting.

"By the time Bruce returned the second time, Papa was…was gone. The sun was so hot, so I had taken off my shirt and laid it over Papa's face. It was the only thing we had to keep Papa…to keep him…I couldn't bear to see him lying there with the hot sun burning…burning into—" She brushed her hands across her face. Even after all these years, Papa's white, lifeless face was etched deep into her memory. Somehow, though, she had to get through the rest of this story. Her head pounded and she could hear her pulse swish in her ears. "When Bruce saw us, Benton had his arm around me and—"

Neal pounded the back of the chair. "If your father was already dead, why did you take off your shirt? Or better yet, why didn't you put it back on when Bruce returned? And why did that old man have his arm around you?" He stood, walked to the kitchen door, and kept his back turned.

Lily jumped to her feet. "You aren't listening, Neal. I just told you. We had no idea Bruce was anywhere around. We weren't doing anything wrong. I had on overalls, so I wasn't completely uncovered. I was more covered than when you and I would go swimming in Lily's Pond. You have to believe me. I couldn't stand to see Papa so…so not there. Benton said I'd cried so hard he was afraid I would faint. He was only trying to comfort me."

"Why didn't you tell me?" Neal crossed his arms but didn't turn around.

"Really, Neal? You haven't even heard the whole story and you've already turned your back."

Neal swiveled, his eyes glaring. "The *whole* story? You mean there's more?"

Joe gripped her hand with both of his. "Go on, Lily. Take a deep breath. You can do this."

Silver specks danced in front of her eyes, but Lily knew she had to continue. "Bruce took a picture of Benton and me with Benton's arm around me. After he got it developed, he sent it to me and also sent one to Benton. After that, if I ever crossed him on anything, he threatened to send it to the newspaper with a story that Papa wouldn't have died if we hadn't been…if…if I had kept my clothes on. He said he'd claim he saw Benton take advantage of me and it would be our word against his. I believed him."

Neal tapped his fingers against his temples. "Oh, I get it now. That's why you said you wouldn't marry me, isn't it? You were afraid of Bruce. It had nothing to do with this crazy farm. I loved you, Lily. Why did I have to wait eight years to hear the truth?"

Her shoulders sagged. "We were eighteen, Neal. Papa died. Mama was so grief-stricken she could hardly get out of bed. And I didn't have a clue how I was ever going to keep the farm going or make sure Bruce finished school. You say you loved me, but you didn't love me enough to stay. Even after eight years, the truth makes you angry. I don't like your questions now and would have hated them then."

"I need some air." The screen door crashed shut behind Neal as he ran down the steps.

"Lily." Amos's hushed voice broke through the tension. "Do you know where the pictures are now?"

She shook her head. "I tore mine up and so did Benton, but that wouldn't keep Bruce from developing more since he has the negative. That's been one of my biggest fears."

Ed Murphy leaned across the table. "Lily, not one person in the search party ever said a word about what they witnessed that night except the tragedy of your papa's untimely death. Paul Archer, Benton Finley, Frank Scott...all solid citizens and men of integrity. There was never a question of wrongdoing."

Joe pulled her to her feet. "Look at me, Lily." He cupped her face in his hands and she met eyes so full of love she could hardly breathe. "Benton's letter stated that Frank Scott found you. Don't you think that if there was any question about impropriety it would have been raised at the scene? The only leverage Bruce had over you was the fear he managed to instill with his threats, and he can never use that power again." He traced her cheek with on finger. "Come here." He pulled her to him, and she went willingly.

NEAL CROSSED HIS arms above his head and leaned his forehead against the barn wall. He'd made a complete fool of himself. It wasn't the first time, but this time mattered most. Hadn't he only hours before come face-to-face with the fact that he still loved Helen? Now he'd spent the last half hour or so making Lily's heart-rendering experience all about him and how he'd loved her and she hadn't told him...

He was too proud to admit that Joe Kendall was indeed the better man. Not better because of what he could materially afford. The man didn't even have a permanent home, for lands sake. But he knew Kendall exhibited an unconditional love that he couldn't provide, maybe never could've provided. Lily marrying him wouldn't have changed Ruth's condition now. He wouldn't have been comfortable sharing a home with any mother-in-law, especially one with Ruth's condition, and Lily would never do anything less than what she was already doing for her mother.

Lily wouldn't like living in town, hosting bank associates, bridge parties, and gardening clubs. And he'd never be a country boy, not even in a home as fine as the Finleys'. He wasn't even sure he was cut out to be a small-town banker. He'd loved Kansas City and all it had to offer…fine restaurants, beautiful parks, infinite shopping choices. While it should thrill him, or at least make him grateful that his parents were willing to gift his childhood home to him, the truth was…he dreaded it.

He'd not heard anything from the realtor, so his home in Kansas City must not have sold yet. Clyde Riley, his old boss, had told him he would always have a job waiting for him if he ever decided to return. Wouldn't Mr. Riley be surprised if he walked in less than a month after he left? Rosie had mentioned several times that she missed her friends, and he'd not yet taken the time to introduce her to new ones in Anderson.

He changed positions, leaning his back on the side of the barn. If he returned to his home and his old job, would that be considered turning tail and running, or could coming back to Anderson in the first place be given that label?

Now what? Should he talk to Father first, or Joe Kendall? Joe would no doubt be relieved. Father would not share the sentiment. He didn't even want to think what leaving and taking Rosie would do to Mother. But in the end, it had to be his decision and a willingness to live with the consequences.

Thirty-One

THE SUN HUNG like a red ball above the horizon as Neal shuffled back to the house. His chin throbbed and his ego was bruised, but after a long afternoon of battle with memories versus reality, he'd finally conceded the fight. Running from the house before Lily finished reliving that terrible afternoon was easy, though cowardly. Returning to face the music, or, in this case, to apologize to Joe Kendall was much harder. Whatever made him think he could out best the best man?

If it were any other man, he'd hate him and fight to the end. But Kendall had proven himself to be one of the good guys. He stopped at the bottom of the steps up to the porch and gripped the pipe rail, still warm from the heat of the day. How many times had he taken these very same steps two at a time to find Lily waiting for him, her nose pressed against the screen door? It was a sweet memory, but today it didn't elicit the butterflies in his gut. Instead—he rotated his neck from side to side—it released the knot between his shoulder blades he'd experienced since realizing he was no longer the kid wonder of Anderson, Kansas. He took a deep breath of air and ascended the steps into Lily's house perhaps for the last time.

Joe looked up as Neal stepped back into the kitchen. "I didn't realize you were still here." He set a plate of scrambled eggs in front of Ruth. "Care to eat with us? I promise I didn't put anything unhealthy in them."

Neal straddled the nearest chair. "No. I guess I missed the train back into town, didn't I? I didn't realize they were all leaving."

Joe sprinkled salt and pepper over Ruth's eggs and handed her a fork. "That happens when you disappear before the meeting is done. Amos wanted to get the wills filed as soon as possible so Lily went with him. Your dad was eager to get home, too."

Neal's shoulders lifted with a sigh. "*Tuck tail and run* seems to be my trademark."

"Doesn't have to be. You can always apply for a new one." Joe filled his plate with the remainder of the eggs and sat beside Ruth. "You want some bread and butter, Mama?"

Neal's nose wrinkled. "Mama? You call her Mama? Wow. That didn't take long."

Joe put his fork full of eggs on his plate. "I'm not sure what you're implying, but you do remember that she thinks I'm Bruce, don't you? What can it hurt to allow her that one memory?"

"I'm sorry, Joe. I really didn't come in here to pick another fight."

"Good thing." Joe laughed. "I'm even stronger after I eat." He buttered a slice of bread and laid it on Ruth's plate.

Neal rubbed his chin. "That wasn't a lucky punch, was it? I deserved it. I was way out of line."

"Nope, it wasn't a lucky punch and yes, you *were* way out of line." Joe cocked his head. "If you didn't come in here to pick a fight, what exactly can I do for you?" He scooped a forkful of eggs.

Neal smacked his lips. "Love her well, Kendall."

Joe's fork clattered onto his plate and eggs splattered across the table. "Wha—"

"You asked what you could for me, and I told you. Love her well. And no, I can't believe I said that."

"One punch on the chin and you declare me the better man?"

"It wasn't the punch on the chin. It was the punch in the gut when I saw the way she looked at you, the way she seemed to fit in your arms…and I didn't miss her reaching for your hand before she started explaining, well, you know. I'm not anywhere near ready to declare you the better man—at least not better than me. But you are the best man for Lily and that's clear." He motioned to Ruth. "I couldn't do it, Joe. Not even for the love of Lily."

Joe patted Mama's arm. "I would do this even if Lily weren't a factor. Let's say I do this because of my love of Hazel—*Aunt* Hazel, if you will." He smiled. "So, what are you going to do now, Neal?"

"First I'm going to sit down and have a long talk with my dad. After that—who knows? I'm learning, though I'm a very, very slow learner, that I have to deal with what I thought I'd left in Kansas City before making further plans."

"Are you going to say anything to Lily?"

Neal punched him in the arm. "What? And make it easy for you? No, big man. I think you'll find the right words to satisfy Lily. Like I said, love her well."

"I will, Neal. I promise. But you know, Lily will have something to say about this."

"Yeah, I know." He saluted Joe. "Make sure it's 'I do'." He walked to the door, then turned and approached Joe, his arm extended. "Friends?"

Joe gripped Neal's hand. "Friends. Always."

"YOU'RE SERIOUS ABOUT moving back to Kansas City?" Neal's father tented his fingers.

Neal perched on the edge of his chair. "I am serious. I know this comes as a shock, and I don't want you to think I'm not grateful for all you've done for us since Rosie and I have been here. I don't want to leave you in a bind, Dad, and I'm willing to stay on at the bank as long as you need to find my replacement. It's just that—"

"I appreciate that, son, but I don't think it will be a problem. In the few weeks you've been home I've come to realize how much I miss going to work each morning. I guess I'm not quite ready to be put out to pasture."

"What about the Finley farm? Will this keep you from moving to your retirement home?"

Father smiled at Mother. "When I retire, we'll still make the move. In the meantime, we'll rent it out. There are plenty of families around who've recently sold their homes and whom I would trust to take good care of the place. What about you? You're sure you can get your old job back? I'd hate to see you move without a job waiting for you."

"I'll call in the morning. I wanted to talk with you first." He reached across the space separating him from his mother's chair. "How about you, Mother? Are you okay with this decision?"

Her hands shook as she gripped his and smiled through her tears. "I will miss you terribly, and Rosie even more. But your father and I have both known that your decision to come home so soon after Helen's death was based more out of pain than logic."

"I thought by—"

"I know." She patted his cheek. "You thought if you got away from everything that reminded you of her, it wouldn't hurt so much. But it doesn't work that way, sweetheart, because memories have a way of traveling with you…in here." She put her hand across her heart.

He chewed on his bottom lip. "I'm not at all sure how I will handle walking into our home again, knowing she's not in the next room."

"You'll hold Rosie tight and walk from room to room, remembering. You'll weep and you'll allow Rosie to cry with you. And it might take a long, long, long time, but you'll come through it stronger and wiser."

He sniffed "When, Mother? How long is *long, long, long*?"

She wiped tears from his cheeks. "I can't answer that question, and don't let anyone else answer it for you. But I can tell you this, you'll know."

"How? How will I know?"

"Well, when you focus more on what you had rather than what you lost. And," she brushed his hair from his forehead, "when you realize that your heart is no longer empty but has made room for a new love. You will love again, Neal. And don't ask when or how long that will take, but you'll know."

He shook his head. "I thought I loved Lily. Was I wrong?"

"Not entirely. You did love Lily. But you loved *high school* Lily…an eighteen-year-old Lily. The only thing that made it wrong is you thinking you could get rid of the hole in your heart left by the finality of Helen's death by filling it with memories of someone else."

"That was unfair to Lily, wasn't it?"

She nodded. "Expectations that involve another person are most generally unfair. They have no idea what you're expecting, and you're disappointed when they don't meet them. That leads to doubt and misunderstanding."

He leaned and kissed her cheek. "Thank you." He stood and faced Father. "I want to apologize for my behavior today, Dad."

Father got to his feet and clamped his hand around Neal's arm. "There was a lot of information to take in and I understand your frustration, but it was out of line. You don't owe me an apology, but I think Lily warrants one."

"I know." Neal's cheeks puffed. "I'm going to write her a long letter tonight."

"That's not the best way to apologize, you know. It would be much better in person."

Neal acknowledged his statement with a nod. "I know. I know. For now, it's all I can do."

Father threw his arms around him and gave him a hug. "Then do what you can do. It's better than nothing."

"Thank you." He pulled Mother to her feet and they stood in a three-way embrace. "Thank you both for everything. Now, is Rosie in her room? I want to tell her...tell her we're going home."

JOE LEANED HIS back against a pile of blanket-covered hay and drew his knees to his chest. "I take it everything went well at the courthouse."

Amos lowered himself to the floor beside him. "Well, the filing went okay. Now we wait to see how quickly we can get it probated. That process can sometimes take up to a year, but I think I can appeal to the powers that be to hurry the process along. Since Ruth is no longer capable for making decisions, and Lily has stayed on the farm these eight years and has managed all the business plus taken care of her mother, there should be no problem in getting things settled in a timely fashion."

"Legally, or are you going to sic Barnabas on them if they don't?"

"What do you mean, legally?" Amos pitched a handful of straw at Joe. "You think for one minute I'd risk Lily losing anything more by doing something underhanded? Although, I've considered releasing my trusty hound on more than one occasion."

"Are you saying that if it isn't settled in a timely fashion, that the deadline the city council has given my company to find a way to save the lake project could well be null and void?"

Amos chewed on a piece of straw. "You didn't think purchasing this property would save the project, did you?"

"I don't know." Joe scratched his head. "I'm not sure what I'm thinking. I know, lake project or not, Lily can't save the farm. I'm more concerned about how long it will take to get some kind of cash flow for her. If the lake project goes under there won't be money to purchase the property."

"Joe, there isn't money now. That's the reason the city council has put the brakes on it."

"If I could come up with a plan that the city will agree to, would that hurry the probate along?"

"It would have to be a good one, but it might help. You have such a plan in mind?"

"I do." Joe scrambled to his feet and grabbed a stick lying loose among the debris on the floor. "Look." He drew a diagram in the dirt. "This is a rough drawing of the projected lake when it's finished." Then he drew small rectangles along both sides of the outline. "What if, and I know this is a big *if,* but what if the city could offer to sell cabin sites along the banks? Kansas is not known for its natural waterways, so to be able to purchase a small vacation home, fishing spot, or perhaps even a permanent dwelling along the shores of a beautiful small lake might draw some attention. What do you think?"

Amos groaned as he heaved himself to his feet. "What I think, Joe, my man, is that you're a genius. Now all you have to do is sell Trinidad and the city council on the idea, but I'll back you up."

Joe screwed his lips to one side. "There's more. Want to hear it?"

"More?" Amos pulled an overturned bucket closer. "Should I be sitting to hear this?"

"I want to move Lily's house to higher ground so Ruth will be in familiar surroundings and Lily can see the lake. I know I can't move her favorite spot, the place she calls Lily's Pond, but maybe I can find a close second."

Amos hooked his hands behind the bib of his overalls. "You do realize moving a house is a project all its own, don't you? And what about the cost? Even with the will, and your company purchasing the property, she owes so much there isn't going to be a lot left. She'll have to have something to live on in the future."

"I know. I've thought of that, too."

Amos's laughter rang through the rafters of the barn. "Oh, I'm quite sure you have. I don't suppose your little scheme includes Lily Archer, does it?"

"I can only hope, Amos. I can only hope."

Amos motioned toward the house. "Maybe you should put feet to that hope. I know for a fact she's sitting on the north side of the porch. You might want to check on her after her very emotional day."

"You think? What if she doesn't...what if she asks me to leave...what should I say?"

"Just check on her, Kendall. I didn't say propose, but you might want to speak in full sentences." He punched Joe on the shoulder. "Go. If nothing else, sit with her. Sometimes one speaks louder by not using words. Trust me."

"*Trust me*, says the man who makes his living by spouting words."

"But you'll have a jury of only one to convince. Piece of cake, my boy. Piece. Of. Cake." He kicked Joe in the seat of his pants. "Get out of here."

Joe's heart tripped as he walked to the house. Oh, if only he had a bottle of orange soda and a bag of peanuts.

Thirty-Two

LILY SLID TO the porch floor and rested her forehead against her bent knees. Fireflies flitted across the yard and somewhere in the distance a mockingbird trilled through its evening repertoire. On most summer evenings, after a long day of work, she found a kind of rest in the normalcy of the night sounds. But not tonight. She couldn't remember a time when she'd been so exhausted. Not the kind of body tiredness that comes from a hard day's work. Rather, a weariness that went beyond the physical expenditure of energy and hunkered down deep in her heart. They'd found the will. It was filed. She was named executor. But what next?

The fragrance of Old Spice and a mumbled 'Hey there, Dog' alerted her to Joe's presence before he stepped around the corner of the porch and sat beside her. "Did you get everything done in town?"

His nearness sent shivers across her shoulders. She quickly lowered her legs, smoothed her skirt, and folded her hands in her lap. "I think so. I'm glad Amos was with me. I just wish…"

He turned his head toward her. "What do you wish, Lily?" He was so close his breath was warm against her face. "*Star light, star bright.*

First start I see tonight. Do you know that little rhyme? Pick a star, Lily, and make a wish."

Was he teasing her? *"If wishes were horses beggars would ride. Do you know that one?"*

His chuckle vibrated against her shoulder. "I do, but you're no beggar, Lily. If you won't wish on a star, then tell me." He reached for her hand and locked his fingers with hers. "What do you wish?"

Heat rushed through her body at the touch of his hands. "Are you my fairy godmother now? 'Tell me, and I'll make your wish come true'?"

"Not your fairly godmother, but someone who cares very much about you and will do anything possible to grant you your heart's desire."

Oh, if only he knew her heart's desire, but she dare not voice that piece of information. "I wish I knew what's going to happen next. Even with the will and the money from the sale of this farm, I won't have enough money to buy another house. I don't know anything but farming. How will I ever—"

"Shh." He put his arm around her shoulders. "I have a plan, but I want you to hear me out before you say anything." He laughed. "I know it will be hard, but try. Okay?"

The excitement in his voice as he told of his plan kept her from interrupting. The silence that followed his narration was even more quieting. After what seemed like hours, he stood and pulled her to her feet. "What are you thinking?"

Thinking? How could she think when he was so close she could hear his heartbeat? "You would do this for Mama?"

He cupped her face in his hands. "Not only for Mama, Lily. For us. You and me."

Her heart hammered against her chest. "There's an *us*?"

He ran both hands through her hair. "That's a question only you can answer. It is, however, *my* heart's desire. There's been an *us* in my heart from the first day I saw that beautiful hair tumble from your straw hat and you shook a newspaper in my face, until this very moment. It's too dark for me to see your face, but I know every curve of it. Your eyes are like brown velvet and I don't allow myself to think of your lips for fear I'll…I'll do…this." He lowered his lips to hers and deepened the kiss when she didn't pull away. Little did he know she was powerless to move from his embrace. If this is what he meant by *us*, she didn't want it to ever end.

"I love you, Lillian Ruth Archer," he murmured against her lips. "I love you and want to spend the rest of my life with you."

She gasped. "Are you asking me to marry you, Joe Kendall?"

"I'm asking, but I have no ring, and I don't want to let you go long enough to get on my knees."

"But what happens if the city council won't accept your plan? What will you do? I can't leave Mama."

He kissed her nose. "I would never ask you to leave your mama, Lily. If my plan isn't accepted, then we'll make new ones. Do you love me, Lily?"

"Yes. Yes, I love you."

"Then listen while I say this one more time. I'm not going anywhere."

She put her arms around his neck. "Remember when you asked me to make a wish?"

"I do, and you said you wished you knew what was going to happen next. And this is your next, Lily."

"But I made another one I didn't tell you about."

He laughed. "Are you going to tell me what it is?"

"I wished I could get married on the banks of Lily's Pond."

"Well, then. Before I can grant you your wish, my dear, I have to have an answer to my question. Will you marry me?"

"On the banks of Lily's Pond?"

"On the banks of Lily's Pond, on the moon, anywhere you wish. Just please say yes."

She raised to her tiptoes and pressed her lips against his. "Yes, I'll marry you, but please don't turn loose of me. My legs are so weak I'd fall in a heap."

He clamped his arms around her waist and swung her off her feet. "Hang on tight, Lily. I won't let you fall."

Long after she reluctantly stepped from Joe's embrace, and he'd returned three times for another kiss before going to the barn, Lily lay awake on her sleeping pallet beside Mama's mattress. It had been eight years since someone proclaimed his love for her. But he'd walked away without looking back. Neal was right. Had they known about the will earlier, she might have accepted his proposal, but it wouldn't have negated the promise she'd made to Papa, nor would it have guaranteed Neal would have agreed to live on the farm.

Now, along came Joe Kendall at the worst time of her life. She'd shook a paper in his face and asked him to never come back, yet here he was always with the promise that he wasn't going anywhere no matter how hard she tried to get rid of him.

She brushed her fingers across her lips. She could still smell him, feel his arms around her, hear his words of love murmured over and over again. She was loved. And she couldn't tell Mama. Oh, she could tell her but she'd never know for sure that she understood.

Lily turned to her side and let the tears flow. Tears of joy for what was, tears of deep sadness for what would never be again. She had no idea what might lie ahead. But she did know with a certainty no number of tears could wash away that, no matter what, she'd not be alone.

Joe Kendall was not going anywhere.

About the Author

Julane lives with her husband of sixty-plus years in a wee cottage beside a small lake nestled in the beautiful flint hills of Kansas. The daughter of a cowboy and named after a character in a story found in a Western magazine, her love of the Kansas prairie and the stories hidden within comes naturally.

Her passion is to present the promises and hope found in God's word through the down-to-earth everyday experiences of her not-too-perfect characters.

While becoming a published author was the fulfillment of a childhood dream, she considers becoming a wife, mother, and grandmother her greatest achievement and treasures the time spent with family above all else...even chocolate.

Made in the USA
Monee, IL
07 May 2021